CROWNER'S CRUSADE

How a humble Devon knight became a king's coroner: the thrilling prequel to the perennially popular Crowner John medieval mystery series.

1192. Returning from the Holy Land at the end of the Third Crusade with Richard the Lionheart, King of England, Sir John de Wolfe, a Devon knight, finds England simmering with rebellion. Discovering a body washed up on the shores of the River Exe, its throat cut, Sir John deduces that he was a king's courier. Tasked by Hubert Walter, the Chief Justiciar, to find out why the man died and who killed him, Sir John de Wolfe finds himself drawn unwillingly into affairs of state. His new career as a king's coroner is about to begin...

CROWNER'S CRUSADE

Bernard Knight

Severn House Large Print
London & New York

This first large print edition published 2014
in Great Britain and the USA by
SEVERN HOUSE PUBLISHERS LTD of
19 Cedar Road, Sutton, Surrey, England, SM2 5DA.
First world regular print edition published 2012 by
Severn House Publishers Ltd., London and New York.

British Library Cataloguing in Publication Data

Knight, Bernard. author.
  Crowner's crusade.
  1. De Wolfe, John, Sir (Fictitious character)--Fiction.
  2. Coroners--Fiction. 3. Devon (England)--History--
  Fiction. 4. Great Britain--History--Richard I,
  1189-1199--Fiction. 5. Detective and mystery stories.
  6. Large type books.
  I. Title
  823.9'14-dc23

  ISBN-13: 9780727897190

Severn House Publishers support the Forest Stewardship Council™
[FSC™], the leading international forest certification organisation. All
our titles that are printed on FSC certified paper carry the FSC logo.

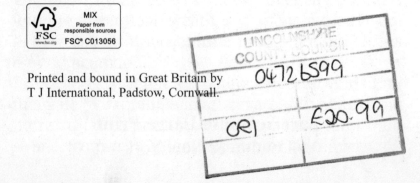

FSC
www.fsc.org   FSC® C013056

MIX
Paper from
responsible sources

Printed and bound in Great Britain by
T J International, Padstow, Cornwall.

Author's Note

Apart from the fact that Sir John de Wolfe is a fictional character, the description given in this book of Richard the Lionheart's disastrous journey home from the Third Crusade is as accurate as can be achieved after an interval of more than eight hundred years. A number of accounts were written soon after the actual event, some taken from men who were with the king at the time, such as his chaplain Anselm, yet details vary considerably from one chronicler to another. The story given here is hopefully a reasonable synthesis of what actually took place on that perilous expedition which, had it ended differently, might have altered the course of English – and indeed European – history. For those readers interested in seeking further details of that fascinating period, some sources are listed at the end of the book.

Historical novelists have to resist the temptation to stuff all the fruits of their research down the throats of their readers. However, though being well aware that novels are meant to be entertainment, not textbooks, the hundreds of comments received by this author after fourteen previous Crowner John sagas, indicate that many readers appreciate 'an easy way of learning some history', as they often put it. This fifteenth story is a result of suggestions from readers that they would welcome a 'prequel', an explanation of how Sir John came to be appointed as the first coroner for the County of Devon.

PART ONE – The Journey

Anno Domini 1192

ONE

The Ninth Day of October

As the evening light faded, the King of England slipped away from the Holy Land like a thief in the night. Though it was quite contrary to his flamboyant nature, which revelled in pomp and ceremony, no trumpets sounded and no flags waved. Neither did any royal pennants stream from the masts of the inconspicuous merchant vessel *Franche Nef,* as she quietly slipped her moorings in Acre's outer harbour and aimed her blunt prow northwards.

Richard the Lionheart stood at the rail of the sterncastle, wrapped in a cloak against the evening sea-chill that could be felt even in the Levantine autumn. He stared pensively at the great walls of the battered citadel as the ship glided past, thinking of the legions of men who had died there in battle or from disease – including more than two thousand Moslem captives that had been beheaded on his orders. His lips moved in an almost silent benediction as the gap widened between the vessel and the shore.

'O Holy Land, I commend you to God,' he murmured. 'In his loving grace, may he grant me such length of life that I might give you such help as he requires.' His tall, burly figure stood for some time as he stared landwards, thinking pensively of the greater part of the original crusading army who would never return home – and to such little result.

Eventually he gave a great sigh and turned away from the fading view of Palestine. 'Is this the last we will ever see of Christ's homeland, Sir John?' His deep voice spoke sombrely to a man almost as tall as himself, who stood protectively at the head of the ladder that led up from the main deck. Though they were now at sea, spies and infiltrators were widespread and, amongst the numerous crew, one could well be an assassin. Sir John de Wolfe, a Devon knight who was one of the king's small bodyguard on this voyage, was having similar thoughts of his own about this bare and bloody land.

'Sire, you swore you would return for another attempt on Jerusalem, but surely that must now wait upon what you find in England and Normandy when we return.'

De Wolfe was stating the obvious, but he sensed that Richard desired someone to talk to on this day of despondency. His king had spent a year and a half fighting his way up and down Palestine against Saladin's army and though he had twice come within sight of Jerusalem, he had known that even if he captured it, he could not hold it for long. Instead, he settled for a three-year truce, which enraged other Crusader kings, during which Christian pilgrims would be allowed to visit the Holy City. In addition, the shrunken Christian kingdom could keep a narrow strip of land along the coast.

The Lionheart did not respond to his retainer's comment, but turned back to watch the barren coast recede into the gloom. He was wondering what hostile eyes might be searching for the vessel that was taking the leader of the Third Crusade away, so that messages could be sent throughout the Mediterranean to waylay the man who had made so many enemies, both Moslem and Christian.

As he pondered on what may lie ahead on the long journey home, the dusk and a thin mist soon obscured the coast. The vessel was gradually pulling farther out to sea, though the Italian sailing master, standing respectfully in the furthest corner of the quarterdeck, would always keep land in sight for as long as he could, navigation being uncertain on the open ocean.

John de Wolfe stood immobile on the other side of the deck, the hilt of his heavy sword poking out from under his black cloak, ready to be drawn at any sign of trouble. Like that of the other retainers on the ship, his armour was stored below deck, well wrapped in oiled hessian. A hauberk of chain mail rusted quickly enough on land, but salt air and spray would ruin it within days.

He stood bareheaded, his black hair a complete contrast to the fair auburn thatch of the king. Different too were the styles, as Richard Plantagenet's was cropped short below a line running round above his ears, in the usual Norman manner. The maverick de Wolfe wore his long, swept back from his forehead to the nape of his neck. With satanic eyebrows of the same jet black as his hair and the dark stubble on his cheeks, it was easy to see why his nickname amongst the soldiery was 'Black John', though this was as much from his dour and unbending nature as from his appearance. His hooked nose and long, grim face were equally forbidding, though women somehow sensed that this was a man who could be a passionate lover.

The Lionheart turned eventually and addressed himself to the sailing master. 'When should we arrive in Cyprus? The wind seems favourable, does it not?'

The Venetian raised a knuckled fist to his head in salute as he answered. 'God willing, on the third day, sire. This breeze will take us well up the coast, then we must weather across westwards to Limassol. I regret that the *Franche Nef* makes no pretence at being a speedy ship.'

Richard and his advisers had chosen an ordinary merchant vessel for the journey, instead of the usual ship-of-war or a fast galley in which kings and princes normally travelled. The journey back to Normandy and England would be fraught with danger, as apart from seaborne Muslims and Mediterranean pirates, most of Europe's rulers were on the lookout for Richard Coeur de Lion, keen to revenge themselves on him for his real or imagined sins against them. Amongst these, Philip Augustus of France and Count Leopold of Austria hated him most, as they had abandoned the Crusade in Palestine and returned home early, outraged at what they considered Richard's slights against them and now his alleged capitulation to the Saracens. Another who would dearly like to get his hands on Richard was Henry of Germany, whose ambitions to conquer Sicily has been frustrated by the Lionheart. He had recently been elevated to Holy Roman Emperor after his father, William Barbarossa, had died falling into a river in Turkey on his way to Palestine at the head of a huge German and Hungarian army, most of whom had abandoned their mission after his death.

An hour later, King Richard was still staring into the growing darkness, reluctant to lose the last fading glimpses of the Holy Land, until feet clattered up the ladder from the main deck and a man appeared alongside de Wolfe.

'Go down and get something to eat, John,' he murmured.

'It's my turn to stand guard over our lord – though it's time he went below, he can't stand there all night in the cold and the dark.'

The new arrival was William de L'Etang, another staunch supporter and close friend of the king. A knight from Le Mans, he was a stocky, red-faced man of about forty, a couple of years older than John, with whom he had fought side by side in many of the campaigns against the Mohammedans.

As part of the king's desire to make his voyage home as unobtrusive as possible, Richard was accompanied only by ten Templar knights and a sergeant, but there were a few others aboard. These included John de Wolfe, William de L'Etang, Baldwin of Bethune, his High Admiral Robert de Turnham, the chaplain Anselm, and his clerk Philip of Poitou. This was a very different journey to the one the previous year, when Richard had set out from Marseilles ahead of a massive convoy bearing his army of thousands of Crusaders.

The big merchant ship, known as a 'buss', was relatively empty, the crew well outnumbering the passengers. There was no cargo, which left plenty of room below decks for the horses that would be needed when they landed, wherever that might be. Richard had still not made up his mind about the safest route through Europe, even though he was anxious to reach Normandy and then England as quickly as possible. This had become even more urgent since he had had repeated messages from his mother, the doughty Queen Eleanor of Aquitaine, warning him of the plot his treacherous brother John had hatched with the French king, for Philip to annexe Normandy and for John to seize the English throne.

William de L'Etang gave de Wolfe a friendly nudge to encourage him to go down for something to eat. 'Your man Gwyn says he brought a joint of mutton from ashore and it's still warm in a box of straw. Enjoy it while you can, John, we'll not eat so well when we get out to sea this late in the season!'

De L'Etang was right about harsher conditions later in the voyage. It was already past the safe date for deep-sea voyages, which were forbidden between October and April by a number of countries around the Mediterranean. Cooking was difficult or impossible in rough weather, as the danger of fire on board was the constant fear of seafarers. Most voyages hugged the coast and the travellers usually went ashore every night, where food could be cooked on a quayside or a beach and fresh water obtained. However, de Wolfe was sure that the king would try to keep well clear of the mainland, both for safety against attack and the attention of spies, as well as wishing to press on with his urgent need to get home, even if it meant sailing day and night.

The *Franche Nef* was broad in the beam, leaving plenty of space on the main deck between the sterncastle and a smaller elevation at the bow. The only cabin on the ship was under the sterncastle, placed between the men who handled the two steering oars, as the old ship had not adopted the more recent invention of the stern rudder. This cabin was strictly the province of the Lionheart, the rest of the ship's company living and sleeping on deck, except in bad weather when they could share the large hold with the horses. De Wolfe's stomach persuaded him to take William's advice and he bowed to the king and clambered down the steep ladder to the main deck below. He found Gwyn squatting against the windward bulwark, sheltering from the cold breeze, busy cutting a loaf of bread in half with his long dagger.

'I saw you coming down, Sir John, so I've started on our supper!'

Gwyn of Polruan was a very large Cornishman, as great a contrast to his master as could be imagined, except in the matter of height. Built like a bull, with a barrel chest and massive shoulders, he had an unruly mop of ginger hair

14

and long drooping moustaches of the same colour. A ruddy face carried a bulbous nose and a lantern jaw, relieved by a pair of twinkling blue eyes.

It was difficult to define his relationship with John de Wolfe, as he was bodyguard, squire and friend all rolled into one. Originally a fisherman from Polruan, a village at the mouth of the Fowey River, he had become a soldier in the Irish wars, where he served under de Wolfe and had developed this curious blend of mutual respect and comradeship that had now lasted for eighteen years. They were both a couple of years short of forty and in campaigns in France, Ireland and lately in the Holy Land, had saved each other's lives several times over.

Gwyn handed his master a hunk of bread, on which were several thick slices of roast mutton, still warm even though it was several hours since they had come off a spit in their billet in Acre. 'Get that down you, Sir John. There's more here when you've finished.'

As de Wolfe squatted down on the deck, Gwyn pushed across a small wineskin and a pottery mug. 'Wash it down with some of that! It's the usual camel piss, but we should be used to it by now. Please God we'll have some decent ale when we get back to Devon.'

When together, they spoke in a mixture of Welsh and Cornish, both very similar dialects of the Celtic tongue spoken widely in Devon and Cornwall. It was Gwyn's native language and de Wolfe, though having a Norman father, had learned Welsh at his mother's knee, for she came from Gwent in southern Wales.

Thankfully, the ship had only a slight roll in these calm waters, though a southerly breeze was moving them along quite briskly. John managed to fill his cup with the rough red wine without spilling much and, as he ate and drank, he looked about him in the growing dusk. Other groups of men sat or lay about the deck, some eating, some praying, especially the Templars. Others played dice, though a few had already rolled themselves in their cloaks and were sleeping either on straw palliasses or on the bare deck planks.

Gwyn hacked away at the joint and before long the two men had eaten all the meat and bread. Tossing the bone over the bulwark into the sea, Gwyn delved into the large leather bag that held his few belongings and pulled out some oranges. Passing two across to John, he began peeling his own as he meditated upon their journey. 'I wonder, Sir John, how are we going to get home? There's no way we can sail westward through the Pillars of Hercules – and even if we could, trying to cross Biscay this late in the year is just an easy way to get drowned!'

Gwyn always traded on his few years as a Cornish fisherman to set himself up as an authority on all things maritime, but John already knew that the current flowing into the Mediterranean past Gibraltar was faster than any sailing ship could overcome, unless they hugged the coasts, both sides of which were in the hands of their Moorish adversaries. In fact, the large Crusading fleet that had set out from Dartmouth back at Easter 1190, carrying the English army that was to rendezvous with the Lionheart at Marseilles, could never return from the Mediterranean. The remnants of the army would have to find their way home through Europe and the king's most trusted general, Hubert Walter, Bishop of Salisbury, had been left behind in Acre to organize their evacuation to Sicily, a kingdom founded by the Normans.

'I know that after Cyprus, the king has decided to follow the coast as far as Rhodes,' replied de Wolfe. 'But I don't think any decision has been made yet as to where we go from there.' He knew the small group who advised Richard, of which he was a member, were concerned about the dangers of virtually all the possible routes back to Normandy and England.

As if reading his mind, a figure rose from one of the nearby groups on the main deck and ambled across to them, still nibbling at a chicken leg until its bare remains were tossed over the side to follow Gwyn's mutton bone.

'Well, John, we're on our way – though only God knows where we'll end up!' Echoing their discussion, Baldwin of Bethune squatted down between them and nodded amiably at Gwyn before continuing. 'At least we can take stock when we reach Limassol in a day or two. The Templars there should have had some news from Sicily or Corfu by now.'

Baldwin came from a prominent family in Artois in north-eastern France and was a couple of years older than de Wolfe. He was a good-looking man with a tendency to dress in mildly dandyish fashion – which did not prevent him from being a fearless fighter when the occasion demanded. Baldwin had become a firm friend of the Lionheart, who valued his help and opinions, especially as Baldwin had trained as a lawyer in his early years.

Gwyn found a spare mug and poured the newcomer some of the indifferent wine. 'We were just speaking of the problems of finding a route home, Sir Baldwin,' he said respectfully. Though the Cornishman was a mere commoner and always deferred to his Norman masters, he was no craven peasant. His well-known devotion to John de Wolfe and his almost manic prowess in battle with sword and mace, had gained him the respect of all the Crusaders.

Baldwin nodded gravely. 'Everyone aboard has the same concerns, Gwyn. The obvious way would be to go back to Marseilles and then ride north into Aquitaine, but now Provence is in the hands of Raymond of Toulouse, who's no friend of ours since the king's brother-in-law Sancho invaded his lands.'

Sancho the Strong of Navarre was the brother of Berengaria, Richard's new, and somewhat neglected queen.

'Could we not land on the Spanish coast and aim for Navarre and then over the mountains into Aquitaine?' asked Gwyn. This large Duchy in south-western France was Richard's homeland, as, though born in Oxford, he was its Duke, where he had been brought up as a young man. The marriage of his mother, the doughty Eleanor, to King Henry II had linked Aquitaine to Normandy and England.

'We've discussed that option in our council,' answered de Wolfe. 'But the east of Spain is all hostile – the Moors in the south and in the north, Aragon and Catalonia favour Philip of France. No doubt they have been bribed by him to arrest Richard if he sets foot anywhere between Barcelona and Provence.'

They sat glumly sipping their wine, unable to think up any more cheerful news than the fact that at least the island of Sicily was a safe haven, thanks to their king's intervention there on the outward voyage. He had supported the new Sicilian ruler Tancred against the prospect of being displaced by Henry of Germany, whose wife Constance was next in line to rule the island after the death of her father, King William of Sicily. In the convoluted liaisons between European rulers, William had been married to the Lionheart's sister Joanna – who Richard had even tried to marry off to Saladin to obtain a treaty, until she flatly refused to be wedded to a Muslim!

The three men sat discussing the problem until the wineskin was empty, by which time it was totally dark. Their king had come down from the sterncastle and was in his spartan cabin, with a pair of Templar knights guarding the door. The *Franche Nef* steadily ploughed northwards, the sailing master steering by the stars and the occasional glimmer of light from headland beacons on the distant shore.

Baldwin of Bethune, already feeling a little sick from the motion of the ship, returned to his

19

other friends, who included Brother Anselm and Philip of Poitou. They settled themselves down for the night, laying on a mixture of blankets, cloaks and thin mattresses, which though not particularly comfortable, were far better than many a night spent in the arid wastes of Palestine.

John de Wolfe and Gwyn, who after many years of campaigning across Europe, could have slept on a bed of nails, soon followed their example. Within minutes they were asleep, Gwyn to dream of playing dice in an Exeter tavern and John to lying in a Devon hay barn, his arms around Hilda, the lover of his youth.

The shipmaster had been correct with his forecast of their arrival at the Cypriot port of Limassol, as it was the early morning of the third day when the *Franche Nef* dropped two of her many anchors in the bay. John de Wolfe leaned on the port bulwark with Gwyn and William de L'Etang, looking across at the small town a quarter of a mile away.

'Not much of a place, but the wine was better,' observed William, recalling the weeks they had spent there on the outward journey. King Richard had rapidly conquered the island to depose the tyrant Isaac Commenus, a renegade Byzantine. Then he sold it to the Templars as a base for their operations, before getting married to Berengaria in the Chapel of St George in Limassol. His bride had arrived from Sicily before him on a different ship, being chaperoned by his sister Joanna. Their honeymoon had been brief, as news arrived from Tyre that Philip of France had already arrived outside Acre. Richard, dubious about Philip's intrigues and abilities, had hurried away in his fast galley, the *Tranche Mer*, to join in the siege, leaving his wife and sister to follow with the main fleet. Now he was back again in Cyprus.

'If our lord is in such a hurry to get home, why did he want to stop here?' asked the ever-curious Gwyn. 'We've surely got supplies enough to last us until Rhodes.'

'Money, that's the reason for most things!' replied William. 'The king will need plenty of coin for hiring and bribing on our journey, as well as for feeding us and our horses.'

'So why come here? asked John de Wolfe, who had also been wondering about this diversion to Limassol. De L'Etang was a closer confidant of the king and knew much more about the intriguing that went on.

'When he sold Cyprus to the Templars, they failed to pay him the full amount. Now that he's given the island to Guy of Lusignan to compensate him for losing the kingship of Jerusalem, Guy owes him the balance of the money, so I'm sure he's called here to collect an instalment.'

'And we need to get the latest news of our enemies,' came a voice from behind them. Baldwin of Bethune had approached to join them, resplendent in a bright green surcoat over his long red tunic. 'Tancred promised to send regular messengers to our main ports of call with reports on what those bastards in France and Germany are up to.'

Gwyn raised his arm to point shoreward. 'There's a boat coming out already. Looks like some Templars are aboard.'

As it came nearer, they could see a skiff pulled by four oarsmen and, in the stern, two men with the familiar red cross on their belted white tunics. Baldwin hurried across to the cabin under the sterncastle, the door guarded by another pair of Templars, a knight in a white surcoat and a sergeant in a brown uniform, both emblazoned with the eight-pointed cross. Baldwin vanished into the king's quarters and within a few minutes, emerged with Richard, dressed more grandly than usual in a long white tunic, a jewelled velvet belt and large sword, with a narrow gold circlet around his head suitable for a visit to the nominal ruler of the island.

Behind him came another of his small band of retainers, Robert de Turnham, an English knight who was the king's High Admiral. A burly man with a pock-marked face, he was an administrator rather than a sailor, responsible for the fleet of vessels that had brought the crusading army to Palestine and was now doing his utmost to see that his monarch was returned safely. His elder brother Stephen was also an admiral, now charged with organizing a fleet to get the remaining troops back to Sicily, together with Richard's new queen and his sister, chaperoned by the Bishop of Salisbury, the king's second-in-command at the Crusade.

The trio went to the rail to join de Wolfe and William de L'Etang, who each gave a quick bow of deference, as Gwyn backed away to a respectful distance, though Richard acknowledged him with a wave and a grin. Aboard ship, with its tight little community cramped together for many weeks, the formalities of the court were greatly relaxed, even more so than during the eighteen-month campaign up and down the Holy Land. Though the Lionheart was a stickler for discipline and etiquette, with moods that swung from light-hearted banter to towering rages, the harshness of life on the battlefield or in the privations of long marches in near-desert conditions, had discouraged a strict adherence to the usual separation between king and subject.

'Sirs, I'm off to visit de Lusignan!' he shouted robustly. 'I'll risk my life in that cockleshell down there and trust to those worthy knights to save me if it sinks!'

The small boat pulled alongside and Robert de Turnham clambered down a ladder hanging over the side, closely followed by an agile king. Though he had been quite ill during the past weeks in Acre, a flux of his bowels bringing him very low, Richard now seemed quite recovered and his six foot two of muscular body, with his notably long arms and legs, swung easily over the rail. He shinned down without mishap, but all those clustered along the bulwarks were relieved to see the boat push off safely.

'Thank God no one was wearing their hauberks,' muttered de Wolfe. A coat of chain mail would send any man straight to the bottom, as the last Holy Roman Emperor had found to his cost after falling from his horse in a Turkish river. No one aboard wore their armour, unless an attack by another hostile ship was anticipated. Even their military monks, the Templars, stuck to their light tunics, as the daytime sun was still hot, even in October. They watched as the boat reached the stone jetty that stuck out from the beach and saw the passengers safely climb ashore. Even at that distance, they could see a reception party, with more Templars forming a strong guard.

As they vanished into the town, John de Wolfe and the other knights settled down to more tedious hours of waiting. Even after only a few days of the voyage, boredom was already the main feature of the journey. Playing chess, cards or dice filled a few hours. Eating and sleeping occupied some of the remainder, together with singing, in which the Lionheart took part lustily, even singing solo, sometimes songs which he had composed himself. Twice a day, the chaplain Anselm held prayers on the main deck, with frequent celebrations of the Mass, where all on board prayed fervently each time for the preservation of their lives on that most dangerous of elements, the sea.

Thankfully, during the first part of the voyage, the calm weather allowed the crew to cook, a charcoal fire being lit in a large iron pan secured on a slab of stone set in the deck. At noon, they would have spit-roasted chicken from the scores of fowls kept in a cage in the forecastle and soon, the enterprising merchants of Limassol were rowing out to the ship to sell fresh meat and fish, as well as bread, wine and a variety of fruits. Another boat provided kegs of fresh water which would keep them and the horses supplied for the next leg of the voyage to Rhodes.

As the day wore on, there was no sign of the king returning and after their dinner of vegetable potage and chicken, de Wolfe, Baldwin, and de L'Etang sat in the shade of the aftercastle, drinking some of the better local wine that they had bought from a bumboat.

'I wonder what we'll find when we get back?' mused Baldwin. 'I live too damned near to the lands of Philip Augustus for comfort. He's got his eye on Artois, just as he has on the whole of Normandy.'

The King of France, though nominally overlord of a large area of the country, actually had control of only a relatively small area around Paris and was always seeking ways to enlarge his territory. Now that Richard Coeur de Lion was far away in the east, Philip Augustus was greedily eyeing Artois, which spread up to the coast at Boulogne and also the Vexin, the northern part of Normandy. Though the lands of absent Crusaders were supposed to be inviolate, Philip had tried to get Pope Celestine to lift the protection, but had so far been rebuffed.

'The same is happening in England,' grunted de Wolfe. 'His treacherous brother John has been hoping that Richard would never return from the Holy Land. I'll wager he prays every night for him to be struck down by a Saracen arrow or a rampant fever, so that he can take his crown.'

They went again through the catalogue of men who wished the Lionheart ill will, from Philip

Augustus and Henry of Germany, through Leopold of Austria to Raymond of Toulouse and the princes of Genoa and Pisa – all the adversaries that were now blocking their pathway home.

The time passed slowly, Gwyn returning to his old profession for a while, as he took to fishing with hook and line over the ship's side. Whether by luck or remembered skill, he landed half a dozen sizeable fish to add to their supper, until in the late afternoon, there was a cry from the lookout up in the barrel lashed to the mast above the spar for the single furled sail.

'They are coming back, sirs!'

Moving to the rail, they saw a procession coming down the main street to the quayside and soon two boats were being rowed towards the *Franche Nef*, the second carrying a small chest.

Once alongside, King Richard hauled himself aboard and when Robert de Turnham followed him, the admiral turned to the crew and threatened them with horrible tortures if they allowed the treasure box in the second skiff to fall into the sea. When it was safely on the deck, a Templar staggered with it into the king's cabin, as Richard watched them with a satisfied smile.

'The contents should see us across Europe, gentlemen. Though only God knows how we're going to achieve it!'

TWO

The voyage onwards to Rhodes was notable only for its tedium. They left Limassol within an hour of the king's return and a favourable wind took them along the south coast of the island. Next morning, they lost sight of land and headed up towards the coast of Asia Minor. When they arrived there, the shipmaster made sure that he could still glimpse the mountains of Anatolia, but kept well offshore, due to the hostility of Byzantium to the Crusaders who had wreaked such damage to their country on the way to Palestine.

They took almost a week to reach the harbour of Emborikos on Rhodes, as the wind had changed and the clumsy ship had to claw its way along by innumerable tacks. Richard refused to go ashore at night and the navigator had to do his best in the dark, when clouds obscured the moon and stars.

John de Wolfe was on duty as the king's guard and companion on one such night, when Richard came up on to the aftercastle. To pass the time, the king seemed inclined to talk for a while. He told John about his abiding interest in ships and how he was convinced that England needed a navy to protect itself, rather than depend on commandeering a few ships when the need arose.

'I have a mind to establish Portsmouth as a base for my navy when I return. It has an excellent harbour, large enough to assemble a fleet and an army to settle affairs with Philip Augustus!'

John could already see himself part of such an army, even though at almost thirty-nine, he was getting a little old for the rigours of the battle-field. He had fought for Richard's father, old King Henry, in Ireland and various parts of France, before taking the Cross for this campaign in the Holy Land. But what else could he do but soldier on? He had no other profession and the country would be awash with unemployed knights after the end of the Crusade. He diffidently expressed these doubts about his future to the king, who seemed in one of his genial moods this evening.

Richard slapped him on the shoulder and gave him a hearty reassurance. 'You are a good man, de Wolfe! A faithful subject and a tenacious fighter! I'll always find a place for you somewhere – and for that mad bull of a Cornishman who watches your back so well.'

Swinging away, the king clattered down the ladder to his cabin, leaving a flattered, but rather pensive de Wolfe to lean on the bulwark and stare into the darkness, wondering whether his monarch really would remember him in a few years time.

They stayed but one day in the harbour of

Rhodes, sending Baldwin of Bethune and William de L'Etang ashore to seek the latest news, while more food and fresh water was taken on board. The king stayed in his cabin for most of the time, not wanting to advertise his presence in a crowded port filled with spies from half a dozen countries, though in fact probably every urchin and lemon seller knew that Richard Coeur de Lion was on the ship.

He spent several hours with his clerk, Philip of Poitou, dictating letters that he hoped could be dispatched at their next port of call, Corfu. He was writing to his mother, the elderly but strong-willed Queen Eleanor, to his Chancellor William Longchamp and to Bishop Hubert Walter, as well as duty letters to his wife Berengaria and his sister Joanne.

As soon as they left Rhodes, the king called a meeting of his shipboard council to discuss what Baldwin and de L'Etang had learned ashore. The Sicilian messengers from Tancred had made themselves known to the newcomers and Baldwin relayed their scant information to the council.

'It is now widely known in the eastern Mediterranean that you are at sea, my lord,' he reported. 'Philip Augustus has urged everyone who owes him fealty to look out for you and seize you if possible.'

William de L'Etang confirmed this and added that Henry of Germany had alerted those in the Italian peninsula, as he was still preparing to march an army south to Sicily to add the island to his Holy Roman Empire, claiming that Richard had illegally deprived his wife Constance of her right to the Sicilian throne by supporting Tancred.

'So we have few friends anywhere!' commented the Lionheart. 'That's not unexpected, but makes it more difficult for us to wriggle our way back to Normandy.'

'Am I to tell the shipmaster to strike westwards from here to reach Sicily?' asked Robert de Turnham, in his capacity as High Admiral.

The king shook his large head decisively. Normally clean-shaven like most Normans, he had joined the others in letting his hair and beard grow since leaving Acre and now had eleven day's worth of golden fuzz on his face.

'No, we'll keep to the original plan of stopping at Corfu, where there will be the most up-to-date intelligence from Italy, just across the straits from there. We can decide then what is the best course to take. It might be up into the Adriatic.'

The journey continued and the weather began to worsen, as the season was now far advanced. Suspicious of the reaction of other Byzantine ports in the region, the king and his officers directed the shipmaster to keep to the south of the chain of islands in the Aegean, passing on the horizon Karpathos, Kasos and then the seemingly endless coastline of Crete. The buss wallowed along in worsening weather and any thought of hot food was banished, as no fire could be lit on the rolling deck. As well as Baldwin, the chaplain was seasick for days on end and Philip of Poitou had to lead the prayers, most of which were heartfelt pleas for deliverance from this slow torment. Thankfully, John de Wolfe was a good sailor and of course, Gwyn relished the motion, having spent much of his youth in cockleshells off the Cornish coast.

'How long d'you think this bad weather will last, Gwyn?' demanded de Wolfe of his squire, as they huddled for shelter under the windward bulwark.

'What bad weather, Sir John?' asked the ginger giant, with a roguishly innocent expression.

'There's a bit of a swell, admittedly, but at least the sea is staying where it's supposed to be – outside the ship!'

His reassurance did not last long, as when the *Franche Nef* eventually passed the western end of Crete, the ship began to pitch as well as roll and spray began to fly back from the bow. Within another day, occasional green waves were crashing over the low main deck and streaming out through the scuppers.

'No sleeping on deck tonight,' said Baldwin mournfully. 'We share the hold with the horses from now on.'

Below deck, under the large hatch sealed with planks and canvas, twenty horses shared the misery with them. The animals were penned in stalls at each side, the whites of their eyes rolling with terror as the ship plunged along. For a further week, the men tried to sleep as best they could. Some climbed into the diminishing piles of hay that were stacked under the forecastle, others tried to wedge their straw pallets between the crates and casks of the food stores that were lashed down in the centre of the hold.

In the daytime, they staggered up on deck, preferring a wetting from the spray to the stink of horse manure and urine that seeped down to the bilges. Their own sanitary arrangements were little better – a bucket was the usual receptacle, as only the nonchalant crew dared use the ring-shaped wooden seat that was clamped to the bulwarks, hanging over the waves below. For obvious reasons, it was always fixed downwind on the 'looward' side, from which it got its nickname, 'the loo seat'.

William de L'Etang stood one day with John and Baldwin at the lee rail, gripping it with dogged determination. 'I trust someone knows where we are,' he shouted, over the moan of the wind and the soughing of the water as it churned ten feet below them. 'One bit of the God-blasted sea looks the same as the next!'

Geography was not the strong point of many on board, though the voyage out had given them some notion of the main way-stations. Maps and charts were speculative, outside local coastal waters.

De Wolfe looked out at the empty sea, now that the islands were far behind. 'I think Greece must be up there somewhere,' he hazarded, waving a hand vaguely northwards.

'That's cheered me greatly!' muttered William, as seawater swirled about his ankles as the deck tilted rhythmically. It was becoming cooler under a grey sky and they began to miss the comfort of hot food. The previous day, one of the crew attempted to boil them some stew over a brazier of charcoal in a sheltered corner of the deck, but the whole thing was overturned, scalding the man's leg. Thankfully, the large wave that had upset it also flooded over the coals and prevented any conflagration.

When a few more days had passed, it was nearing the end of October and the horizon was still empty, but as the ship laboured further northwards, they saw land again far away on their starboard bow, the wild mountains of the Greek Peloponnesus. A day or two later, as land closed in on both sides, the strong winds abated somewhat. They entered a wide strait between an island and the mainland, almost a score of miles across. John de Wolfe and Gwyn watched from the aftercastle as they passed between the rugged land on either side.

'Where are we now, master?' demanded John of the Venetian who navigated the vessel. The man spoke enough French for them to converse and told him that the island was Zakynthos and that ahead of them was an inland sea.

'We come through these islands to gain shelter, even though they have dangerous currents and jagged reefs,' replied the man, turning away to yell something in a strange language at some of his seamen struggling with ropes attached to the single large sail that was driving them along.

'Much as I love the sea, I've had my fill of it for now!' complained Gwyn, hunched over the rail in his scuffed jerkin, made of stiff boiled leather that was almost as good as armour. Other than in the hottest weather, he seemed to live in it, thought John. It had a pointed hood hanging down the back, which when worn, made him look like a huge Cornish pixie, especially as he also had coarse worsted breeches tucked into wrinkled ankle-length boots. Whereas all the others had given in and allowed their beards to grow unchecked, Gwyn periodically scraped off most of his stubble with a sharp knife, leaving his bushy red moustaches to droop down to his collar.

'You'll not recognize your two boys when we get home, Gwyn,' observed his master. 'They'll be a couple of years older by then.'

The Cornishman grinned. 'As long as there are not more than two there when I get home, I'll be happy!' he said mischievously. 'And what about your own lady, Sir John? You've not seen her for the same length of time.'

De Wolfe scowled at him, his long, saturnine face glowering under the nascent black beard. 'You know damned well that the less I see of her, the better I'm pleased! I came on this Crusade more to get away from her, than from any great desire to slaughter Saracens!' Everyone in Exeter knew that the relationship between John and Matilda de Revelle was anything but a love match. Pushed into a marriage of convenience by their respective parents some fourteen years earlier, they lived in a state of smouldering antagonism. During that time, de Wolfe had spent less than a year living with her, managing to find a war somewhere in Ireland or across the Channel to give him a legitimate reason for his absence. It had also gained him a sizeable store of silver, which he added to his winnings and ransom money from his success at tournaments, all wisely invested in a joint wool-exporting enterprise with a prominent merchant friend in Exeter.

'Where is she living while you are away?' asked Gwyn, in an innocent tone, though he well knew the answer.

'With her bloody brother, who she considers is only slightly less sanctified than Almighty God himself!' growled de Wolfe, cynically. 'She's either at his house in North Street or up at his estate in Tiverton.'

His brother-in-law was Sir Richard de Revelle, a wealthy knight with aspirations as a politician. He had estates in several counties in the West Country and had been sheriff of Somerset for a short time. John detested him even more than he disliked his own wife. De Revelle had carefully avoided joining the king in either his French wars or in taking the Cross for service in the Holy Land. De Wolfe strongly suspected him of being a covert supporter of Prince John's intrigues to unseat the Lionheart from the throne, as he had been cultivating a close association with some of the canons of the cathedral, who were in favour of the prince as the new king.

'My wife wants me to buy a house in the city when I return,' grumbled de Wolfe. 'She was content for us to live with her cousin in Fore Street for the past few years, but managed to insinuate herself into her brother's household when I left for Palestine. God knows how she gets on with his wife, the icy Eleanor, for they dislike each other intensely.'

Gwyn nodded his shaggy head understandingly. 'Thank Jesus I don't have that sort of trouble. My good wife Agnes manages to survive on the loot I left her last time I was home, though she also keeps a cow, some fowls and a goat in our backyard to make a few more pennies.' Gwyn rented a small cottage in the village of St Sidwell, just outside Exeter's East Gate.

Their discussion of family matters was ended by the gong which summoned them to their midday dinner. By now, a crewman had taken advantage of the calmer weather to light a charcoal brazier and as all the meat had long been eaten or gone rotten, fish was on the menu, bought from a small boat that came out to them from the islands. At least it was fresh, a great improvement on the dried stuff that came from casks in the hold. The last of the bread from Rhodes had gone mouldy but there was plenty of hard, unleavened biscuit. The fish were grilled on skewers over the brazier and a passable meal was handed around, washed down by either brackish water or the indifferent wine from Acre.

The passage across the gap between Zathynkos and Ithaca took a couple of days, the erudite chaplain Anselm informing anyone who would listen that the latter island was the home of Odysseus, news which was lost on all his flock, none of whom had ever heard of *The Odyssey*.

The king was becoming more impatient as time went on, urging the shipmaster and his High Admiral to push on with greater speed, something which the clumsy buss was incapable of doing. Richard was anxious for more up-to-date news of what his enemies were doing, both in their efforts to block his return home and what avaricious designs Philip Augustus now had on Normandy. Before leaving Acre, he had sent a fast galley to Messina to inform Tancred that he expected to be in Corfu in a few weeks' time and fervently hoped that the Sicilian would honour his promise to send couriers with the latest information.

Out beyond the shelter of the coast, the sea became rougher again and it was with relief that the hazy outline of Corfu became visible on the morning of the ninth day of November.

Next day, they had clawed their way up the inner side of the large island to reach Kirkira, the main city and port, where with great thankfulness, they dropped anchor. Corfu was also part of the Byzantine Empire ruled from Constantinople and Richard and his advisers were unsure of the reception they would get there. Philip of France had also called at Corfu on his way home the previous year and Richard was not sure of what poisonous lies he had left behind him about his rival. It was known that he had been proclaiming all over Europe that the Norman king had been trying to kill him and also the lie that he had ordered the fatal stabbing of Conrad Montferrat, ruler of the Kingdom of Jerusalem. However, it was imperative that they learned what they could from Tancred's messengers, as well as taking on food and water for the next leg of the voyage, as by now their stores were seriously depleted.

'You go with William and Baldwin, John,' commanded the Lionheart, as the ship's boat was lowered over the side. 'Seek out these men from Sicily, if God willing, they have arrived. Take Gwyn with you, he is worth any three men if you have to fight your way back!'

They dressed in sober clothing with no rich adornments, so as not to attract undue attention, and left the Templars on board, as they were not always welcomed by the Orthodox communities. They clambered gingerly into the small boat and two crewmen rowed them the half mile to the long curving beach with its stone jetty. Many ships were drawn up on the strand, including Venetian trading vessels hibernating for the coming winter.

The boat grounded on the sand near the base of the jetty and the three knights waded ashore, Gwyn following behind, his old sword scabbard slung across his back from a leather strap. They climbed a slope up to the town, where several streets rambled away, lined with a mixture of wooden and stone buildings, the latter gleaming in the autumn sun. The people in those streets were even more mixed than the buildings. Some of them wore Moorish robes, others dressed like farm peasants and yet more were obviously merchants, artisans and labourers.

The four men attracted curious glances and some hostile glares, for it seemed that everyone knew that it was the ship belonging to the King of England that lay at anchor in their bay.

'Keep your hands near your weapons,' advised William de L'Etang. 'Some of these fellows don't seem all that pleased to see us.'

They strode up the main street away from the

sea and it seemed to John that the crowds parted to let them pass, as if they might have some contagious disease.

Gwyn moved up to walk alongside de Wolfe and muttered in his ear. 'How are we supposed to find these Sicilian messengers? We know no one here to enquire, do we?'

'I understand that they will find us, if they are here. If not, we must return to the ship after a couple of hours.'

As they walked farther from the more open area near the beach, the main street closed in, with many narrow, crooked alleys running off on each side. The smell of a town grew stronger, a mixture of cooking, sewage, rubbish and un- washed humanity. Though well used to similar odours in almost every town they had ever visit- ed, after weeks at sea in clean, open air, the stink affected their nostrils more than usual. Shops and stalls lined the road, a haphazard collection selling all manner of goods, as Corfu was a meeting place of several cultures. Venice had strong trading links with it and Italy was not far over the western horizon. Merchants from North Africa and the Levant added a Muslim flavour, the various styles of clothing of all these people making a bewildering mixture.

'No one has approached us yet,' said Baldwin, looking around expectantly. 'Maybe those couri- ers from Tancred never arrived. Shipwrecked perhaps, if they were as foolish as us to venture on the high seas at this time of year.'

Soon the road widened out into a marketplace, even more crowded and chaotic than the main street. Amid the stalls and booths, old women sat on the ground amid piles of vegetables and fruit, donkeys and packhorses trod between them and roaming dogs and urchins added to the general confusion.

'Now where in hell do we look?' demanded de Wolfe, stopping to view the congested square with distaste.

A voice from his right answered him in perfect Norman-French. 'I think you may be seeking me, sirs!' A short man stepped out from behind a canvas booth selling fish. He was dressed in drab, but good-quality clothes, a short tunic and baggy breeches, a floppy wide-brimmed hat on his head. His light cloak carried several religious badges and he held a long staff in his hand, giving him the general appearance of a pilgrim. He had a smooth, bland face, one that John thought was instantly forgettable, perhaps an advantage in a secret courier.

Baldwin advanced on him, glad that the quest seemed to have ended. 'You have business with the king's men?' he asked.

The man nodded and introduced himself as Brother Lawrence. 'In spite of my appearance, I am a priest and one of King Tancred's chaplains, though I seem to spend more time serving him than the Almighty!' He turned and beckoned to another figure, who was still lurking behind the fish-stall. 'This is Gilbert, a lay brother and my protector on covert missions such as this.'

A large and ugly man appeared, grasping a cudgel and wearing a short sword on his belt. He nodded curtly, but said nothing, looking about him as if ready to fend off any attack.

'You have intelligence for us?' William demanded of the Sicilian priest. 'King Richard is most anxious to learn of any news about those that wish to confound him.'

'We have, sir. But this is no place to impart it.' He looked around, just as his bodyguard was doing. 'Since the scurrilous accusations put about by the French and the Germans, many in these islands are ill-disposed to your king. They know who you are, so I suggest returning with us to your ship as soon as we can.'

As they retraced their steps through the crowded streets, de Wolfe was well aware of the scowls and muttering that some of the populace directed at them. As they neared the harbour, a small group of younger men shouted some unintelligible abuse at them from across the lane and then a stone was flung at them, which hit Gwyn on the leg. The big Cornishman was not one to suffer insults and with a roar, he launched himself across the street, pushing bystanders aside as he slipped his scabbard from his shoulder and pulled out his sword. The youths instantly scattered, but not before Gwyn had landed a few blows with the flat of his long blade and whacked another man with the heavy scabbard. They vanished into a side lane as Gwyn sheathed his weapon and walked back to the others.

'Well done!' growled de Wolfe. 'But the local populace don't seem so pleased with us.'

A number of the people in the crowded street were glaring at the strangers and several shook their fists and shouted, though they were careful not to come within range of Gwyn's sword.

'Let's get back to the ship before we start a riot,' advised Baldwin and they moved more briskly towards the beach where their skiff was waiting.

As they clambered aboard, several men and a couple of small boys followed them at a safe distance, shouting insults and, when the boat was safely afloat, they began throwing pebbles at the departing visitors.

'How will you fare with them when you go back ashore?' asked William of Brother Lawrence.

The priest shook his head. 'We are not going back, sir. We will have to travel with you to Sicily, as I know you will need to land there for provisions and to hear any more news that has come to the ears of King Tancred.'

Once aboard the *Franche Nef,* Gwyn took the silent Gilbert to find something to eat and a place to lay a mattress, leaving the three knights and the Sicilian messenger to go straight to Richard in his cramped cabin, where Robert de Turnham and the senior of the Templar knights, Gerald de Clare, were closeted with the Lionheart. After they bent their knee to the king, Richard motioned them to sit on the narrow benches fixed to the bulkheads. His clerk, Philip of Poitou, poured wine for everyone and the envoy from Messina delivered his message.

'It is not good news, my lord! Henry of Germany is now camped halfway up Italy with an inadequate army, angry at his inability to fight his way further south to attack Sicily – and blaming you for much of the problem. He has been in contact by courier with King Philip and since we sent messages to you at Limassol, we hear that they met together in Milan. Our spies report that they have sent warnings to Leopold of Austria and their allies and vassals along the coasts of Provence and northern Italy, to be on the lookout for you landing in those territories and to seize you if you are found.'

Lawrence elaborated on the details, emphasizing how the city states of Genoa and Messina, previously favourable to the crusading king, had been turned against him by the propaganda and probably bribes of Philip and Henry. 'Your only haven in Italy would be Rome, where the Holy Father is naturally protective of those who so ably defended the Cross,' he said. 'I can also report that the galley carrying your gracious queen and your noble sister arrived safely just as I left the island. By now, your admiral, Stephen de Turnham, will have taken them up the coast to Rome, where the Vatican will give them shelter.'

Richard nodded, but did not seem too worried about the safety of his queen. Berengaria had tended him carefully when he was so ill in Acre just before he left, but he seemed content to leave her welfare in the hands of his mother and sister. He looked around the anxious faces ranged around the cabin. 'So if the Mediterranean coast is closed to me from Pisa to Perpignan, where do you gentlemen suggest we aim for? What about Spain, in spite of the difficulties there?'

There was a rumble of discussion, then John

de Wolfe, who had fought for old King Henry down in the south of Aquitaine, spoke up. 'In terms of distance, it would seem an advantage to land somewhere on the northern coast of Spain and strike up over the mountains to Navarre and hence into Aquitaine.'

'What about continuing up the Adriatic from here?' suggested Robert de Turnham. 'We have no quarrel with Hungary, which controls much of the eastern coast north of Ragusa.'

Richard smiled rather bleakly. 'It's a possibility, though I'm not sure how well I am in favour with King Bela these days, as although he is married to my sister-in-law Marguerite, she is the sister of Philip of France – and Bela was not happy when I broke off my engagement to her other sister Alice, to marry Berengaria!'

De Wolfe never ceased to be intrigued at the convoluted marital manoeuvres of the royal houses of Europe, which all seemed to revolve around politics and territorial gains, rather than affection or love. At the end of yet another unsatisfactory discussion, all that could be decided was that they would brave the wintry weather once again and make for Sicily, to get the latest news on the situation before committing themselves to aiming for the Spanish coast. The king gave Robert de Turnham the order to sail at dawn and make all speed to the next stop on this hazardous journey.

THREE

The next leg of the voyage was tedious and uncomfortable, as the weather, though free from storms, was uniformly windy and often wet. The sea was choppy and the buss pitched and rolled all the way to Sicily. Often the rain forced the passengers to sleep in the stinking hold, where the poor horses were having a bad time. After weeks in near-darkness, with only old hay for fodder, many were thin and listless, exhausted from the strain of trying to keep upright in the endless gyrations of the vessel. Two animals had died and had to be hauled up and pushed overboard.

'When we eventually do manage to get to land, in the state they're in, they'll be damned near useless for riding,' fumed Gwyn, a devoted animal lover, especially of dogs and horses. The issue was the subject of the next meeting of the king's advisers and it was decided to sell them when they reached Sicily.

'Better to hire new mounts with the money when we get ashore,' advised de Wolfe after the conference was over. 'Though from the way we may be dodging all over the Middle Sea, we may need camels instead!'

They were sighted at sea by another vessel

during the first few days, as the shipmaster had to claw his way across the Strait of Otranto to within sight of the Italian coast near Brindisi. A coasting vessel carrying pilgrims up to Assisi via Ancona, passed within a mile of the *Franche Nef* and Richard had no doubt that the identity of the large buss was recognized after all the unwelcome publicity of past weeks.

'Perhaps it's no bad thing that they saw us,' he boomed, as he leaned on the rail of the aftercastle, staring after the other vessel. 'When their tongues wag at the next port, it may mislead our enemies into thinking that we are making for the top of the Adriatic.'

In a few weeks' time, the Lionheart may have cause to ponder on this prophetic remark, but at the moment, everyone was praying for a change in the wind and currents that would take them south and west. Thankfully, by next day their prayers were answered by a north-easterly wind the locals called the *gregale* and now sailing more rapidly, they rounded the heel of Italy and aimed down towards the toe. It grew warmer and calmer as they approached Sicily and the Lionheart held a council meeting on the poop, following Sunday Mass. All of them now had beards, the king's being a reddish-blond, merging with the curly hair which had now covered his usual cropped neck. John de Wolfe's normal black stubble had turned into a villainous-looking bush, but he said that he was damned if he was going to attack it with his specially honed knife until he could get some hot water and tallow soap to soften it.

'We must soon make a firm decision on our route,' the Lionheart declared, leaning against the taffrail with his advisers in a half-circle before him.

The first advice came from Brother Lawrence, the Sicilian envoy. 'We should not try to pass through the Straits of Messina, as those on the Italian side are not well-disposed to us – and also, fighting ships from Genoa and Pisa, now in thrall to the Emperor Henry, often lurk far to the south of Sardinia.'

'So you suggest keeping to the south side of Sicily?' asked Robert de Turnham, who as the king's admiral, felt responsible for the ship's progress.

Lawrence nodded vigorously. 'Most definitely! Also, King Tancred said that he would send messengers to the major ports along that coast, to give you the latest intelligence about those who are arrayed against you.'

They had left Corfu on the eleventh of November and due to the favourable wind, they saw the tip of Mount Etna lift above the horizon on the twentieth of the month. Gwyn and de Wolfe stood watching for the next few hours as the coast came nearer and saw a wisp of smoke around the summit, something which highly intrigued the Cornishman.

Baldwin came across to them and for a time they watched the distant plume of smoke, then talk turned to more personal matters. 'John, you come from Devonshire, which I have heard some say is the end of the known world!' Baldwin was being cheerfully provocative and neither of the two West Countrymen took offence.

'That's not Devonshire, but Cornwall, which sticks out like a sore thumb into the western ocean,' retorted de Wolfe, with one of his rare grins. 'That is truly the end of the world, peopled by giants with red hair!'

Gwyn beamed amiably at the taunt. 'Giants who had long been Christian when the Normans were still pagans clad in animal skins!'

Baldwin roared with laughter and clapped the big man on the shoulder, before turning again to his master. 'How came you to be in this Devonshire, John? Were you born there?'

'I was indeed, and my father and grandfather before me. My great-grandfather came from Normandy with Duke William at the time of the Conquest and was granted a parcel of land which the family has worked into a manor over the generations. My father was Simon de Wolfe, son of Odo, but he was killed twelve years ago in a skirmish in Ireland.'

The noble from Artois nodded. 'But where does your "Wolfe" come from? I bear Bethune as a name, for that is my town. I know of nowhere called "Wolfe".'

John shook his dark head. 'That was the battle name of my great-grandfather, given to him by his fellows because of his rabid madness when he had an axe in his hand. He was originally a landless knight, born near Caen, so the family became named after the wolf's head device on his shield.'

A wide smile split Gwyn's face. 'The same rabid blood still runs in Sir John's veins, only now he prefers a sword to a battleaxe!'

'Have you been in England, Baldwin?' asked John.

'Only to Westminster and Winchester, on royal business,' admitted the bland-featured knight. 'That must be far from your home, I suspect.'

De Wolfe explained that his home was more than a week's ride from London, at Stoke-in-Teignhead, near the coast beyond Exeter.

'And you have family there?' persisted Baldwin, who seemed curious about these natives from the remote west of the Isle of Britain.

'My mother Enyd is still hale and hearty, and I have a younger sister and an elder brother who manages the manors, for we also have a smaller estate some miles distant.' He felt it unnecessary to add that his generous brother William, as well as supporting their mother and sister, gave John a quarter of the manorial profits.

They watched Etna's cone slowly diminish in the distance as they continued to sail down the east coast of Sicily. When they rounded Cape Passero, the wind sharpened and the *Franche Nef* began to pitch again. Everyone on board was thankful when they entered the harbour of Licata next morning. This was a small port on the island's south coast, where Brother Lawrence said a courier from Messina would be waiting. There was deep enough water in that almost tideless sea for the shipmaster to bring the buss against the quay that projected from the town.

For once, King Richard stifled his desire for speed and agreed that all his entourage could disembark for the first time since leaving Acre, as Sicily was a Norman country, the only safe haven for them in the whole Mediterranean. With unsteady legs, the Templars and the other companions of the king went thankfully down the gangplank and entered the little town. Here they could at least eat and drink in the taverns, while the Lionheart went with Baldwin, de L'Etang and Brother Lawrence to the portreeve's house where Tancred's messenger would be waiting.

Here arrangements were made to transfer the horses ashore and to leave them to be sold after they had left. The portreeve was willing to pay the king for them from the town's treasury, but at a price little more than half their original worth, because of their poor condition. The king's clerk, Philip, was eager to bolster the contents of the strongbox in Richard's cabin, for no one knew what the remainder of the long journey home would cost.

John and Gwyn gladly took the chance of a few hours on dry land, the first they had enjoyed since their brief excursion on Corfu. They stocked up on some palatable food for themselves as a relief from the ship's provender. Fruit, cheese, figs and honey was bought from stalls in the single street, then they joined several of the Templar knights who were eating and drinking in a nearby tavern. Gwyn bemoaned the absence of ale, but at least found that the wine was a better quality than in Palestine. They watched as the horses, thin and bedraggled, were hauled out in slings from the ship and herded off on tottering legs to pasture outside the town.

Sitting outside the tavern on a plank laid across two logs, the warm Sicilian sunshine and the wine were conducive to nostalgic reflection.

'I wonder what my good wife is doing now?' mused Gwyn. 'Feeding the fowls or clipping my naughty lads around the ear?'

John de Wolfe had no such fond thoughts about his own spouse. Matilda was probably on her knees in some church or other, praying to God to send a thunderbolt down on her wayward husband. His wandering thoughts shifted from a certain passionate widow in Sidmouth to a willowy blonde in Dawlish. Gwyn broke in again on John's mildly erotic reverie.

'I'll wager Gabriel is either playing dice in the castle gatehouse or down in the Bush Inn drinking good Devon ale brewed by your friend Nesta.'

Gabriel was the sergeant of the garrison in Rougemont, the nickname for Exeter castle, from the ruddy colour of its sandstone walls. His mention of the Bush and of Nesta sent John's reverie off on a tangent. She was the young wife of the landlord, Meredydd, a Welsh archer who de Wolfe had known during the last campaign in Touraine. Not long before John had left for the Crusade, Meredydd, wounded in the leg, had bought the tavern in the lower part of Exeter with the money he saved and looted during his years of service. He had brought his wife from Gwent, the cradle of archery and started to revive the fortunes of the down-at-heel alehouse. Nesta was a very pretty and vivacious redhead and the pair were working hard to make their new venture a success when John left.

'I hope the Welsh couple are doing well in the Bush, Gwyn' he said, as he downed the rest of his wine. 'They deserve to. She brews a great drop of ale and the archer was a popular landlord.'

Gwyn's yellow teeth showed beneath his great moustache as he grinned at his master. 'I think you quite fancy her, Sir John! She's a fine woman, that's a fact!'

John scowled at him. 'What normal man wouldn't fancy her? But she's married to a good friend, so she's out of bounds. Meredydd was a staunch comrade to both of us in France. And a damned fine archer, too.'

The Welsh were much sought after all over Europe as mercenaries, both as archers and foot soldiers. They even fought against fellow Welshmen, if the pay was good enough.

The two men lapsed into idle somnolence in the sunshine until late in the afternoon when Richard reappeared and reluctantly, the exodus to the ship began.

After evening prayers, the king again assembled his inner circle of counsellors up on the afterdeck. 'There was little new information to be gained and what there was was not cheerful,' he announced in a sombre voice. 'Count Raymond of Toulouse is reported as being incensed at the attack on his lands by my brother-in-law, Sancho of Navarre.'

'Sire, that will surely make our chances of crossing into Aquitaine from any part of the French or Spanish coast all the more hazardous,' commented Baldwin, who was now against a Spanish landing.

The Lionheart nodded his agreement. 'But what else can we do? Italy is closed to us, and we heard in Corfu that Philip Augustus and Henry of Germany met in Milan and agreed on joining forces to defeat me.'

Robert de Turnham shook his head despondently. 'The more I hear, the less I like the idea of pushing on into the western part of this sea, my lord. The north coast of Africa is infested with Moorish pirates and many more use Majorca as a base to terrorize shipping in Spanish waters.'

Once again, the discussion went around in circles, with an increasing feeling that continuing westwards was courting disaster. Next day saw a development that at least brought them to a decision, for better or worse.

Late next day, with the sun dropping near the horizon, the hills of Sicily had faded from sight and the *Franche Nef* was alone on an empty sea. The wind was from the north-west and the ungainly buss was tacking to try to make headway.

John, who had a vague notion of the geography of the Middle Sea, wondered how near they were to Africa and had visions of them having to fight Mohammedans all over again! As if his thoughts were the mother to the event, at that moment there was a cry from the lookout up on the main mast, yelling that he could see two vessels coming up over the horizon from the south.

Everyone came to look, either lining the port

bulwarks or clambering up on to the forecastle. Though from deck level there was nothing yet to be seen, within little more than an hour a pair of single-masted ships were visible.

'They must be galleys,' declared Gwyn. 'No sailing vessel could approach that quickly with the wind in this quarter!'

The same conclusion had been reached up on the afterdeck, where the shipmaster, the admiral and Richard Coeur de Lion were in urgent discussion. Within minutes, shouted orders sent crewmen scurrying to haul around the sloping yards of the two sails and the two steersmen were heaving at the huge steering oar. The buss lumbered around and as the now more favourable wind filled out the great triangular sails, the buss soon doubled her speed.

'We're running away from the bastards!' grunted Gwyn, almost saddened that he was being deprived of a fight.

Baldwin was beckoning to John to come up to the quarterdeck and soon the half-dozen royal retainers were clustered around their king.

'They are Moorish corsairs!' snapped Robert de Turnham, pointing over his shoulder at the two sleek galleys that were now only a couple of miles astern. 'But now that we are running before the wind at this fair pace, they'll not catch up with us before darkness closes in.'

It was already twilight, the sun having sunk well below the horizon.

'We are not going to fight them off, then?' asked de Wolfe, who like Gwyn had a natural distaste for running away from Saracens.

The king shook his head regretfully. 'No doubt we could overcome them, but to what end? I am not interested in slaying a few pirates. We could lose a few lives and suffer injuries. I have more urgent business – we need to get home!'

'So where are we going now, my lord?' asked William, who was the closest to the king and best able to speak frankly.

'This has made up my mind – perhaps God sent these vermin to end our indecision!' boomed Richard, his fingers playing with the novelty of his beard. 'We will return to Corfu and then head up the Adriatic to seek a landing in Hungary. What happens after that is in the hands of the Almighty, but it seems most sensible to pass through King Bela's kingdom into Saxony, where we will be welcomed by my kinsman Henry the Lion.'

The Prince of Saxony had married Matilda, the Lionheart's late sister. Their son Otto was both a nephew and close friend of Richard, having spent several years in England when young.

At dawn next day, the sea was empty, the galleys obviously having abandoned the chase when darkness fell. The wind remained favourable for travelling eastwards and, two days later, with some guesswork and not a little luck, the shipmaster was relieved to see Cape Passero again, on the corner of Sicily.

From there, they retraced their route of the previous week, keeping within distant sight of the heel and toe of Italy until they reached the straits across which lay Corfu. The wind was fairly kind to them, giving the lie to the prohibitions of sailing in late autumn. Without the horses, conditions were much better down in the hold on the few days and nights where rough seas kept them below deck.

John and Gwyn suffered the boredom and the endless rolling and pitching of the ship with resignation, having endured far worse conditions on dry land over many years. They ate the communal rations supplied by the crew and their own figs, dates and citrus fruit that they had bought in Licata. These lasted them almost a week, leaving only a few more days on dismal food until they reached Corfu. At dawn one morning the hilly western coast of that island came into view and the weary passengers lined the rail to welcome it as yet another stage on their erratic journey.

'Are we keeping this vessel to go up the Adriatic?' asked John, who was standing next to Robert de Turnham.

'It would take a month in this old tub if the winds are against us,' grunted the High Admiral. 'They're mainly from the north-east in the winter, the worst of them being the notorious *bora*.'

'So what should we do?' Gerald de Clare, the senior knight of the Templar contingent, sounded anxious. He was a tall, thin man, with a bushy grey beard. One eye was half closed by a livid scar running across his forehead on to his cheek, the legacy of a spear thrust at the battle of Arsuf the previous year, when Richard's forces defeated a massive attack by Saladin. The Templars had played a crucial role in the victory, but paid a heavy price in dead and wounded.

'We need a ship that will sail better than this one,' replied de Turnham. 'It can be much smaller, now that we no longer have the horses. There are coastal currents up the east coast that will help, as well as many islands that will offer shelter to a small vessel in this devilish time of year.'

Once again, it seemed that God was listening to the admiral, though at first the intervention of the Almighty looked more like a disaster than a blessing. Their discussion was suddenly brought to an end by a shout from a lookout on the forecastle, who was pointing towards the distant hills, just visible above the horizon. As he spoke a patois peculiar to the eastern Adriatic, they had no idea what he was saying, but his frantic gesticulations alerted the shipmaster, who yelled back at him in the same language.

'What's going on?' shouted John, as several of the other knights began climbing on to the poop for a better view.

'A galley coming out from the island!' yelled the Venetian. 'Almost certainly another corsair or a pirate.' The difference was slight, though a corsair was supposed to have the blessing of the local Christian ruler to prey on Moorish ships, whilst a pirate would attack anyone.

There was a bang below as the king's cabin door slammed open and Richard appeared to see what the fuss was about. Baldwin of Bethune rapidly told him that an attack was likely and immediately the Lionheart took charge, almost eager to get involved in some violence to ease the tedium of the voyage.

'Shipmaster, how long before they can reach us?' he bellowed.

On learning that they had more than an hour, the king called everyone to arms. 'Every man get your hauberks, shields and helmets from the hold and buckle on your swords!'

There was a rapid, but orderly scramble as the experienced soldiers prepared for a fight and the crew also went to their stations, fetching cross-bows and spears from the forecastle. The king disappeared into his cabin and with the help of the Templar sergeant, soon came out attired in his long coat of chain mail over which was a scarlet linen surcoat with two golden lions* emblazoned across the chest. He wore a round iron helmet with a narrow gilt crown around the brim. From a broad belt and baldric, a massive sword hung almost to his feet.

John joined his fellows in recovering his armour from the hold and after unwrapping the oily cloth, Gwyn helped him lower the hauberk over his shoulders and gave him the plain helmet with a nose guard.

'I'll leave that off until I know we are actually going to fight,' growled John, tucking the helmet under his arm.

There was no time to unpack the gambesons for the knights, the thick padded tunics that were normally worn under armour to soften the shock

*It was 1198 before Richard adopted a third lion, which is still seen in the present-day coat of arms.

of heavy blows, but this was not to be a battle-field combat, with thundering horses and the impact of long lances.

Gwyn pulled a battered helmet on to his unruly ginger hair, but had no armour. For years, he had depended on the half-inch thick boiled leather of his jerkin to absorb or deflect most of the sword clashes and arrow points that came his way.

Back on deck, fifteen knights now assembled, together with the sergeant and many of the crew who had armed themselves with a variety of weapons. They lined the bulwarks on the side facing the approaching galley, Richard being up on the poop with Robert de Turnham and de L'Etang, the rest either on the main deck or up on the forecastle. On the king's instructions, the Templars stood in the most prominent positions, so that the universally known red crosses on their white surcoats could clearly be seen.

As the galley came nearer, they saw it was of medium size, with a single tier of rowers, about twenty oars each side.

'At least its pennant shows it's Christian, not Moorish!' shouted the shipmaster.

The sail was furled, as it was moving against the wind, but the rhythmical beat of the oarsmen was sending it along at a brisk pace. The high prow, which curved forward at the waterline to form a ram, carried a fighting platform. On this were a few dozen men waving spears and swords, while others had coils of rope and grapnels. The galley curved around behind them to move in the same direction.

'They can't come alongside to attack us,'

explained Gwyn, their maritime oracle. 'The oars would be snapped off – and if all the boarders ran to one side, they'd capsize, as these narrow vessels are top-heavy!'

He knew that the usual technique was to ram the victim ship with the armoured spike under the bow, then swarm aboard from the forecastle, the ships being held together by grappling irons thrown on first impact.

Across the water, they could now hear the regular beat of the drum which gave the time to the rowers and soon added to this were yells and screams of defiance, designed to terrify the prospective victims. They had picked the wrong ship this time, as the Templars stood stoically at the rail, looking impassively at the approaching galley, which began to overtake, coming up on the buss's port quarter.

When it was just within crossbow range, the Lionheart gave a great bellow and hauled out his sword which he brandished in the air. As one man, the rest of the knights did the same, holding aloft a forest of blades which glittered in the sun. Then up on the aftercastle, the Templar sergeant took careful aim with his bow and pulled the trigger. A few seconds later, they saw one of the crowd on the nose of the galley stagger and clutch his arm. A scream was added to the tirade of threats, which rapidly faltered as the rhythm of the drum altered, then ceased. The galley lost way as the oarsmen stopped pulling and it glided parallel to the *Franche Nef,* but now just out of arrow shot. The buss was still moving at her usual speed, but by deft movements of their steering oar and yelled commands to the oarsmen, the sleek galley kept pace at a respectable distance. The watchers on the buss could see animated gestures going on between the figures on the fighting platform of the other vessel and very soon a man began shouting at them through cupped hands.

'What's he saying?' the king demanded of the shipmaster.

The Venetian put a hand to his ear, then translated. 'He has seen the crosses and wants to know if we are returning Crusaders, sire. He cannot be a local man or he would have learned that already from Corfu.'

The Lionheart leapt up on to the rail of the poop, grabbing a mizzen stay to support himself. Raising his arm to better display the golden lions on his surcoat, he brandished his large sword at the galley. 'Tell him this ship carries King Richard of England back from the Holy Land!' he yelled at the master. 'And if he dares interfere with us, I will kill him and his crew – and the Pope will send all their souls to hell!'

It was impossible to tell if the Venetian gave a literal translation in the local language, but it was immediately obvious that the aggressive mood of the pirates rapidly subsided. Weapons were lowered and the boarding party on the forecastle began to disperse following some commands from their leader. A few moments later, there were more unintelligible shouts between the two ships. The buss's master explained that the galley chief was allowing them to pass unhindered, as they were the soldiers of the

Almighty.

'Sensible man, for we would have cut them to pieces and then sunk their lousy ship!' growled Gwyn, who stood protectively behind John de Wolfe.

But Richard Coeur de Lion had not finished with the pirates. After a rapid discussion with his admiral and Baldwin of Bethune, he yelled again at the shipmaster to pass a surprising message to the galley.

'Tell him I wish to hire his vessel to take us to Zara – there's good Italian silver waiting for him if he agrees!'

FOUR

Later that day, the two ships anchored together in the bay off Kerkyra on the side of Corfu facing the mainland, while the bargaining and then transfer of supplies took place. The home port of the *Franche Nef* was Limassol, but the shipmaster was not going to risk taking her back there in mid-November and decided to winter in Corfu. The king's clerk paid him the remainder of the passage money from Acre and next morning all the belongings of the passengers and most of their provisions were moved across to the galley.

'We're going to be sleeping with our feet in the next man's mouth!' grumbled de Wolfe to Gwyn, as they clambered aboard the narrow vessel and surveyed the limited space for their eighteen men. The oarsmen were on a lower deck, not far above water level and above this was a flat main deck with a single mast carrying a triangular sail on a long sloping yard. Towards the stern, there was a wooden canopy arching over the deck to form a rudimentary shelter.

'I suppose this is where we must live for a week or so,' said Richard cheerfully, revelling in the discomfort and the glum expressions on the faces of his retainers. He marched ahead of them and bent his big body to peer into the low deck-house. 'Come on, sirs, think of the adventures you will be able to relate to your grandchildren!' he chided them, ignoring the fact that the Templars were celibate monks.

They managed to squeeze a dozen mattresses into the shelter and the remaining Templars elected to go to the lower deck and find some-where to lodge right at the stern, near where the two steersmen manoeuvred the long steering oar.

The haggling with the corsair's master for their hire of the galley was carried out partly through the buss's captain, who spoke a little of the Dal-matian language and also through the galley's mate, a villainous-looking Sicilian. He could speak fair Norman-French, so the king, Philip his clerk and Baldwin hammered out an agree-ment that for two hundred lira, the galley would deliver them to the Hungarian port of Zara, halfway up the Adriatic. These silver coins from Richard's treasure chest were minted in the Italian city state of Lucca and were used all over the Mediterranean lands, especially by Crusad-ers who used them as a common currency.

After Anselm had said prayers that evening, the new passengers had a remarkably good meal as the vessel sat in the calm anchorage. On the deck below, there was a gap halfway down the rowing benches where on one side the ship's skiff was stored. On the other was a large cook-ing brazier, where several of the pirate crew grilled scores of skewers carrying hunks of meat, onions and garlic. A couple of these, eaten with olives and flatbread made a satisfying meal, washed down with water and a local wine brought from ashore with the rest of the food.

As darkness fell, they crawled into the deck house to lie on the straw palliasses, squeezed in side by side. Even the king had the same meagre space, as there was no cabin for him on this vessel. With Baldwin on one side and de L'Etang on the other, all royal protocol was banished in the circumstances which had been thrust upon them. However, Richard seemed quite happy to be treated like one of his fellow soldiers and, as he had often done on campaign in Palestine, he shared their discomforts without complaint. Indeed, he seemed to revel in them, as if this was a welcome respite from the cares which had plagued him in the Holy Land and the travails that would face him at home.

John de Wolfe and Gwyn of Polruan were right at the open mouth of the shelter, but driving rain seemed unlikely that night and covered by their cloaks, they were soon sound asleep. When they awoke at dawn, the motion of the ship told them that they were already under way and the unfamiliar rhythmic swish of the oars and the thump of the drum seemed strange after being under sail for so long on the *Franche Nef*. The galley moved rapidly northwards, hugging the barren coast for many miles. Once out of the lee of Corfu island, the motion of the sea increased, but it was nothing like as rough as they had experienced on the trip to Sicily and back. The corsair captain, a sly-looking man with greasy black hair and a dark complexion which defied any guess as to his origins, wanted to follow the usual habit and pull into a bay to spend each night ashore, but the king dipped into his travel fund once more and bribed the man with a few more lira to keep going. They had lost over a week in the futile diversion beyond Sicily and the Lionheart had recurring visions of Philip of France advancing into Normandy in his absence. They were now in the first days of December and he had originally hoped to be home sometime in January, a hope that was now utterly unrealistic.

During the third day, a fresh wind blew from the south-east and the rowers shipped their oars, as the great sail was unfurled and they made just as good progress as from the efforts of the men on the benches below. After two nights spent at sea, the captain flatly refused to again forego their usual practice of going ashore, claiming that the crew would mutiny if made to spend another night on the benches. At dusk, the galley pulled into the shelter of a small bay. The captain was obviously quite familiar with this inlet and at dusk the galley was rowed up on to a soft sandy beach behind the headland. The crew disembarked and at the top of the beach they began building a fire to cook a meal. There were a few fishermen's huts nearby with some small boats drawn up into the bushes. The Sicilian vanished into one of the huts and soon came out to invite the passengers to use some outhouses as shelter for the night. These sheds stank of fish, but at least were stationary, not bobbing up and down and rolling as on the previous two nights when few of the travellers could get much sleep.

On the instructions of the Sicilian, the king's clerk distributed a few Lucca coins to the fishermen for their accommodation and for an ample supply of fresh fish. This was grilled on the fire and with some coarse bread, olives and dried figs, made a welcome meal before settling down to sleep. Next morning the galley was slid back into the sea and they set off northwards once again. Though the sea had become more choppy the previous day, a strong easterly wind now churned it even more and to avoid being blown out to sea, the sail was lowered and they resorted to the oars.

By noon, the weather worsened as the wind shifted more to the north-east and brought a chill with it that warned them that warm Mediterranean days were now well behind them. The Sicilian and the galley master were becoming more animated as they argued and gesticulated towards the land, now about seven miles away on their starboard side. Eventually, the mate came across to speak in his tortured French to Richard and his admiral.

'It is the *bora*, sirs, and it is getting worse. We cannot carry on, or we will founder. We must seek shelter until it dies down.'

'And how long might that be?' demanded the king, anxious to get to their landfall in Hungarian territory.

The Sicilian shrugged. 'Maybe a day – maybe a week. But we must make for Ragusa and hope that God preserves us that far.'

'How distant is that?' bellowed the Lionheart, his now luxuriant golden beard bristling in his frustration.

'A few leagues further, sire. A safe harbour, if we can get into it in this weather.'

'And if not?' demanded Richard.

For answer, the Sicilian crossed himself.

The *bora* worsened during the afternoon and the galley laboured against it, the oarsmen weakening with the sustained effort. The master steered much further towards the coast to try to gain some shelter, but de Wolfe failed to notice much advantage. He was beginning to fear for his life as the rolling and pitching increased and the cries of the rowers below became more strident as they struggled with oars that were deep below water one moment and pointing at the sky the next, water pouring over the low bulwarks as the hull corkscrewed along.

'A hell of way to die after all we've been through, Gwyn!' John muttered to his squire and friend, as he clung to the rail and stared anxiously at the grey cliffs that were now only a mile away.

The former fisherman, who had spent years off the Atlantic cliffs of Cornwall, was philosophical about it, as were so many sailors, few of whom ever learned to swim. 'Never say die until you draw that last breath, Sir John!' he advised. 'This master, bloody pirate though he be, seems a good seaman.'

As the early dusk of winter began to close in, the galley captain and his mate seemed to get more agitated, pointing ahead where a faint light shone from a headland a mile or two away. As they laboured nearer, they could see a flickering flame from a fire burning in a large brazier high on the cliff.

'Just beyond that beacon is the bay of Ragusa,' yelled the Sicilian, pointing at it. 'But the wind will be worse when we pass the shelter of the cliffs.'

He staggered back along the deck and went down the ladder to survey the shambles below where stores and provisions were rolling about. The oarsmen were desperately trying to keep stroke with the drum, even though the inboard ends of the sweeps were fighting them at every heave.

Within an hour, the mate's forecast proved correct, as when the galley turned east to enter the bay, the full force of the gale struck them, coming straight off the snow-covered mountains of the Balkans.

All the passengers, now wet through with spray, either clung on to the top of the bulwarks or lay in the shelter, hanging on to the ribs at the sides to avoid being rolled across the deck. De Wolfe and Gwyn stood hunched, clinging to the rail, looking ahead into the gloom, the wind tearing at their hair and clothing. It came in gusts, sometimes dying down for a few moments, allowing the oarsmen to recover some semblance of rhythm. But a moment later, a gust like a hammer blow would come again and, several times, John feared that the vessel would capsize.

King Richard, standing a few yards away, was obviously of the same opinion. 'If God wills us to survive,' he cried, 'I solemnly promise to pay

69

for a church on the spot where we land, in grateful thanks for His compassion!' Turning to his chaplain, who stood alongside him with his clerk Philip, he made sure that the Almighty heard his promise. 'Mark my words well, Anselm, and ensure that my soul be damned if I do not fulfil this heartfelt vow!'

He crossed himself as he spoke and the priest followed suit. The other knights heard him swear his oath, but were more concerned with muttering their own prayers for survival as they anxiously scanned the coast for any sign of the harbour.

'There's an island coming up, with a light on it,' yelled Baldwin, who as a self-confessed landlubber, had suffered badly from seasickness throughout the voyage. However, when the violence of a gale was this bad, *mal de mer* was banished by the prospect of impending doom.

'That's the Isle of Lokrum, just outside Ragusa,' replied Robert de Turnham, who had been here before on a voyage from Venice.

'I can see faint lights beyond it, in the distance,' shouted Gwyn. 'That must be the port. Another mile or two and we'll be safe!'

They passed the wooded island, now just visible in the gloom and headed for the flares of the distant harbour in what was momentarily, a lull in the gale. But just as everyone was thanking Jesus Christ, the Virgin and every saint in the calendar for their deliverance, a violent squall roared across the water and hit them on the port side. There were yells and screams from below as the inboard ends of the long oars swept men from their benches, then the galley heeled over, water pouring over the lee bulwarks of the lower deck. For a moment, the vessel was poised on the very brink of capsizing, but at the last second, the force of the wind on the hull slewed it around and drove it careering back towards Lokrum, now only a few hundred yards distant. Either their combined prayers – or the Lionheart's vow to endow a new church – must have persuaded the Almighty to preserve them, for the galley was driven straight on to the only safe patch of beach which lay between large boulders at the foot of a wooded hill. Though it was not soft sand, it was at least pebble and shingle, free of any large rocks. The shallow draught of the hull slid up with a grinding noise that could be heard even above the howling of the gale.

'Get yourselves off as fast as you can!' yelled Gwyn, whose stentorian voice was a match for even the worst weather. 'Get ashore in case she's sucked back by the undertow.'

There was a scramble for the ladders down to the rowing deck, with the king's inner circle and the Templars making sure that Richard was safe – though his own bull-like roar made it equally sure that his small treasure chest was carried along with them. Thankfully, the almost flat keel of the vessel kept her upright and though a wind-lashed surf was rolling up the beach, the castaways found that by moving almost to the bows before jumping over the low sides, the water was then only waist-deep. There was still a glimmer of twilight in the far western sky, enough to let them stumble from the waves that sucked at their legs and to crunch their way up the beach. The shipmaster and the Sicilian were yelling at their crew to take ropes from the bows and trail them up the beach to secure the galley to the nearest trees.

The pines grew almost down to the pebbles and once free of the water, John de Wolfe looked up in the dim light at the steep hill that was Lokrum. 'There's a light up there at the top,' he growled at Gwyn, as they stood shivering and shaking water from themselves like dogs.

'Let's hope there's also a good fire up there as well. I'm as cold as a whore's heart,' replied his companion, squeezing water from his wild hair and long moustaches.

'Over here, all my good men!' shouted the king, rallying his exhausted entourage around him under the trees. 'Are we all here, safe and sound?'

The energetic Baldwin checked their party and found every soul present, albeit drenched and bedraggled. Philip of Poitou also confirmed that the small treasure chest was safe, inside which was another box which carried Richard's narrow battle crown and his Great Seal.

'That poor thing has been shipwrecked twice now,' bellowed the king. 'It must have the nine lives of a cat!'

His official seal, which was impressed on to the wax of all documents to confirm that they bore his royal will, had been lost on the outward journey to the Holy Land. His seal-bearer, Roger Malcael, was drowned when his ship, part of the flotilla that also carried Berengaria and the king's sister Joanne, was wrecked off Cyprus. Miraculously, his dead body was washed ashore with the seal still hanging from a chain around his neck.

'We've already lost our horses, now we've no chance of saving our armour either,' lamented William de L'Etang, peering back at where the galley was bucking and rolling in the surf at the end of rope tethers. Several score of drenched shipmen and rowers were milling about the beach, being harangued by the captain and his mate.

'We've got our lives and our swords, rusty though they'll be after this soaking,' cried Richard heartily. 'Now we need fire, food and shelter, for which I will more than amply repay with the church I vowed to build on this blessed isle!'

FIVE

The promised church was never built on Lokrum, but the generous – many would say profligate – Richard Coeur de Lion gave a large donation towards the rebuilding of the cathedral in Ragusa itself. He had been persuaded by the city fathers that the money would be better spent that way and his only condition was that as long as the sanction of the Pope was obtained to this amendment of his vow, a small part of it must be used to renovate the dilapidated priory on the island. The four hermetic monks there had given them food and shelter in the hours after the shipwreck.

The king's generosity was not universally welcomed.

'Though I love him dearly,' grumbled John de Wolfe, 'I must acknowledge that he can be overly free with other people's money.'

He was standing with Baldwin, William and Brother Anselm some three days after their shipwreck. They were once again at the rail of yet another vessel, staring out at bleak mountains a few miles away, the further peaks now dusted with the first snows of winter. The knight from Bethune looked quizzically at de Wolfe, as even the mildest of criticism of their sovereign was a novelty coming from the doggedly faithful man from Devonshire.

'What do you mean, John – "other people's money"? Legally, he owns everything in his kingdom.'

De Wolfe shrugged. 'I know that, but the chancellor and the *Curia Regis* seized every spare penny to fund the Crusade. Not only in England, but Normandy and Aquitaine as well. They squeezed the merchants and taxed the common people until they howled and then bled the Church as dry as a bone, taking their gold plates and chalices and their wool and corn.'

'And all in God's great cause!' retorted Anselm, defensively. 'To recover Jerusalem from the grip of the infidel Saracens.'

John sighed and wished he had kept his mouth shut. 'Well, we failed in that didn't we? But what I mean is that all that money was scraped together to equip and feed a great army and pay for a fleet of ships to transport them to Palestine. It was not for lavishing on a new cathedral in some obscure foreign city.'

William de L'Etang slapped his friend on the back. 'But, John, it's typical of our lord and master! Fierce and even cruel at one moment, then hearty and boisterous at the next, throwing gold around as if it grew on trees. It's what makes him what he is and we all love him for it.'

Anselm nodded his agreement, but partly sided with de Wolfe. 'Yet I admit he is sometimes too impulsive and often fails to think of the consequences. Look at how yesterday he went with the Templars to the Treasury in Ragusa and borrowed thousands of Venetian ducats against a Templar promissory note. Chancellor Longchamp will have a stroke when all these bills come home to roost.'

John held his tongue, but William threw in a half-jocular comment. 'And what did he do with some of that new money? Spent it on three expensive jewelled rings for himself!'

Baldwin came to Richard's defence over this apparent extravagance. 'Our lord is a great king, ruling lands that stretch from the Pyrenees almost to Scotland. He needs the appurtenances of a king, such as these ostentatious jewels, to display his power and influence in the world!'

'Well, I wish he had used his power and influence to get us a better vessel than this,' grumbled de Wolfe, looking down the deck to where Gwyn was contentedly fishing over the side, his ever-unruly hair blowing in the wind.

'There's little wrong with the *Medusa*, John,' remarked Robert de Turnham, who had joined the group from his place up on the aftercastle. 'She's getting along quite well with this new southerly wind behind her.'

The *Medusa* was an ordinary merchant ship called a 'cog', which was much smaller than the more bulky *Franche Nef*. With a single mast and square sail, she was a maid-of-all-work similar to hundreds of others in the Mediterranean – though virtually all of those were now laid up for the winter. Only the generosity of the Lionheart to the bishop and city council of Ragusa had persuaded this shipmaster to venture up the coast of Dalmatia in December.

The violent *bora* had subsided as quickly as it had arisen and after two nights in Ragusa, with blissful sleep in the guest house of the monastery, the travellers were sent on their way towards Zara, about a hundred and sixty miles up the coast, well into Hungarian territory.

'With this wind, we should reach Zara the day after tomorrow,' prophesied the High Admiral. 'The route lies behind the many islands that line this coast, so we should be protected from any westerly storms. Pray God we don't suffer another *bora*.' He crossed himself virtuously as he spoke.

At the king's council held earlier that day, it was agreed that they would buy horses in Zara and make the long ride to the court of King Bela, who had a grand palace in Estergom on the Danube. There Richard would trade on his kinship with Bela's queen, to seek hospitality and advice on how best to return to Normandy and England. Though most of the knights had only a hazy idea of the geography of Central Europe, both Richard and Baldwin knew enough to debate possible routes.

'Either we aim for Saxony and the undoubted welcome of Henry the Lion,' declared the king. 'Or perhaps we could ride north to reach the Baltic and take ship to the German Ocean.'

Baldwin was dubious about the latter plan. 'It would mean riding many hundreds of miles across turbulent territory. The Polish lands are in turmoil and we would not be welcome amongst them, even as returning Crusaders.'

Robert de Turnham had been equally pessi-

mistic about the idea. 'Sire, as you have discovered from our recent experiences of sea
voyaging, we would be much too late in the
season for safety. To attempt such a long journey
across the northern waters in the depth of winter
would be foolhardy in the extreme.'

The meeting broke up with a decision to wait
until they reached the Hungarian capital, to hear
what their opinion would be.

The king had a cubbyhole to himself on this
vessel, too small to be called a cabin, just a large
box built under the poop. The rest of them
squeezed into other spaces under the aftercastle
and the forecastle, sharing the deck boards with
the dozen crew. None of these spoke a single
word of any language they could recognize,
other than the shipmaster who could manage a
little Latin. The mattresses from the galley had
been lost, along with their armour and most of
their possessions, so new palliasses were provided in Ragusa, along with a change of clothing.

'We'll arrive home like beggars,' muttered
Gwyn, as they huddled under cloaks on the
slowly rolling deck. 'No spoils of war on this
trip, that's for sure.'

John de Wolfe told him what had been said at
the council as they lay on the thin straw bags that
were their beds, and Gwyn wanted to know
more. 'Who's this King Bela, then?'

'A powerful ruler and one of the richest in
Europe, thanks to the minerals and salt in his
country. Thankfully, he's no friend of Henry, the
Holy Roman Emperor, whom we're trying to
avoid.'

The Cornishman digested this and probed again. 'But I heard that he's related to our king. Is that true?'

John turned over with a grunt to relieve the pressure of his hip on the deck boards. 'By marriages, at least. Bela's wife is Margaret of France, who was the widow of Richard's older brother, Henry the Young King who died years ago.'

Gwyn chuckled into his cloak. 'I know of her all right! It was common knowledge that she was William Marshal's mistress.'

He was talking about the Marshal of England, a great warrior and tourney champion.

'Better not voice that about too loudly when we get to Hungary,' advised de Wolfe. 'She is also sister-in-law of Philip of France, which is a point not in our favour!'

Gwyn clucked his disgust with all these imperial entanglements. 'These royal folk are like rabbits in a box, mating with someone different every five minutes! I'm not sure I want to go to Hungary!'

Perhaps God was listening once again.

Though the Lionheart had bribed the shipmaster to carry on sailing through the first night, the second was spent on shore, as they needed food and water. In addition, the helpful southerly wind had freshened markedly during the day and the motion of the *Medusa* became far too lively for much sleep to be had on deck.

They stopped in a bay on the mainland side of the island of Zirje, though the captain informed de Turnham in his halting Latin, that he had wanted to land on the opposite mainland.

'It seems that the wind and the currents made it too difficult to cross the strait,' Robert explained to the other knights. 'He is also worried that tomorrow might bring a worsening of the wind, though, thank St Christopher, there seems no sign of that damned *bora*, which could take us back to Ragusa or even beyond.'

The cold, grey dawn showed them that the shipmaster was right. Once they left the shelter of Zirje, they were hit by a blustery half-gale, which took them towards the north-west, in spite of the crew's efforts to get them back into the narrow channels between the mainland and the offshore islands of Kornat and Pasman.

The cog was far more seaworthy than the galley, but it was hopeless at sailing more than a few points off the wind. By mid-afternoon, the shipmaster admitted that they had no chance now of getting back into the archipelago that lay outside Zara.

As they raced on out into the open sea before the relentless south wind, Richard's admiral, who was best at understanding the captain's garbled speech, relayed the bad news. 'He says there is no hope of getting to Zara, unless you wish to wait for days to get back to it after this gale stops.'

The Lionheart rapidly lost his recent good mood in his frustration at being repeatedly thwarted from getting back to his Norman dominions. After a string of choice oaths, he demanded to know where they were going now.

80

'The shipmaster says that there is another port called Pola further up the Adriatic, on the peninsula of Istria opposite Venice. It is still within the Kingdom of Hungary and in fact, would be nearer King Bela's capital than Zara.'

Slightly appeased, the king grunted a demand to know how long it would take to get there.

'If this wind holds, we should be there this time tomorrow,' replied de Turnham. He decided it would be wiser not to repeat that the captain had added 'If the vessel doesn't founder on the way!'

The rest of that day and the night were yet another miserable time for the weary travellers. The wind grew progressively stronger and as it was dead astern, the *Medusa* pitched rather than rolled, its blunt bow dipping into the waves, then hauling itself up to point at the sky. Big rollers coming up behind them in the narrowing funnel of the Adriatic constantly threatened to 'poop' the vessel. Poor Baldwin of Bethune had a return of his sickness and spent all his time hunched over the scuppers, retching until nothing came up except a trace of bile. At dawn, the cog still raced on, the gale not abating in the slightest, though its direction backed slightly so that it came from the south-east, which was even worse for them.

'If this keeps up, we'll land in Venice, not Hungary,' said de Turnham, as he squatted in the shelter of the aftercastle with the others. 'Though the master has just admitted to me that he has no idea where we are at the moment, only that we are being driven northwards – which any ten-year-old deck boy could have told me!'

'So how are we going to find this Pola place?' demanded de Wolfe.

The admiral shrugged. 'It's in the hands of God and his angels – the shipmaster doesn't know! He's used to hugging the coastline and going ashore every night, so the open sea is a mystery to him.'

Even though the crew had lashed up the sail closely to its yard, the *Medusa* was careering along under a bare pole from the pressure of the wind on its blunt stern and the relentless progress of the rollers that endlessly see-sawed the hull.

Once again, few slept for more than a hour or two that night and Gwyn, with his fisherman's senses, sat up in the early hours and listened for a moment. He knew from de Wolfe's breathing that he too was awake and touched him on his shoulder. 'The wind has dropped a little, but I can smell land!'

Growling, John struggled to a sitting position and sniffed, but smelt nothing but the unwashed bodies around him.

'And I can hear something, too,' grunted Gwyn. 'It sounds like surf on a beach.'

At that moment, there were shouts from the crew on watch and simultaneously, the pitching of the cog ceased and was replaced by a rapid careering motion as the hull was seized by breaking waves and hurled towards the land.

Pandemonium broke out as sleepers awoke and the rest leaped to their feet as the ship was driven on to a muddy shore in the darkness. It heeled over slightly and as it came to rest, the door to the king's cuddy banged open and a stentorian voice overcame even the sound of the gale.

'Jesus and Mary, don't tell me it's another shipwreck!'

SIX

At the first light of dawn, John de Wolfe stood with Gwyn on a stretch of coarse grass above a muddy shore. He had a momentary sensation of all this having happened before, but then realized that instead of a pebbled beach below a wooded hill in Ragusa Bay, they were stranded on the edge of an apparently limitless marsh, which stretched inland for miles. In the far distance, the jagged peaks of snow-covered mountains lined the northern horizon, whilst nearby, gullies and runnels of brown water meandered between reeds and bullrushes.

The survivors were clustered around the king in a ragged group, each clutching a bundle of their personal possessions carried from the *Medusa,* which now sat leaning over on the mud in a couple of feet of water. The wind had dropped markedly as it hit the land, but there was still a stiff breeze strong enough to whip their cloaks about their legs. Robert de Turnham had just squelched up the beach to join them, having been questioning the shipmaster, who had stayed aboard the cog with his crew.

'The man says the vessel is undamaged and he can float it off in a couple of days when the moon brings a higher tide,' he reported. 'He is willing take us back to Pola or Zara if we want to wait.'

King Richard's frustration turned his voice into an angry snarl. 'To hell with that, I'm staying on dry land! Not that this poxy swamp is dry ... wherever it is!'

Baldwin, equally thankful to be off the heaving sea, also wanted to know where they had landed. 'Does the shipman know where this place might be?'

'He says he thinks it is east of Venice, in the marshes beyond the mouth of the Tagliamento. Further east is Istria, which is where Hungary begins.'

The learned clerk, Philip of Poitou, standing shivering in his wet cloak, had a better knowledge of geography that the others. 'Then Aquileia must be hereabouts,' he said. 'At least, it was in Roman times, when it was one of the greatest cities in the world.'

'Can we seek aid there?' demanded the king, his bushy auburn beard jutting dangerously, as his temper shortened.

The clerk shook his head sadly. 'The city was destroyed many centuries ago by Attila the Hun, sire. But the local counts who rule this region still hold the titles of *Advocates of Aquileia,* so there may still be some sort of settlement there.'

The Lionheart nodded brusquely, anxious for action. 'Right, then let us seek out these Advocates and impress upon them that we are Crusaders returning from the Holy Land, deserving of their hospitality and assistance, as the Pope directs all men to provide on pain of excommunication.'

'The Truce of God!' intoned the chaplain reverently, crossing himself.

Baldwin of Bethune, who had been an ambassador to the Flemish Court and knew much about European politics, broke in with a caution. 'We must be careful, sire. These counts now hold their lands in fealty to the Holy Roman Empire, so if Emperor Henry's warnings to watch out for you have reached here, these local lords may present a real danger to us.'

William de L'Etang agreed. 'Our long journey must have made half of Europe aware that you are travelling home with an escort of Templars. And the news of two visits to Corfu and then your generous endowment to Ragusa Cathedral must have spread widely and places you firmly in the Adriatic. I doubt we can slip by them into Hungary without being recognized for who we are.'

'So what do you suggest we do?' asked the king. 'By hook or by crook, we need to reach sanctuary with Henry the Lion in Saxony.' Richard was the supreme tactician when it came to fighting battles, but this particular problem was unfamiliar to him.

'My Lord, our Templar brothers here are the most obvious pointer to our identity,' ventured John de Wolfe. 'If they would discard their revealing surcoats, we could all pose as shipwrecked pilgrims returning from, say the Virgin Mary's house in Ephesus. We all obtained anonymous clothing after the wrecking in Ragusa, so with our long hair and beards that

86

would fit in well with the deceit.'

Richard looked dubious, as his natural desire to flaunt his kingship battled with necessity. 'And who am I supposed to be in this mummer's pageant you suggest?'

The diplomatic Baldwin jumped into the breach, sensing the king's reluctance to hide his royal light under a bushel. 'You could pose as a rich merchant, my lord, with a retinue of a few servants leading a band of pilgrims back to France.'

Richard's mercurial temperament seized on the novelty of this plan, which as he always demanded, made him the leader. 'Very well, I shall call myself Hugo of Tours. First, we shall need horses, if they have such things in this God-forsaken place.'

They looked despondently around at the miles of empty marshland, until one of the Templars spotted thin smoke rising from behind a small mound about a mile to the east.

'We'll try there first, if we can make the natives understand a single word,' commanded the king. 'Philip, have you any notion of what tongue they would speak here?'

The clerk considered this problem. 'I would think that west of here, it would be some dialect of the north of Italy. But we must be in or certainly near Carinthia and the lands of the Archbishop of Salzburg, so the Germanic languages would prevail.'

'And we speak none of them?' replied Richard, sardonically. 'But no doubt money speaks all tongues, given in sufficient quantity!'

Before they set off to walk in search of a habitation, the six Templar knights who still had their surcoats with the distinctive red crosses, reluctantly discarded them. Of the eighteen men, a dozen still had their swords, the rest having lost them in the confusion of two shipwrecks. John still had his under his long grey mantle and Gwyn had kept his battered weapon slung in its scabbard across his broad back.

The king's remark about money opening mouths, led to another ceremony before they moved off the head of the beach. The small treasure chest was opened and Richard directed William to distribute much of the remaining coinage amongst the company.

'We cannot lug this heavy box across Europe,' he announced. 'And it is very likely that we shall be split up at some stage, so I am giving each man sufficient for his sustenance, keeping the remainder for horses and whatever situations may arise.'

Each of the knights received a handful of silver lira which they stuffed into the scrips on their belts, Gwyn and the Templar sergeant being given the same. The rest was distributed for safe keeping between the king's inner circle of clerk, chaplain, admiral, Baldwin, William and de Wolfe. As well as the silver coins from Lucca, there were some heavy gold *bezants*, the more valuable coins from Constantinople. Richard kept many of these for himself, but included a few in the dole to his closest retainers. He secreted his slim coronial circlet and his Great Seal into a wide pocket inside his cloak, then the empty chest was thrown into the nearest gully, stuffed with the discarded Templar garments.

The small band of fugitives then set off across the marshes – it was December the tenth, two months and a day since they had slipped away from Acre.

The smoke came from a miserable hamlet built slightly above the flood level of the plain. Too small to be called a village, the dozen huts thatched with reeds contained a frightened handful of peasants, none of whom could speak or understand anything the travellers said. Terrified by the arrival of almost a score of large foreigners, all that could be gained from the headman was the word 'Aquileia', accompanied by vigorous pointing north-eastwards.

At least there was a track leading away from the hamlet, better than the endless stumbling through reeds and jumping across ditches that they had endured coming from the beach. Within a couple more hours, they had covered about six miles and arrived at a dilapidated town built amongst the crumbling ruins of what had been a vast settlement. There were still columns and walls that marked it as the ancient Roman metropolis, though an odd feature for such a modest town was a large and much more recent basilica with a tall bell tower. What was of more interest to the king's party was the sight of a small priory adjacent to the basilica, built of old red bricks salvaged from the Roman ruins.

Brother Anselm went inside and found someone with whom he could speak Latin and soon, with the stimulus of some of the royal silver, they were being fed in the refectory that catered for the dozen monks. The rich merchant 'Hugo' and his 'steward' Baldwin, offered the prior a fictitious account of their pilgrimage to Ephesus and the more honest account of their latest ship-wreck. They learned that the basilica was the seat of the Patriarch of Aquileia, who was cur-rently in Venice, having been chased out again by the Counts of Gorz, vassals of the Holy Roman Emperor.

The prior informed them that the nearest large town was Gorizia, where Count Englebert III was one of the Advocates, his brother-in-law Meinhart II being the other, residing in the more northerly town of Udine, up towards the edge of the Alps.

The next problem was horses and John de Wolfe and Gwyn volunteered to go with one of the monks to scour the little town for steeds. Though John was unable to either read or write any language, over years of campaigning he had picked up a rudimentary knowledge of dog-Latin, so was able to stumble through some basic words to do with horses. To find enough of them for sale in a place this size was asking a great deal, but they were fortunate in that it was a market day and amongst the goats, sheep and skinny cattle being sold, they found ten horses and four ponies. The monk arranged for the animals to be brought to the priory, where the king grandly dispensed his silver to pay for the overpriced steeds, in spite of the muted protests of his clerk at yet another example of the royal extravagance. It was now about noon, according to the position of the watery sun seen between the scudding clouds.

'How far is this place called Gorizia? Can we ride there before darkness falls?' demanded the Lionheart, who spoke excellent Latin, though he had never bothered to learn a word of the native language of his English kingdom.

He was assured that if they set off at once, they should cover the nineteen miles by time the winter dusk set in, as the remains of the old Roman road was straight and still in fair condition.

The next problem was conveying eighteen bodies on only fourteen horses. The senior Templar, Sir Gerald de Clare, wryly observed that four of his fellow knights could demonstrate the original full title of their Order – *The Poor Soldiers of Christ and the Temple of Solomon* – and ride two to a horse to emphasize their poverty. The Great Seal of the Templars actually depicted two knights squeezed on to the back of a single beast.

They set off, with four of the larger horses carrying a pair of the thinnest knights. None of the mounts had saddles, only a blanket and a simple bridle, but all the riders were very experienced and they had little trouble in keeping up a steady pace on the flat, straight track, where much of the old Roman paving was still in place.

'Thank God for a horse under my legs, instead of a heaving ship,' de Wolfe exclaimed, as he rode alongside Gwyn. Their steeds were skinny, but seemed healthy, as were the mountain ponies

91

ridden by the clerk, chaplain and a couple of the Templars. The king naturally had the best of the beasts and rode proudly at their head, as if he was riding to battle at the head of his army.

As they rode, John could not help comparing this journey with riding through the leafy lanes of his native Devon. Though there was a large area of tide-marsh along the estuary of the River Exe, its green turf was nothing like this vast expanse of greyish-brown reeds and dead grass. There were certainly no snow-covered peaks standing on the horizon like jagged teeth – at home, he would have seen the rolling heaths of distant Dartmoor, with their curious granite tors heaped up on the skyline. Having been away for so much of his adult life, he was never homesick as such – with Matilda as a wife, home was a place to be avoided. But as he grew older, he found that the places of his childhood and youth crept more often into his consciousness. As he rode across this dreary marshland, he saw in his mind the manor of Stoke-in-Teignhead where he was born, in its little dell a short distance from the River Teign. The sea cliffs were a mile away, as was the sandy harbour of Teignmouth. He could see again his parents and his brother and sister – and unbidden, the face of the beautiful Hilda came to him, the daughter of the reeve at their other manor at Holcombe, just up the coast.

'Don't fall asleep, Sir John! Without a saddle, you'll fall off that bloody horse!' Gwyn's rough voice jerked him out of his reverie. The big Cornishman looked after him better than any wife, whether it be saving him from an Irish pike or a Saracen's sword – or just preventing him from falling from his horse. As he pulled his attention back to his present surroundings, he wondered if Gwyn's brand of Cornish-Welsh had ever been heard here since time began.

The prior in Aquileia had been somewhat optimistic about reaching Gorizia before dark, but the city with its prominent castle on a hill was still visible in the distance just before the last of the day faded. Starlight and a gibbous moon low on the horizon got them to the gate in the city wall, which as usual was firmly closed at nightfall. However, there was an inn outside, which was used to catering for latecomers. At the sight of Hugo's silver, the taverner, who spoke a halting Italian variety of Latin, was happy to accommodate them. He showed them a large loft which occupied the whole upper storey and said that he could supply straw-bags for sleeping. Their horses were fed and tethered in a paddock at the back and the enterprising landlord sold them another four animals to make up the numbers.

Inside the wooden building, they were given a meal of indifferent potage followed by boiled mutton and beans, washed down with a raw local wine.

After eating, the king called them to a conference around the firepit. 'So far, we have made good progress, but where do we go from here? The choice is still either to ride east into Hungary – or try to cross the mountains and reach Moravia and then Bohemia, where Prince

Ottakar is at odds with Emperor Henry and should look sympathetically on us. From there we can easily move into Saxony.'

John de Wolfe's knowledge of Central Europe was not enough to follow this and certainly Gwyn had never heard of either of those countries, but Baldwin spoke up. 'Given that we are unsure of the reception we might get from King Bela – and the very long journey from here to Estergom, I suggest that we consider riding north, even though it is likely to be more hostile country.'

William de L'Etang agreed with Baldwin, though Robert de Turnham was very dubious about crossing into Austria, given the bad blood that had arisen in Palestine between Richard and Duke Leopold. The Lionheart had thrown down Leopold's banner from the walls of Acre and had refused him a share of the loot, on the grounds that the Austrian had contributed little to the successful siege. De Wolfe had nothing to contribute to the discussion, but could sense that the Lionheart was already set on trying to get directly to Saxony.

'Sire, are we to make ourselves known to the ruler of this city, or is that too dangerous?' asked William de L'Etang. 'Some local knowledge of the route and perhaps the help of a guide would be of great help to us.'

They discussed this for a while, Robert de Turnham and a few others feeling that it would be too dangerous to approach a vassal of the Empire, in case orders had already reached them that the royal party was to be seized on sight.

However, the idea attracted Richard, who seemed to find it hard to imagine that his kingly status would not overawe a mere count.

'Baldwin, dear friend, you are the most diplomatic among us. Take this ruby ring I purchased in Ragusa and go up to the castle to present it with my compliments as a gift to this local chieftain. Your silver tongue will no doubt persuade him to offer us safe conduct and guidance tomorrow.' Richard pulled off the wide gold band carrying the precious stone and passed it to his courtier.

With misgivings on the part of some of the others, the man from Bethune sought out the innkeeper and, with a few more coins, persuaded him to take him to the town gate, where yet more silver got them entry through a wicket.

The group waited uneasily in the gloom of the tavern for his return. They were all dog-tired after being shipwrecked and then walking and riding across miles of unfamiliar countryside.

John de Wolfe, though a phlegmatic and somewhat unimaginative man, pondered on their being adrift in potentially hostile territory. They had only the clothes they wore, a few weapons and a pouchful of money, with many hundreds of miles between them and home. Though he had spent many months, indeed years, in foreign lands, he had always been part of an army, not isolated like this, with the great responsibility of protecting his king.

After two hours, John began to wonder if Baldwin had been seized at the castle, but finally he appeared at the door, looking anxious and agitated as he hurried to bend his knee to the king.

'My Lord, dark though it is, I think we should leave at once. I do not trust the man I met to keep his word!'

SEVEN

By the afternoon of the next day, the weary fugitives had reached Udine, the main town of the province. This was another twenty miles to the north, where the stark outline of the Julian Alps were now clearly within view. The town, like so many, consisted of a fortress built on a central mound, surrounded by burgages inside an outer wall. This time, the gates were open, but today Richard was more cautious and sent William de L'Etang and seven others inside on foot to seek an inn, whilst he and the rest of the party remained outside at a tavern built amongst the straggle of dwellings that overflowed the city boundary. 'When you are settled, come back and lead us to a different hostelry, for we are too conspicuous in one group,' he commanded.

William, Geoffrey de Clare and six of his Templars strode away while the king and his remaining escort waited uneasily in the outer tavern. They sprawled in exhaustion on benches in the taproom, where Baldwin used Latin mixed with miming signs to order ale and food from a surly potman.

'There seems no sign of pursuit, sire,' observed John de Wolfe, as they used their knives to attack thick bread trenchers covered with gristly boiled pork and fried onions. 'I feared that we would have been seized before we could leave Gorizia last night.'

The Lionheart extended his right hand to look at the ruby ring, which Baldwin had brought back from his abortive visit to Count Englebert the previous evening. The courtier again wished that the king would not flash such a striking jewel around in public.

'He sounded an honourable man, given the circumstances,' declared Richard. 'I've got my ring back and we still have our freedom.'

Their precipitate departure from Gorizia the previous evening had been in response to Baldwin's urgent concerns. He had been granted an audience with the count and offered him the ring as a goodwill gift from the rich merchant 'Hugo of Tours' as an overture to requesting a guide for the journey north through the mountains. However, Englebert had handed it back and sardonically told Baldwin that he was well aware that 'Hugo' was Richard, King of England, for whom half of Europe was searching. Fully expecting to be seized on the spot, Baldwin was astounded when Engelbert told him that both his party and the Lionheart himself were free to depart. The count declared that although he had the duty to arrest him on behalf of his Emperor, the honour King Richard had done him by offering such a valuable gift, made it unchivalrous for him to lay hands upon him in his own city.

When Baldwin brought this news back to the inn, there was no demur when the Lionheart

ordered an immediate evacuation, in case Engelbert changed his mind. Paying their bill and
forfeiting a night's lodging, they took to their
horses and hurriedly rode off in the moonlight,
feeling their way along the high road to the
north. At least every man now had his own
horse, and when Gorizia was five miles behind
them, they turned aside into a lonely wooded
glen. Here they rolled themselves into their
cloaks and lay on the damp turf. Though
exhausted, they slept fitfully until dawn, with
ears cocked for sounds of pursuit. Unfed, they
set off again at first light and still on a good
Roman road, reached Udine soon after midday.

They now rested in the tavern outside the
town, where to Gwyn's relief, he found that
being now in a Germanic region, the inn provided ale as well as wine, even if it tasted quite
different to the English variety. Though hardened soldiers, used to extremes of discomfort
and privation, the two months at sea and little
sleep for several nights had taken their toll on
John de Wolfe and his squire. They slumped on
hard benches in the tavern, waiting to hear from
William about him having obtained accommodation within the city. They drank a few pints
of the local brew and promised themselves an
early retreat to the mattresses laid out in the loft
above, as the early winter dusk was already setting in under an overcast sky.

'God alone knows what's ahead of us on this
journey,' growled de Wolfe. 'So we'd best get as
much rest as we can now.'

Both he and Gwyn had always subscribed to

the campaigner's principle that you should eat, sleep and fornicate whenever the opportunity arose, as you never knew when the next chance might come along – especially as perhaps it would never come, given the uncertainties of warfare.

There was also a single room for hire at this inn and Richard had installed himself in it, feeling that even a token display of his true status was long overdue for a king. He had taken himself to it to have a meal brought and then get some sleep, leaving the others of his diminished group in the taproom. Baldwin of Bethune and Philip of Poitou sat on the bench next to John and worried about their royal master's inability to keep a low profile.

'He grossly overpaid the landlord for the room and food,' fretted Baldwin. 'And when he handed over the coin, I saw the man's eyes glint when he saw the profusion of gold and jewels on his fingers.'

'It makes it hard to sustain this pretence that we are travelling pilgrims when our lord persists in such ostentation,' agreed the royal clerk. 'I wish he would keep those damned rings in his pouch.'

Their grumbling was suddenly interrupted by Gwyn, the one with the keenest ears. 'What's going on outside?' he growled. 'I hear the clinking of harness and the rattle of steel?'

'Probably a messenger from William telling us he's found somewhere better to stay the night,' grunted de Wolfe.

Before he could get up to investigate, a figure

appeared in the street doorway. A tall man, dressed in a mailed hauberk and a Norman-style helmet with a nose guard, stared intently around the room. As the 'pilgrims' scrambled to their feet, the new arrival held up a hand to placate them, as his eyes roved across their faces.

'Which one of you is Hugo the merchant?' he demanded. To their surprise, he spoke in French, with an accent that was undoubtedly from Normandy.

Baldwin, eyeing the swords that they had stacked in a corner of the room, took a step towards the newcomer. 'Our master is resting in another room,' he replied, indicating a door in the back wall. 'But who are you, sir, who speaks the language of my homeland so well?'

The Norman turned and slammed the door shut, but not before the men inside saw two armed soldiers standing in the street. 'I am Roger of Argentan, a servant of Count Meinhard, the ruler of this region. He has sent me to investigate reports of travellers coming to his city. I need to speak with your leader.'

The inner door opened and the Lionheart appeared, disturbed by the raised voices. 'Who wants me? And who are you?' he demanded of the man in armour.

If they had been surprised by the man's accent, they were even more astonished when he dropped to his knee before Richard and bent his head in obeisance. 'My Lord King, it is many years since I saw you that Christmas at Argentan, but I know full well that you are no pilgrim merchant, but Richard Coeur de Lion!'

Two nights later, the depleted band of exhausted fugitives had their first undisturbed sleep since the storm in the Adriatic.

With only ten of them left, they had walked their tired horses up the long track to reach the monastery of Moggio, high above the long valley that cleft the Julian Alps from west to east. Carrying the old *Via Julia Augusta* alongside a wide, stony river bed, the Val Canale joined Italy to Austria, with only the relatively easy Pontebba Pass as a barrier at its western end.

After once again fleeing from Udine, the king and his small party had spent the hours of darkness hiding deep in the forest off the high road. They rode all the next day, afraid to visit inns for food, their horses having to survive on cropping the sparse winter grass in woodland clearings. All they had to eat was some coarse bread that their inconspicuous chaplain and clerk were sent to buy in one of the villages through which they had passed. There was the daunting prospect of yet another night spent in the open, this time well into the cold mountains. Thankfully it had not yet snowed, though plenty lay high up on the peaks on either side of the valley. They survived that night, burrowing under drifts of dry leaves beneath the trees and next day, riding from dawn till dusk, they covered many more miles. As the light faded, the sight of a monastery high on its rock on the valley side was too tempting to be ignored.

'For the Blessed Christ's sake, we are returning Crusaders, under the Pope's protection!' shouted Richard from his horse. 'If we can't trust holy men to honour the Truce of God, then I'll stop saying my prayers!'

As they turned off the main road and began to climb the last mile up the mountain track, the cautious Baldwin suggested that they first try their 'Hugo the pilgrim' ruse, in case the monks had a strong political loyalty and the chaplain agreed with him.

'The bishops of Bamberg and Salzburg are masters of huge areas of Carinthia and Austria,' advised Anselm. 'They are almost certainly sympathetic to both Duke Leopold and the Emperor.'

When they reached the monastery, the abbot and his dozen monks seemed to accept their cover story without question and they were given food and a place to sleep in the guest house of the grim edifice. In return, Richard made a generous donation to the abbey coffers, the size of which again made Baldwin and the others concerned that he was drawing unnecessary attention to himself. After the meal, they sat with the abbot and some of the monks in the warming room, the only chamber to have a fire between November and April. The abbot was keen to hear details of their pilgrimage and again it was fortunate that Anselm had actually been to Ephesus and visited the alleged House of the Virgin, so that he was able to spin a convincing tale. They went on to describe their intention of returning to France by way of Moravia and the difficulties of travelling in this region when none of their number spoke German. It was either this friendly conversation or the size of Hugo's gift that must have prompted the abbot to offer them the services of an orphan youth who had been in Moggio since being left there as a baby.

'He has no interest in serving God as a monk and if he stays here, he will always remain a lay-brother,' explained the abbot. 'This boy, Joldan, is a clever lad, having picked up Latin from us, as well as having his native German. It seems a waste for him to spend the rest of his life herding goats and hoeing turnips.'

The abbot paused to top up Richard's cup from a jug of hot, spiced wine, before continuing. 'Joldan has become impressed by travellers' tales of life in the cities and would like nothing better than the chance to seek his fortune in one. He is a wily lad, and would survive and prosper wherever he settled. You could drop him with a few coins at somewhere like Villach or even Judenberg. He can always find his way back here if he so wishes.'

Joldan was brought before them – a wiry boy of about twelve, with a thin, foxy face in which quick, intelligent eyes roved around warily. The old abbot put the proposition to him and the lad eagerly accepted the chance to escape this mountain prison for his imagined paradise of urban life. Richard agreed to take the boy with them when they left in the morning.

'He can ride up behind you, Gwyn,' he added jovially, the royal spirits restored after a good meal and the prospect of a bed for the night. 'Your horse will never notice his featherweight, compared to your bulk!'

The Cornishman grinned amiably, as with two boys of his own back in Exeter, he was quite happy to play godfather for a few days. After prayers in the abbey church, to which Anselm willingly contributed, the travellers retired to the guest dormitory and before collapsing on to their pallets, the chaplain led them in private prayers for the safety of their compatriots left behind in Udine.

The king was quite sanguine about their prospects in captivity. 'Almost all were Templars, returning from the Crusade,' he declared. 'They belong to a powerful order and will come to no harm. I am the only one that is being sought by those bastards Philip, Henry and Leopold!'

'What about William de L'Etang?' worried Baldwin. 'He's no Templar.'

'But he's another staunch soldier of Christ, under the protection of the Pope. And his rich family will have no trouble in raising a ransom, if needs be.'

They had lost the other part of their group to the searchers sent by Count Meinhard to scour the city inns for King Richard, as a fast messenger had just come from his cousin Englebert to say that the royal party had been in Gorizia and were probably headed for Udine. Only good fortune or the Grace of God had directed one of the searchers, Roger of Argentan, to the hostel outside the south gate. The Lionheart explained that as a youth, he had several times visited Argentan, a lordship in southern Normandy, with his parents, King Henry and Queen Eleanor. Though he could not remember him, this Roger must have been present at one of their Christmas festivities and had retained some lasting loyalty to the Angevin royal line. In fact, Roger had become quite emotional whilst on his knees before Richard, weeping and imploring him to ride away at once to avoid capture – even offering him his own superior horse.

He promised to return to his master Meinhard – whose niece Roger had married – and tell him that 'Hugo' was genuinely a rich merchant, not the King of England. It was too late to save the other group, surprised by another search party of the Count, who even if they had tried to resist, could not have got past the city gates which had been closed against them.

Now, in the early morning three days later, Richard Coeur de Lion led his party of ten men and a boy out under the arch of the abbey gatehouse and down towards the bleak valley that cut through the Alps. It was December the thirteenth, twelve days before Christ Mass.

EIGHT

The next three days went well, apart from increasingly cold weather. The snow held off, though the interminably grey skies showed no break, with cloud often obscuring the mountains on either side. The horses, some of whom had been exchanged at the abbey for better ones, performed well, covering over twenty miles each day on the ancient road. The small group in their travel-worn pilgrims' attire and with the small lad clinging on to Gwyn's broad back, drew little attention and certainly offered no hint that this was a royal cavalcade.

They stopped outside villages and sent Joldan ahead to buy bread, cheese and sometimes meat pies from the stalls and to seek any news passing along the *Via Julia* proclaiming their presence in the area. At dusk, the lad would try to find an inn that could accommodate the travellers or, failing that, a farmer who, for a silver coin, would let them sleep on the hay in his barn.

Eventually, they came out from amongst the high mountains into a countryside of hills, valleys and lakes beyond Villach. The abbot had described the route they needed to take to pass northwards through Carinthia and Austria to reach the border with Moravia, also telling the lad Joldan the names of the towns they needed to pass through, finally skirting Vienna to cross the Danube.

The approaching winter kept most people off the road, but there was sufficient traffic for a band of pilgrims not to look out of place, even if they did have a rather military bearing as they rode along. After the small towns of Feldkirchen and St Veit, the next significant place ahead of them, according to Joldan's latest enquiry in a baker's shop, was Friesach. From what they told him about the place, the boy was looking forward to seeing a metropolis of many hundred inhabitants. It had a silver mine and a mint, producing the famous Friesacher *pfennig* and as the boy had never before been more than five miles away from lonely Moggio, he was excited at the prospect. Gwyn was sorry that he possessed no more than a dozen words of Latin, as he would like to have talked to the lad who had been clinging to him like a limpet these past few days.

In the event, Friesach turned out to be another – and worse – disaster. They neared the town in the early twilight, seeing in the distance yet another castle on a hill. The dense forest through which they had been passing gave way to farmed strip fields for the final two miles, but on the right-hand side of the track, a tongue of woodland survived, still joined to the mass of dark trees that rolled away to the horizon.

Richard was in the lead as usual, the ten tired horses now at walking pace, after trotting for much of the afternoon. His tall figure sat erect, his long fair hair curling from under his broad-brimmed hat, tied with a lace under his chin. Suddenly, he held up an imperious hand and reined in his black mare, the small cavalcade coming to an abrupt halt behind him. 'Horsemen ahead!' he snapped. 'Coming at a trot towards us.'

The anxious eyes of the group stared ahead at a cloud of dust half a mile away, thrown up from the dry road by a large number of hooves.

'I fear this is not healthy for us!' called Robert de Turnham, from the third rank behind the king. 'It looks as if we are going to have a fight on our hands.'

'There are well over a score of them,' shouted de Wolfe. 'We cannot prevail against so many, warriors though we are!'

As usual, Baldwin took the initiative. 'The king must be saved, above all other considerations!' he cried. 'Sire, ride off into the forest there, the rest of us will delay them until you have vanished into the trees.'

'What? And leave you to be vanquished!' roared Richard, turning on his horse's back, red in the face with anger. 'Never! The King of England does not run away like a scared rabbit!'

'My Lord, you are all that matters in this venture,' Baldwin beseeched desperately. 'If you are taken, God alone knows what will happen to Normandy and England without you. We are of no consequence, we can fight and if seized, we can be ransomed. Your adversaries have no interest in us, it is only you they seek! Save yourself, sire!'

His voice was vibrant with urgency and John de Wolfe added to it, 'Whatever is to happen, it had better be very soon!' he yelled. 'They'll be upon us in a few moments. If he goes now, they may never guess that the king was here at all.'

In Richard's mind, there flashed a vision of Philip of France tearing into all his possessions in France and of his treacherous brother John ruining the prosperity of England, as well as the ignominy of capture, imprisonment and possibly death at the hands of his jealous rivals. Wheeling his horse around, he made for the edge of the forest, a mere twenty yards way.

'Then God be with you, brave friends! If you defeat these swine, I'll rejoin you somehow. I'll take the boy, otherwise I'll not know enough of this heathen language to beg a crust of bread!'

Baldwin, ever the organizer, shouted for Gwyn to follow the king, with Joldan clinging to his back. 'And you go with them, de Wolfe!' he yelled. 'May God help you to guard our lord king well!'

NINE

The king never did rejoin the others, as an hour later, Gwyn cautiously threaded his way back through a mile of trees to the road and found it deserted. Apart from a confused pattern of many hooves having milled about in the dusty track, there was no sign of a fight and thankfully, no dried bloodstains on the ground.

The Cornishman saw from crushed undergrowth and ripped branches, that there had been a search amongst the trees for a few hundred yards from the road, but with such a vast area of forest, it would have been a hopeless task in the failing light, even if the searchers had known that Richard had been present and had escaped that way.

Gwyn made his way back to where he had left the three remaining fugitives, using as a guide the small stream that they had followed, using it as a path to obscure their hoof prints.

'I fear they have been taken, my lord,' he reported when he reached the small clearing where the king sat on a fallen tree in the deepening dusk. 'But there is no sign of violence and I suspect that they were unharmed.'

Richard nodded sadly. 'If I know Baldwin, he would have spent half an hour trying to convince them that *he* was Hugo the merchant, to give us as long as possible to get clear.'

'What do we do now, Sire?' asked John de Wolfe, from the edge of the clearing. He was hobbling the three horses with their bridles, so that they could graze in the clearing and drink at the stream without wandering away.

'Carry on as before, that's all we can do,' replied Richard, stretching his long legs. 'It's almost dark, so we must sleep if we can and then take stock in the morning. Moravia is our target, but all I know is that it's north of here – though only God knows how far!'

Thankfully Gwyn, always fond of his stomach, had kept back half a loaf of coarse rye bread from their previous meal and also had a lump of hard cheese, the size and texture of half a brick.

They shared this and drank water from the stream, using cow-horns which the lad had bought at one of the towns on the road.

Joldan seemed to be enjoying the adventure, especially as it was only now he had gathered that Hugo was no merchant, but the King of England. He was enthralled to be in such grand company, even if he had never previously heard of England. Richard was the only one able to converse with the boy, as neither John nor Gwyn had sufficient Latin and he now explained to the boy the predicament they were in. Joldan seemed to hold no allegiance to his own Germanic rulers and entered into the spirit of their escape plans.

'This is the smallest court that has ever attended upon me,' declared the Lionheart in a jocular tone, looking at his three courtiers in the gloom. 'At dawn, we must find some way of getting around this poxy town and continuing on our way.'

As he lay under the stars, his mind roved over a dozen problems, none of which would be solved until he could get home. Richard also wondered where his wife Berengaria was now. He knew he had neglected her shamefully and mildly chided himself for it, but he was a busy man and it was hardly a love match on his side, though she seemed to adore him. The queen had tended him solicitously when he had the recurrent fever that laid him low in Acre. He determined to shower her with gifts when they next met, though he could not promise that he would spend much time with her. She had never been to England, the country of which she was now queen – and if he had but known it, she never would.

Then his restless thoughts moved to wondering how they had been surprised by such a large, organized band today. They had been lucky in Udine to get away with half their contingent, but now it seemed impossible, without a miracle, for just three men and a boy to cross the rest of these hostile lands to safety in either Hungary or Moravia. He crossed himself in the darkness and began to pray for such a miracle as the cold night air began to bite into his bones.

The following days became a blur in John's mind, an endless journey through forested valleys, around towns and through small villages

113

huddled down ready for the winter. After circuitously making their way through the forest back to the road well beyond Friesach, they had learned to avoid any large settlements, where other law officers and state officials might be waiting, now aware that somewhere, Richard Coeur de Lion was on the loose.

It would be some time before the king learned that the ambush in Friesach had been carried out by one of Duke Leopold's barons, Friedrich of Pettau. One of the many swift messengers sent out by the Counts of Gorz had reached Salzburg, where the wily Friedrich guessed that the fugitive king must be somewhere on the main road north and hastened across country to intercept the returning Crusaders at Freisach. Now the sadly diminished royal party persisted in their routine of sending the lad ahead to buy food in villages and seeking a safe place to spend the night, now more often in farm barns than the more risky inns. Since the king's retinue had shrunk to two men and a boy, all pretence at royal protocol had vanished, though Gwyn and de Wolfe still addressed the king as respectfully as ever.

The nights were bitingly cold, though most days were mild enough in the weak sunshine. The only snow they had seen so far was a few flurries swirling in the east wind, but the mornings now showed ice on the puddles in the track.

'By my reckoning, sire, it will be the day of Christ's Mass very soon,' observed John, as they rode along some days later. 'But there'll be no holly branches above the door for us this year!'

Richard, huddled in his cloak and large hat against the chill breeze, translated this into Latin at the top of his voice for the benefit of Joldan.

The lad replied in the same language and Richard laughed. 'That comes of being brought up in a monastery! The boy knows every date in the Christian calendar ... He says the Feast of Our Lord's birth is now only seven nights away.'

According to Joldan's enquiries at a village pie stall, the last town they had skirted was Neunkirchen, with Vienna only a day's ride away, but that night, the king was seized with a recurrence of the dysentery which had plagued him intermittently for months, prostrating him for several weeks before they left Acre. Now he spent half the night squatting behind the barn of a solitary farm, where they had bought accommodation in the hayloft. Even in the icy conditions, his brow was bathed in sweat and he groaned at the colic in his guts. Between these bouts, John de Wolfe and Gwyn hovered over him solicitously, though there was nothing useful which they could do to aid him.

'Damn these bowels of mine,' snarled Richard. 'A year of that Arabic food has done this, unless Saladin has somehow managed to poison me!'

John thought this unlikely as the Saracen leader had even sent presents of fruit to Richard when he was ill, in a curious gesture of mutual respect between deadly enemies.

By morning, the Lionheart had recovered somewhat, when pale and silent, he climbed on his horse and led them off once again. Some time back, they had bought saddles at a horse fair in one of the villages they had passed through, so the riding was easier. The boy still clung on behind Gwyn, but now he had a folded blanket to sit on behind the cantle.

Richard still had to stop at intervals and strain himself behind a bush at the side of the road. That afternoon, he was spectacularly sick, vomiting the bread and cheese bought for their dinner.

'We must get a decent bed for him tonight, not burrow into a heap of straw like rats,' growled John to his henchman. 'Whatever the risk we must seek a hostelry somewhere.'

Scraping together his pitifully few words of Latin, aided by gestures, he managed to convey this to Joldan while the king was again crouched in the undergrowth. The sharp young fellow nodded his understanding and an hour later left them in a copse of alder while he ran off to a village seen a mile ahead of them.

They could see the smoke of a city ahead of them, with a large river to their right meandering past it in a number of channels.

The king, pale and shivering, but determined to put on an air of normality, gestured to the distant collection of wooden buildings, with a vaguely seen palace in the centre. 'That has to be Vienna, standing on such a river,' he muttered. 'A miserable-looking place, not even a city wall to protect that bastard Leopold's court!'

Had he but known it then, a city wall would soon be built, paid for with Leopold's share of Richard's ransom money.

* * *

As far as John could make out from the German boy, the village was called Erdberg, one of the several hamlets dotted around Vienna. This southern one, near the western bank of one of the river channels, seemed to consist mainly of a large market, a cattle pound and a wooden church, surrounded by a few dozen mean dwellings. Judging by the tattered condition of the thatched roofs and the squalid middens between the cottages, Erdberg had very little civic pride.

There were several inns and taverns, consistent with the village's function as a place of agricultural business, much of which was transacted in alehouses. Under cover of twilight, Joldan led them to an inn in a side lane off the main street. It was a poor place, one big room with a central firepit inside a ring of whitewashed stones. A few rough-looking men were standing around the fire, drinking from pottery mugs and they made way for the newcomers when they entered. Joldan had already told the landlord, a remarkably thin man of consumptive appearance, that the guests were three French pilgrims returning home – and that the leader was ill with a flux of his bowels. Richard certainly looked ill, even worse than the ailing landlord. Two of the patrons at the fire dragged a bench forward and gestured for Richard to sit near the warmth, recognizing that he was seriously sick. They attempted to talk to him, but their thick German only caused him to smile wanly at them and shrug his non-comprehension. Joldan stepped into the breach and even John could gather that he was telling them that their master was ill, after the long journey from visiting holy shrines in the East.

At this, a fat woman waddled from a back door leading to the yard behind. She caught the lad's explanation and in a motherly fashion, pointed to the door, obviously telling him where the privy was situated, whenever he was in dire need of it. Through Joldan's request, the woman brought them some food, though all the king could eat was some hot potage and some bread. The others sat at a trestle and wolfed down a large meal of boiled beans, mutton and onions, followed by bread and cheese.

After they had eaten, their young translator had a long conversation with the fat woman, who turned out to be the emaciated landlord's mother. Given the poor state of Richard, she told the lad that his master could sleep alone in the hay above the stables, where their own three horses were now confined, rather than in the communal loft over the taproom.

John saw him safely up the wide steps and got him bedded down in the soft hay, though the landlady, who had become maternal over the plight of the handsome foreigner, brought him a hessian sack to stuff with hay and a coarse blanket. When their sovereign was as comfortable as possible, they left him, but Gwyn announced his intention of spending the night in the stall with the horse below, to make sure that nothing unwelcome occurred during the night. John offered to share the vigil with him, but Gwyn was adamant.

'I'll be quite happy alongside my old gelding

here,' he said with an amiable grin. 'I've got quite fond of the old nag after all these miles – and when our master needs the privy, he may need a helping hand down those stairs, the state he's in.'

In fact, the night passed uneventfully, though Gwyn reported that he had to make a few journeys with the King of England to the stinking shanty that housed the privy pit. By morning, Richard was still weak, but able to eat some gruel. He went back to the stable loft and lay quietly for the rest of the day, Gwyn taking him some more food about noon. Later, he sat drinking the passable ale with de Wolfe in the bar-room, though the bar was nothing more than a plank laid across two empty casks.

'The last thing we needed was for our lord to fall ill like this,' growled Gwyn, using the back of his hand to wipe the ale that dripped from his drooping moustaches. Though he normally had no beard, the privations of the past weeks had allowed a profuse ginger growth to sprout from his lower jaw.

John glumly nodded his agreement. 'With Christ knows how many hundreds of miles between us and home, it was bad enough with a fit man. How we are going to manage it now, I just do not know!'

'He seems better today after resting,' observed Gwyn, hopefully. 'Thank Saint Christopher that we have the boy with us – without him, we would never have got this far, let alone contemplated getting all the way to England.'

John took a large swallow of ale and looked

out of the street door, which had just opened to let in a farmer who smelt strongly of pigs. Beyond him he could see that it was beginning to snow. 'That's another problem – Joldan! What's going to happen to him? We said we would drop him off at a town way back nearer Moggio. We've already brought him to this damned Vienna place – are we going to drag the poor lad all across Europe with us? Perhaps your good wife would like to adopt him when we get to Exeter!'

Gwyn shrugged. 'He seems quite content to tag along with us. Where is he, by the way? I haven't seen him since we ate at first light?'

John squinted through the slatted shutter at the big white snowflakes whispering to the ground. 'I trust he will be safe in this weather. He said he was going to get some provender for our journey, hoping that we can set off again tomorrow. He said the market should have some dried meat, as well as cheese and oatmeal.'

'Has he got money? I've not yet touched any of that which the king divided between us.'

John nodded. 'Richard gave him coins from his own pouch. Too lavishly, as usual. He seems to have no idea of how much things cost.'

Hours later, Joldan had not returned and Gwyn fretted over him so much that John sent him out to look for the lad. He returned an hour later, saying that there was no sign of him, even though he had walked every lane and alley in Erdberg. 'There seems nowhere for him to have vanished into. Apart from miserable dwellings and a few alehouses, the only other places are

120

the market hall and a long building, which seems full of hunting dogs, by the noise coming from it.'

They went out to the stable to report the loss of their guide to the king. Richard was concerned, as the boy was their only means of communication with the locals. 'We must wait another day, to see if he returns,' he decided. 'I am feeling much improved, thank God. We must move from here first thing the day after tomorrow, whether he returns or not.'

By means of gestures and miming, they managed to tell the buxom landlady that Joldan had gone away, and that they would stay two more nights. In the morning there was still no sign of him and reluctantly, they gave up any hope of seeing him again.

'No doubt the attractions of the dismal city have seduced him,' grunted John. 'I suppose we must be grateful to him for getting us as far as this.'

When they went to tell the Lionheart about the loss of their young navigator, Richard decided he was well enough to get up and sit near the fire in the taproom. 'I'll have to be up and about by tomorrow,' he declared. 'We must be on our way, it's but four days to Christ Mass now. At this rate, it will be Easter before we reach home.'

When they reminded him that Joldan had gone out to buy food for the journey, Richard advised them to do the same, ready for their departure next day. Again he gave them a dozen silver coins from his scrip, disregarding their protests that they could buy half the village with that number.

Rather reluctantly, they left him near the fire, where the motherly landlady thrust a wire fork into his hand and some slices of mutton, to grill against the embers. Though Gwyn secretly grinned at the sight, de Wolfe looked rather shocked at the sight of the monarch of the richest lands in Europe being turned into a kitchen boy.

They checked on their horses in the stable and found that John's grey mare had a loose shoe. After some pantomime with the ten-year-old who mucked out and fed the beasts, he led them through a powdering of snow on the ground to a farrier in a nearby lane where they left the horse to have the shoe renailed, while they went to the market. This was a large ramshackle shed in the main street, filled with a chaotic jostling of workmen, wives and urchins, all bargaining and buying a variety of produce. Some was being sold from stalls and booths, but mostly from peasants and old women sitting on the ground, with their wares all about them. Live geese, ducks and hens were alongside cheeses, river fish, meat, rye bread, bags of rough-milled flour and some winter vegetables.

With much pointing and gesturing, together with the display of quartered coins, Gwyn bought bread, cheese, and smoked beef and pork that would keep for many days in this cold weather. Together with a small skin of local wine, which like the food, was probably double the cost to them as foreigners, they made their way back to the farrier and picked up their mare, now with a restored hoof.

As they walked the animal back along the back lane towards the inn, Gwyn suddenly stopped. 'I hear harness jingling and men shouting!' he said, his big head tilted to catch the sounds. Since Udine, such noises had a sinister significance. 'I'll go ahead and see what's going on!'

De Wolfe put out a hand to stop him. Giving him the bridle of his mare, he pulled up the hood of his grey cloak to shield his face. 'No, that red hair and bush of a beard stands out a mile! I'll go, you stay in the shelter of this hut and wait.'

With an ominous presentiment of disaster in his mind, John crossed the lane to another muddy alley opposite and made his way back towards the tavern from another direction. Standing unobtrusively on the corner, he looked down towards the inn and his worst fears were confirmed. A dozen mounted men and a similar number on foot were clustered outside the front door. They all had some sort of uniform, short green jerkins and brown breeches, with round iron helmets on their heads. The ones on horses carried swords or maces and the foot soldiers had *guisarmes*, like a billhook on a pole. To the rear of the armed men, two more elaborately dressed courtiers sat on horses, one each side of an august, portly man on a white mare. He was dressed in a fur-trimmed cloak and had a gold chain around his neck.

John's horror was increased when he saw that one of the soldiers was holding Joldan, gripping him by the hair and forcing him to look towards the entrance to the inn. The lad had a black eye and bruises on his face and it was all John could do to restrain himself from a hopeless attempt to rescue the boy.

There was much shouting and jostling amongst the gape-mouthed onlookers who had materialized from somewhere. Then a more concerted shout went up and the soldiers stepped back a little from the doorway as two more men, one with a wide, flat cap with a large feather, came out, escorting an all-too-familiar figure between them. An icy hand seemed to reach inside John's chest as he saw it was his king. A feeling of utter failure swept over him as he saw Richard, standing erect and proud, being taken to a waiting horse. The man with the feathered cap attempted to help him into the saddle, but the Lionheart pushed him aside imperiously and, in spite of his previous weakness, hauled himself up on to the horse's back.

All the escort now closed around the prisoner and the whole group moved off towards the main street, roughly pushing the gaping crowd out of the way. As they disappeared from view, John de Wolfe was left standing in bitter anguish, the realization of his own failure weighing down his conscience like a ton of lead. He berated himself silently. He should have been there to save his king, to fight to the death if need be. Never would he forgive himself for leaving the great man alone, especially when he was ill. With leaden feet, he turned and trudged back to his squire.

'Our king is taken, Gwyn! I should have stayed to fight them, though there were more than a score!'

The Cornishman was too aghast to answer and stood staring at his master, his normally ruddy face pale as John spoke again.

'So we are alone, good friend! We must make the best of it, as there is nothing we can do for him now.'

On 28 December 1192, the Holy Roman Emperor, Henry the Sixth of Germany, sent the following letter to King Philip Augustus of France:

Because our imperial majesty has no doubt that your royal highness will take pleasure in all of these providences of God which exalt us and our empire, we have thought it proper to inform you what happened to Richard, king of England, the enemy of our empire and the disturber of your kingdom, as he was crossing the sea on his way back to his dominions. His ship was driven by winds on to the Istrian coast and there it was wrecked at a place between Aquileia and Venice. By God's will, he and a few others escaped. A loyal subject of ours, Count Meinhard of Gorz and the people of the district, hearing that Richard was in their territory and calling to mind the treason, treachery and mischief of which he had been guilty in the Holy Land, went to arrest him. They captured eight knights from his retinue, but he escaped. He reached a town called Friesach in the archbishopric of Salzburg, where Friedrich of Pettau arrested six more of his knights. Richard himself escaped yet again, this time with just three companions and rode hard in the direction of Austria. But the roads were watched and guarded and our dearly beloved cousin Leopold, duke of Austria, captured the king in a disreputable house near Vienna, He is now in our power. We know that this news will bring you great happiness.

This letter is remarkable as it is between two European monarchs rejoicing over the capture of a third king, Their actions brazenly ignored the Papal directives that the persons and property of Crusaders were inviolate and though Pope Celestine III threatened to excommunicate Philip if he invaded Richard's lands in Normandy, the French king went ahead with his plans.

PART TWO – The Homecoming

Devonshire, July 1193

TEN

The trading cog *Mary and Child Jesus* glided the last few yards on the smooth flood tide of the River Exe and came to a stop with a slight bump as her prow touched the stone wharf at Topsham, five miles downstream from Exeter. Her bow hawser was thrown ashore to be lashed to a post, so that the tide could swing her around to keep her steerboard side away from the quay. As the half-dozen crew sang their traditional arrival hymn of thanks to the Virgin, three men stood on the aftercastle watching them, two of them mightily pleased that their voyaging was over.

'Glad to be home, are you?' asked the third, a leather-faced mariner who was both the shipmaster and owner of the vessel.

'Thorgils, nothing personal, but I never want to set foot on a bloody ship ever again!' replied John de Wolfe fervently. Alongside him, Gwyn grinned mischievously. 'But we had six months on land before this little pleasure cruise across the Channel.'

It had been a rough trip from Antwerp, in John's memory as bad as anything they had suffered in the Adriatic. Now he just wanted to forget the whole episode, both on sea and shore, though his failure to save his king was something which he could never forget – nor forgive himself for. Lifting his pack on to his shoulder, he gripped Thorgils by the forearm in farewell. 'Once again, I am in your debt, good friend. God knows how otherwise we could have got from Flanders across the French lands.'

As Gwyn was giving his own thanks to the old seafarer, John had a second pang of conscience – this time because he had cuckolded the shipman many times in the past, as for years Thorgil's wife Hilda had been one of John's lovers.

As soon as the cog was secured, they clambered ashore and with one mind, made directly for an alehouse in Topsham's single street.

'As I recall, the Crown made a good brew,' said Gwyn, already salivating at the thought of his first quart of Devon ale since sailing with the Crusading fleet from Dartmouth over three years earlier. Soon they sat in the summer sunshine on a bench outside the tavern, getting used to the feeling of solid ground under their feet after two weeks at sea. It was strange to be back in familiar surroundings and de Wolfe rapidly felt as if he had never been away.

'What will you do now, Sir John? Your wife can have no idea that you are back.' Gwyn lifted his pot and drank most of a pint without drawing breath.

'She probably thinks – or hopes – that I am long dead,' growled the knight. 'I'll stay at the Bush until I discover where she's living. I doubt her brother – and certainly his wife – would have put up with her for all this time.' She had gone there three years ago, when they had given up their rented house near the East Gate.

Gwyn finished his ale and stretched his legs luxuriously. 'What about horses? We need to get up to Exeter, unless you fancy a long walk.'

John signalled the alewife for another jug, while they waited for some food. 'I'll hire a couple of rounseys from the stables up the street. I'll leave yours with Andrew the farrier in St Martin's Lane. He can bring it back here sometime. You won't need one at home, will you?'

Gwyn shook his head emphatically. 'I left my old mare with Sergeant Gabriel at the castle stables. I'm going to spend a week or two pestering my wife and playing with the boys, if they can remember who I am!' he said happily. 'Then I'll go up to Rougemont every day for a game of chance with Gabriel and his merry men. I don't need a damned horse for that. But how are you going to manage?'

John filled their pottery mugs from the new jug. 'I left both Bran and Brutus down with my family at Stoke,' he said. 'I'll ride down there tomorrow on the hired horse and fetch Bran back to be stabled with Andrew.'

Bran was a destrier, a large stallion and former warhorse that John had won from an opponent defeated in a tournament some years ago, while Brutus was a hound of uncertain breed that he had had since a pup. Both were getting on in years, but he was very attached to them both.

'Can you and your wife not stay with your family down at Stoke?' asked Gwyn.

De Wolfe grimaced at the thought. 'Holy Mary, that would be asking for trouble! She can't stand my mother or my sister. To her, they are Welsh savages – and they are not too keen on her, with her airs and graces.'

The landlady brought them bowls of leek soup, followed by a scrubbed board carrying two large mutton shanks in onion gravy, with boiled parsnips and cabbage. These occupied them for a good few minutes and made them feel that at last they were back in civilization.

'I wonder where Sir Baldwin and William de L'Etang are now?' mused Gwyn, after squeezing gravy from his magnificent moustache. 'And the High Admiral and Philip the clerk, too?'

John picked meat from between his teeth with a splinter from the board. 'They'll have been ransomed by now, I'll wager. The priest Anselm will have been freed rapidly, no doubt. The Pope would have called down the wrath of God on anyone who kidnapped a man in Holy Orders.'

They both carefully avoided mentioning the Lionheart, as their failure to protect him from the Mayor of Vienna still weighed heavily on their hearts. They had heard almost nothing of him since that fateful day when the last they saw of their king was him being hustled off in Erdberg as a prisoner. During their arduous six-month journey across Europe, all they had heard was that he was a captive somewhere and that negotiations were going on to try to release him for a huge ransom.

Shaking off their recurring concerns, they finished the food, then walked to the livery stable beyond the church. Here John hired a pair of docile geldings, promising to return them within a few days. The proprietor looked rather askance at the worn and shabby clothing they wore, until John told him who he was and explained that they were returning Crusaders. The man was now effusive in his praise for them and refused to accept any deposit for the safe return of his steeds. De Wolfe knew that the news would be all over Topsham within the hour and probably would have reached Exeter almost as soon as themselves.

'It's shameful news that the king is now cast into prison in Germany!' said the farrier. 'No one knows where he is, but that bastard Emperor Henry is said to have bought him from the Austrians!'

Without disclosing their part in the affair, John pressed him for more details, but he knew nothing more than the rumours that took months to percolate to Devon from across the Channel. On the short jog to the city, he discussed this scant information with Gwyn, but hoped to get better news from his old friend and business partner, Hugh de Relaga – or from Ralph Morin, the constable of Rougemont. As the castellan of a royal castle, Ralph was a king's officer and had good contacts in Winchester and London.

They trotted up the country road alongside the river and when they came within sight of the great twin towers of the cathedral rising above the city wall, John enquired about Gwyn's intentions for the future.

'I don't know what's in store for me, good friend,' said de Wolfe. 'We're both getting too old in the bones to go off campaigning for much longer. But I'll not see you and your family go short of anything, you can depend on it.'

Gwyn nodded appreciatively. 'We can both still wield a sword or a mace if needs be, but I agree we've seen enough of foreign parts for a while. Don't worry about me, I've got a few bits of silver tucked away for a rainy day.'

De Wolfe frowned at the memory of the king's liberality to them. 'That money he shared out with us in Istria lasted us well, thank Christ. It kept us fed all the way to Antwerp. Without it, we'd have starved, unless we'd turned to high-way robbery!'

His squire grinned. 'But it was not enough to buy us new clothes, eh? No wonder that farrier back there looked a bit dubious until he dis-covered who you were!'

De Wolfe, never a smart dresser at the best of times, looked very down-at-heel in the black cloak he had worn since Dubrovnik. Travel-worn, mud-stained at the hem and torn in several places, it covered a limp calf-length tunic of grey serge, stained with old sweat under the arm-pits. His boots were just about serviceable, but looked as if they were more than ready for the rubbish midden. John had lost his pilgrim's hat long ago and now wore a simple coif, a cloth helmet of grey linen, tied with laces under his bearded chin. He could imagine, with some grim delight, what Matilda would say if she saw him now, with her snobbish insistence on keeping up appearances. Gwyn still wore his indestructible leather jerkin, but the knees had worn through on his worsted breeches and one buttock sported a large patch sewn on by a sympathetic alewife in Saxony.

When they reached Exeter's South Gate, both men felt as if their arduous journey was over at last. They passed under the arch into crowded Southgate Street, lined with booths and stalls fronting the houses and shops, most selling cloth and clothing in this lower end. Higher up, the slaughtermen were swilling away the blood and entrails from the street, following the daily public massacre of animals that supplied the butchers' stalls that led up to the central crossroads of Carfoix.

Turning right into the High Street, John rode the few yards up to the new Guildhall, where Gwyn left him to carry on to the East Gate and out into St Sidwells, where he would surprise his wife and children with his sudden appearance. Hitching the rounsey to a rail, John went into the Guildhall, recently rebuilt in stone as Exeter was thriving on its burgeoning trade in wool and tin. Though most of the houses were still timber, the new prosperity was evident in the masonry buildings springing up. The hall was crowded with people carrying on their business, buying, selling and making deals of all sorts. At the far end, several doors opened into rooms where the guilds and city administrators held court and in one of these, John sought his friend, Hugh de Relaga. He was one of the two portreeves, the leaders of the city council, as Exeter had not yet followed the new continental fashion of electing mayors.

As he threaded his way through the crowded

hall, John received some cold looks from the richer merchants in their fur-edged cotes and mantles. This disreputable figure in a dirty cloak and unkempt black beard, was not the usual type of visitor to the trading floor of Exeter's Guild-hall. No one recognized him as Sir John de Wolfe, though he had been well-known in the city before he left for Palestine.

At the door of the portreeve's chamber, a steward held up a hand to challenge him, but a baleful glare from John's deep-set eyes made him stand back. Inside the room, a short, rotund man, some ten years older than de Wolfe, sat behind a table cluttered with manuscripts, attended by a stooped clerk with more bills in his hand. Dressed in a bright green tunic with a scarlet surcoat, the dandyish Hugh de Relaga looked up in irritation, which turned to annoyance when he saw this black scarecrow advancing towards him. Then a grin from the apparition broke the spell and Hugh's normally cheerful face lit up with surprise and pleasure.

'By God's bones, tell me it's you, John!' he cried, rising from his seat. 'We thought you were long dead!'

They embraced, an unusual gesture for the un-demonstrative knight and the next few minutes were spent in a rapid exchange of news between them. Hugh sent his clerk out to get wine and pastries, pushing his parchments aside to make room on his table for cups and a platter. De Wolfe told him of the momentous events he had been involved in and made no attempt to cover up his own mortification at his failure to prevent the capture of the king.

'There is little hard news of Richard's fate,' said Hugh, his round face serious for once. 'Exeter is a long way from Winchester or Rouen and we get more rumour than fact, especially with this county under the yoke of the Count of Mortain.'

This was the title bestowed on Prince John by brother Richard at his coronation in 1189, along with the gift of six English counties, including Devon.

'But have you heard anything of Richard's whereabouts?' asked John, anxiously. 'We only heard that he had been taken from Austria to Germany, where he is in the clutches of Emperor Henry.'

De Relaga shrugged. 'We know little more than that, John. It seems that he was first dragged to some grim castle on the Danube near Vienna, then taken to Germany. Philip of France is trying to get his hands on him, but the Emperor knows he is too great a prize to be given up. Bishop Hubert Walter is leading a deputation to seek his release – and already stoking up a vast tax-raising campaign to pay for it!'

As a businessman, he added wryly, 'That will probably affect us sorely, John, as our enterprise has flourished greatly since you left. Still, we have made a lot of money, so can hardly begrudge some of it to get our sovereign released.'

Hugh stood back and surveyed John critically. 'And we can't begrudge a little more to get you some new clothing and a haircut. I doubt you've washed or shaved since leaving the Holy Land!'

He soon learned that John was virtually penniless, the money given by the king having been almost exhausted. He called his clerk in again and they unlocked a large iron-banded chest in the corner, from which he took a leather bag of silver coins and dumped it into de Wolfe's hands.

'Take this as a start and restore yourself to your former glory! Your wife will have apoplexy if she sees you in this state.'

In the next few minutes, John learned that Matilda was back in Exeter, staying with her cousin in Fore Street. He also discovered that he was now a comparatively rich man, as the sleeping partnership he had with Hugh in a wool-exporting venture had prospered remarkably. Also, his brother William, having heard nothing of John for three years, had deposited his share of the estate income from the manor at Stoke-in-Teignhead with de Relaga, which had added considerably to the profits. With fervent congratulations at having survived the campaign, he ushered John out, repeating his stern command for him to visit a clothiers without delay.

But John had a prior appointment, apart from not knowing where to find somewhere to buy new garments. He wanted to go down to the Bush Inn, to see how Meredydd and his very attractive wife were faring. Some years ago, he had loaned the former archer enough money to make up the price of the tavern when Meredydd purchased it on John's recommendation and he now wanted to see how his gift had been used.

Though he now knew that his wife was back in the city, he had no sense of urgency in going to seek her out. 'The bloody woman will be a millstone around my neck soon enough,' he muttered to himself, as he untied his horse. 'Another hour or two of freedom won't come amiss!'

ELEVEN

The Bush Inn was in the lower part of the city, which sloped downwards from the high point of Rougemont castle in the north-east to the riverside in the south-west. It lay on Idle Lane, which linked two streets than ran down to the western wall. The name came from the waste ground that lay around the inn, left unused after a devastating fire some years earlier.

A large thatched roof sat on a square of wall at little more than head height, with a yard behind with the usual huts for the kitchen, brewery, stable and privy. The front door had a withered bush of twigs hanging over it from a projecting beam, the sign of a tavern since Roman times. This was appropriate, as Exeter's street plan was laid out by the Romans and much of the town wall was built by them, added to later by Saxons and Normans.

De Wolfe tied up his hired horse near a water trough at the side of the inn, as the July weather was becoming very warm. When he went round to the front door, he frowned as he noticed that the limed walls were in dire need of their annual whitewash and the thatch above was becoming tattered and frayed. Three years ago, when he was last here, the place was spruce and fresh, as

Meredydd and Nesta had made great improvements to what had been a scruffy old alehouse.

He went inside and again was dismayed to see broken benches and dirty rushes on the floor. The place smelt strongly of urine, mould and spilled ale. A slatternly girl of about twelve was bringing earthenware mugs of ale from the casks at the back of the large room to a few men seated on the benches. There were no more than half a dozen of them, far fewer patrons than he remembered from three years ago. John beckoned the girl and asked for a quart of ale.

'Where's Meredydd, your master?' he asked her. The child, for she was little more than that, stared at him from big eyes in a thin, pale face. As she backed away, she shook her head, but made no reply. Afraid that his scruffy appearance had scared her, he asked her gently to fetch Mistress Nesta. This time she nodded, then vanished through the back door into the yard behind.

John sat on an empty bench at a table near the central firepit, now filled with dead ashes within its ring of whitewashed stones. Again he noticed the neglected state of everything, so different from its former state. As he pondered the possible reasons for the decline in the Bush, a pot of ale was put on the table before him.

'You asked for my husband?' came a well-remembered voice. He lifted his face and saw Nesta staring down at him. Then with dawning comprehension, she gasped as she saw his features instead of the dirty straggle of black hair on top of his head. 'John? Is it really you, John?'

140

Her face showed amazement, her hazel eyes enormous as they opened wide in disbelief.

John smiled wryly at her. 'Sorry, I expect I look more like John the Baptist than John de Wolfe, but I've come more than a thousand miles! So where is Meredydd?'

To his surprise and utter embarrassment, the landlady slumped down on to the bench alongside him and leaning into his shoulder, promptly burst into tears. Awkwardly, he put an arm around her shoulders, ignoring the curious glances of several other drinkers across the room.

'Mistress, what is it that troubles you? Where's Meredydd?'

For answer, she buried her face in his cloak, oblivious of the dank smell.

'Dead!' she sobbed. 'Dead of a fever, last Michaelmas. I am at my wit's end, John.'

Gently, he sat her upright and sat with one hand lying on hers on the table. 'Nesta, I am here now, I will do all I can to help you. Tell me from the beginning what happened?'

Taking Hugh's advice, when John eventually left the inn he went straight to several clothiers' booths recommended by Nesta after her weeping had stopped, following his assurances that he would come to her aid. In a matter of an hour, he equipped himself with a couple of undershirts, two grey tunics, long hose, worsted breeches, a pair of riding boots and some house shoes. No longer masquerading as a pilgrim, he had no need yet of a hat in this clement weather, as he preferred going bareheaded.

Stuffing his purchases into a saddlebag, he went in search of Gwyn's cottage in the small village of St Sidwell's, virtually a suburb of the city just beyond the East Gate. Here he interrupted the celebrations of his squire's homecoming to give Gwyn and his plump wife a share of the money he had been given by Hugh de Relaga and to ask them if he could use their yard to have a wash!

With Gwyn and two delighted lads assisting, he stripped off before the ruminant gaze of their house cow and had leather buckets of water from the well thrown over him. Agnes produced some soap she had made from goose fat mixed with wood ash and, ignoring his nakedness, lathered and scrubbed him clean. Afterwards, before donning his new clothes, he hacked off his beard and scraped the stubble with the specially honed little knife he carried in his scrip. Finishing off with Agnes trimming his black locks to a manageable length, he felt like a new man. Still putting off his search for Matilda, he sat in their one-room cottage and over a bowl of potage and some ale, told them of the crisis in the Bush.

'Nesta said their business was doing well until Meredydd fell ill last year with a purulent cough and fever. He was dead inside a week and since then she has been struggling to carry on.'

'Does she not have assistance there?' demanded Agnes, instantly sympathetic to another working woman in distress. 'I thought they had a pot-man and a couple of girls to help with the cooking and serving.'

'They did have – but the man tried to make

lewd advances after her husband died and she dismissed him. Then her cookmaid got herself with child and Nesta found she could not afford to hire new people.'

Gwyn frowned. 'But I thought the Bush had become very profitable since Meredydd and Nesta took it over. It was thought of as the best tavern in the city – clean, with good food and excellent ale, thanks to Nesta's brewing.'

John nodded sadly. 'It was, but when she became hard-pressed from working alone, things went downhill. Less income meant less to spend on good food and brewing materials. The customers began to dwindle, especially those from out of town, like the travellers and carters who used to stay there when visiting the city.'

Agnes clucked her tongue in dismay. 'Such a pity, Sir John, after all the work they put into making it a success, especially as you helped them so much.'

'I recall you lending them a fair sum when they bought the place,' observed Gwyn. 'You told me Meredydd needed some silver to make up the price and you gave it him to save him paying usurious interest to the moneylenders.'

De Wolfe grunted, his usual response to anything that might embarrass him.

'He paid me back quickly. It was just a helping hand to an old comrade. Meredydd was a damned good archer when he was with us in France.'

'So is there anything we can do to help the poor girl?' asked the ever-practical Agnes. 'Gwyn could go down there for a bit, to help her. Now that he's come home, I don't want him under my feet here all day, I can tell you!' She smiled affectionately at her large, clumsy husband.

He nodded amiably. 'Sure, I can tidy the place up a bit and mend anything broken. Help with the brewing and that.'

'You'll drink more than you'll brew, but never mind,' scolded Agnes.

'What about the cooking and looking after the lodgers?'

John ran a hand through his newly cleaned hair. 'She'll need a potman and another maid, one that can cook and is more experienced than the poor child that's there now. Do you know anyone?'

Gwyn tugged at his moustache and frowned as he considered the problem.

'What about old Edwin down the street?' he suggested to his wife.

Agnes thought for a moment, then nodded. 'He lives with his married daughter and she says he also gets under her feet, just like you, Gwyn. They might both be glad to see him off the premises.'

Gwyn turned to de Wolfe. 'You'll recall Edwin, he was a pikeman with us at Wexford years ago. Lost an eye and part of a foot there. Terrible old gossip, but reliable enough. He might like to earn a few pennies.'

Agnes, who knew everyone for a mile around, said that her second cousin's daughter Molly was a good cook and an honest girl who might consider the job.

After some more gossip, John felt that he

could not put off his filial duties any longer, so leaving Gwyn and his wife to follow up their suggestions about help for Nesta, he left to walk the short distance back into the city. He had left his horse with Andrew, the farrier in St Martin's Lane, as in town a large animal was more of an encumbrance than a help in getting around.

In his new clothes and feeling clean for the first time since Acre, he set off through the city gate and down the High Street past the Guildhall once more. At Carfoix, where the roads from the four main gates crossed, thanks to the Roman general Vespasian's town planning, John carried straight on down Fore Street, which went downhill towards the West Gate. On the right, he passed the little church of St Olave, where his wife spent so much time on her knees and then came to her cousin's house. This was a small, but well-kept two-storey dwelling built of cob plastered between frames of old oak.

When he rapped on the iron knocker, he expected it to be answered either by the cousin Edith or her miserable old maidservant. It was quite a surprise when the door flew open and the irate visage of Matilda de Wolfe appeared.

The reception he got was in stark contrast to that of Nesta in the Bush. Instead of collapsing against him in tears, his wife stared at him for a moment while her mind grappled with this unexpected situation.

'Oh, it's you John! I thought it was those cursed children again, playing "knock and run away",' she said evenly, as if he had just returned from visiting his mother, rather than an absence

145

of over three years.

'At least she didn't say she thought I was dead,' muttered John, as she stood aside and let him into the short passage that led to the kitchen, with two rooms leading off each side of the front door.

He considered giving her a discreet kiss of welcome for form's sake, but as she waddled in front of him with her back turned, he thought better of it. In the kitchen, a lean-to on the back of the house, Matilda motioned him to a stool at the table and produced two wine cups and a flask. After pouring the wine, she sat down heavily opposite her husband and glared at him. 'So where have you been since gallivanting off with your precious king, leaving me alone to fend for myself?'

It took an hour and the rest of the flask of wine for John to tell his wife of his adventures. Though initially she affected to be disinterested in his selfish affairs, her fascination with things religious gradually thawed her – along with more than a pint of Anjou red wine. Matilda was devoted to all things related to the Church and its priests – along with an almost equal love of food, wine and good clothing. The fact that he had been to Christ's homeland, had actually seen Jerusalem, albeit at a distance and had trodden the hallowed shores of the Sea of Galilee, fascinated her. She began to look at this gaunt, dark man in a new light, just because he had actually breathed the air of the Holy Land and had done his best to free the sacred places from the grip of the infidel Saracens.

She was far less interested in hearing of his arduous journey home, though she was patriotic enough to condemn the capture of a Crusading king by dirty foreigners from Germany. Matilda had been born in Devon, as had her parents and grandparents, but she firmly considered herself to be a true Norman, though she had only once set foot in Normandy, visiting distant relatives. To her, the English were an inferior race – and as for those locals who were remnants of the original Celtic peoples, especially the Cornish, to Matilda they were little better than savages. The fact that her husband had a half-Welsh mother had always been a thorn in her side.

His story told, he enquired what had befallen her whilst he was away. Amid the expected recriminations of leaving her alone and penniless – a blatant untruth, as her father had settled a comfortable sum upon her at his death – John gathered that she had alternated between living with her brother at his estates in Revelstoke and Tiverton and staying with her cousin in Exeter, where the attractions of both the cathedral and St Olave's were greater than the boredom of the countryside.

'So are you staying or are you disappearing again with that uncouth Cornishman to carouse on some distant campaign where you can drink and wench to your heart's content?' she demanded.

From long familiarity, John ignored her acidulous tongue and shook his head. 'I've had a bellyful of wandering, good wife!' he replied.

'I've seen too much of foreign parts now, I need to enjoy the county of my birth for a while. I thought you wanted to settle in your own house at last?'

He went on to tell her of the profits that Hugh de Relaga had earned for him during his absence and the gains from the manors at Stoke and Holcombe. 'Together with what I have in my treasure chest at my brother's house, we are very well provided for, Matilda. I know you prefer the city, so why do we not purchase a house here?'

Even her ungracious nature could hardly turn this offer down and she celebrated this improvement in their relationship by fetching another flask of wine and discussing the merits and faults of various streets in Exeter. As an energetic social climber, she favoured the best areas, either up towards the North Gate or even better, between the cathedral and the east gate, where the wealthiest merchants lived.

Eventually, the wine got the better of her and she rose unsteadily and said she must take her usual afternoon rest. 'But you cannot stay here now, John. I came to help my cousin, as she has a daughter here waiting for childbed in a few weeks' time. I have to share a room with Edith, so you must go elsewhere until we find our own house.'

This was music to John's ears, as he liked her cousin even less than Matilda herself and would be delighted to lodge elsewhere.

'I must first go to my family in Stoke, I will stay with them for a while. But first I have business to settle with Hugh de Relaga, so will board at an inn for a few days. Meanwhile, while you are staying in Exeter, you can discover what dwellings are for sale or lease in the town.'

When he left Matilda, with a feeling of relief in spite of their fairly amicable reunion, he went up to Rougemont, the castle built soon after the Conquest by William the Bastard himself. An inner wall of the red sandstone that gave the fortress its name, carved off the upper corner of the Roman wall at the highest point of the city. Outside this was a much wider arc of wooden palisade mounted on an earthen bank, forming the outer ward where the garrison and their families lived in what was essentially a hutted village. The inner ward was guarded by a high gatehouse, its arched entrance having a draw-bridge across a dry moat. Inside the inner ward were the keep, a small chapel and the barn-like Shire Hall which functioned as the court.

John strode up to the gatehouse and when challenged about his business by a young soldier who had obviously never heard of Black John, he gruffly demanded that Sergeant Gabriel be called.

The lad vanished into the guardroom inside the archway and a moment later, a grizzled man in a short belted tunic and breeches hurried out, a wide smile on his leathery face. 'Blessed be to God Almighty, it is you, Sir John!' He grasped him by both upper arms and shook him in an exuberance of delight.

'Don't say "I thought you must be dead," for Christ's sake!' growled John, but his own wide grin showed his pleasure at seeing his old friend again. Years before they had served together in the North Country and he would trust Gabriel with his life. He rapidly gave him a summary of his doings these past three years, then asked if the castle constable was about. 'We can sit together over a jar of ale and I'll tell you more about my time with the king,' he promised.

A few minutes later, they climbed the wooden stairs to the entrance to the keep, a squat tower which was built over the prison and storehouse, on the further side of the inner ward. Inside, most of the first floor was one large hall, with a few small chambers along one side. This was the meeting place where most of the official business of Devonshire was done, the hall often being crowded with soldiers, nobles, clerks and merchants, all seeking something from the officials who occupied the castle.

A firepit occupied the centre, but was unlit on this warm summer day. However, food was being carried in by servants from a kitchen hut at the back and ale was flowing as required from barrels in one corner. A few rough tables and benches occupied part of the hall and a number of men were eating and drinking at them amongst a babble of noise.

'There he is, though his beard is greyer than when I last saw him!' said de Wolfe, marching across to a table and clapping a hand on the shoulder of a very large man. Sir Ralph Morin looked like one of his Viking ancestors, with a nose as big as John's and a forked beard that jutted out like the prow of a ship. As Gabriel had done, he went through the routine of surprise and delight when he saw who it was – and thankfully avoided telling John that he had expected him to be dead!

John and the sergeant sat down and a servant brought them quarts of ale, as de Wolfe once again went through a summary of the fateful voyage from Acre. Ralph listened avidly, as he was tiring of the inactivity of peaceful Devon, after years where he had campaigned as actively as John. Also like John, he was a devoted king's man, being the military commander of the castle and its garrison. Rougemont was one of the two West Country fortresses to be held by the king, the other being Launceston in Cornwall – a wise precaution as it turned out.

'So how did you and that great lump Gwyn get home after that treacherous seizing of King Richard?' Ralph wanted to know.

'We walked most of the bloody way!' growled John. 'Took us over six months. Neither of us had a word of German between us and that lad had been seized as well, so as we both spoke the language, we posed as Welsh mercenaries, cut off from our main company.'

Ralph Morin grinned, in spite of the seriousness of their plight. 'Plenty of those knocking about in Europe,' he said. 'Did you meet any there?'

De Wolfe nodded ruefully. 'We did indeed, and fought with them for a time in a dispute between two German princedoms. We had sold our horses after a month when our money ran low and walked into Bavaria where there was a local war going on. A company of ruffians from

151

Powys took us on. Thank God they were not from Gwent, for we are of little use with a long-bow.'

He described how they fought for one city alongside Brabantian and Provencal mercenaries against some other German princedom. 'After ten weeks, we had collected enough loot to slip away and walk west again, eventually reaching the Low Countries.'

'How did you get home from there?' queried Gabriel.

'I knew from the business we have with Hugh de Relaga that Thorgils the Boatman regularly came to Antwerp with wool. We waited almost a month there until he showed up, then came home to Topsham with a cargo of finished cloth. We only arrived on this morning's tide.'

After his elaboration on the story had finished, John asked what had been happening here at home.

Ralph rolled up his eyes beneath his bushy eyebrows. 'The West Country has gone to the dogs under that bastard Prince John!' he declared. 'I fear we are in for civil war unless someone can bring him to heel.'

Gabriel shook his head in gloomy agreement. John knew that after his coronation in 1189, the Lionheart had rashly – and in many people's opinion, foolishly – given his younger brother six counties, including Devon and Cornwall, as his own property. Their father, Henry II, had wisely kept his feckless son short of possessions, so that he was known contemptuously as 'John Lackland'. The over-generous Richard more than made up for this and as virtual king over a large area of England, John kept all the taxes and ran the administration personally. There were no sheriffs, as nominally he himself held the shrievalties.

'So who's in there now?' he asked, jerking a thumb at the door of the first chamber on the side wall. 'William Brewer was the sheriff before I left.'

The constable's face darkened. 'No, he's gone on to higher things in Winchester and London. He's a royal justice and one of the King's Justiciars. At the moment, I hear he is in Germany negotiating for Hubert Walter over Richard's ransom. So guess who our dear Count of Mortain has put in as his *locum* sheriff?'

De Wolfe stared at his friend blankly. 'Old Henry de Furnellis, perhaps?' he suggested.

Ralph laughed scornfully. 'No, it's your damned brother-in-law, Richard de Revelle!'

John was aghast. 'God's blood! I think I'll turn around and go back to being a mercenary in Germany! Why would the prince want to do that? De Revelle will bleed the county dry to his own advantage.'

Though it was his own domain, Morin looked over his shoulder in an almost furtive way. 'There's treason afoot, in my opinion. With our king away for years and now locked up in Germany, Prince John sees an opportunity to seize the crown for himself. Many thought that the Lionheart would be killed in battle or die of a fever; when he didn't, John began to think of overthrowing him by force, which is why he's been seeking an alliance with Philip of France and plotting with others at home.'

'What others?' demanded John, concerned at this confirmation of the fears the Lionheart expressed on the journey from Palestine.

'The rumour is that Hugh Nonant, Bishop of Coventry, is his main supporter, along with other senior churchmen, including some of the senior canons of Exeter.'

De Wolfe digested this worrying information with a scowl. 'And you reckon my dear brother-in-law may also be a traitor, if he is thick enough with the prince for him to be given this chance to milk the county revenues?'

The burly constable shrugged. 'We all know what a shifty, devious character de Revelle is, John. I'd not trust him an inch, which is why I'm not letting him nibble away at my royal authority over this castle.'

Gabriel leaned forward. 'I recall that when the king ill-advisedly gave the prince these six counties and a lot more besides, he forbade him to set foot in England for the next three years, as a safeguard while he was on Crusade. But their mother, the old queen, talked Richard out of it, so John has been here most of the time, making trouble from his bases in Gloucester and Bristol.'

De Wolfe jerked his head towards the closed door of the sheriff's chamber. 'Is de Revelle in there now? I suppose I had better tell the bastard that I'm home again. That'll spoil his day, no doubt!'

'He's not there, he's gone to his manor in

Revelstoke, probably to count all his money,' replied Ralph, sarcastically.

John hauled himself to his feet. 'That's something I must do myself, go to my manor. I've not seen my family for three years, so I'll be off to Stoke-in-Teignhead first thing in the morning.'

When they heard he would be staying in the Bush until he could find a town house, Gabriel and Morin expressed their concern at the death of the landlord, whom they had both known as a fellow soldier.

'The place has gone downhill badly since Meredydd died,' bemoaned Gabriel. 'Poor Nesta can't keep it up alone and she's become short of money.'

'I heard that de Revelle wanted to buy the Bush, but offered her a paltry price,' said Morin. 'I expect if she gets even more desperate, he'll get it for a pittance in the end.'

'Over my dead body!' muttered John. 'The Bush is about to regain its former glory!'

TWELVE

It was early evening when John arrived back at the Bush and even after only a few hours, the atmosphere there had changed remarkably. Gwyn was there, heartily organizing a couple of men he had got in to clean up and change the rushes on the floor and throw out any broken benches.

Already, two new staff had arrived. Old Edwin was there, eager to earn twopence a day and all the ale he could drink, together with Molly, the girl from St Sidwell who Agnes had claimed was a good cook.

Nesta looked a different woman, with a linen coif over her red-gold hair, a clean apron and a bright-eyed eagerness in her face. John's promise to help had rapidly transformed both her and the failing tavern and even some of the regular patrons were helping by killing rats and mice that ran from the dirty rushes as it was raked up.

'Great to have you back, cap'n,' quavered Edwin, who had served in Ireland years before and still gave John his rank as leader of their company of pikemen. He had a horrible dead eye from an injury during that campaign, the fish-white eyeball rolling up in the socket when he moved his other eye. In addition, he limped badly, as he had lost all the toes and half the foot in the same conflict.

'Come and sit down for a while, good lady' John said to the Welsh woman. 'We must talk about how we restore your fortunes here.'

As they sat across a table while the bustle went on around them, he proposed his plan of action. 'I'll clear all your debts and lend you whatever is needed to get this fine inn back on its feet. For the time being, I'll pay the wages of the three you have working here. I also think you should have a boy as ostler to look after horses in the yard behind, for it's been a popular lodging for travellers, bringing in much business for you.'

Nesta laid a hand on his and whispered her thanks, her eyes filling with tears of gratitude. 'Why are you being so good to me, Sir John? I know Meredydd thought the world of you, but he's gone, God rest him.'

De Wolfe squirmed a little with embarrassment. Emotion and especially a woman's tears, struck fear into him as much as a dozen Saracen swords. 'Your man was a good soldier and a good friend,' he muttered. 'That's more than sufficient for me to salute his memory by caring for his wife.'

Gwyn ambled up at this moment, obviously enjoying this new challenge as a change from trekking across half the known world. 'The brew-shed is mortally short of materials for making ale,' he rumbled. 'And the kitchen is equally bare. Can I go out tomorrow and buy enough to stock us up?'

For answer, John reached into the pouch on his

belt and slid a leather bag across the table towards the landlady, part of the earnings he had received from Hugh de Relaga. 'That's to be getting on with, Nesta. Give Gwyn what he needs for the market tomorrow. Good food and clean mattresses will soon bring back the customers.'

'And I'll find a couple of men to start whiteliming the walls, inside and out – and get the thatch repaired,' promised the big Cornishman, as he stumped off again to supervise the cleaners.

Nesta laid a hand on the purse of silver, hesitant about accepting it. 'How can I repay you, Sir John?' she murmured.

He gave her one of his rare smiles, his dour face lightening and momentarily making him a youth again. 'Forget the "Sir", Nesta! I've had six months living like a common mercenary, it will take a while for me to feel like a knight again!'

She beamed at him and he suddenly realized what an attractive woman she was. John was a great admirer of the fair sex, but as she was the wife of an old friend, he had genuinely never had any amorous or lascivious thoughts about Nesta. However, he had always enjoyed her vivacious company in the inn, especially as he could speak to her in Welsh. He looked with new appreciation at her heart-shaped face, the pert snub nose and the big hazel eyes. She was a small woman, with a tiny waist but a full, curvaceous bosom. Her auburn hair was her crowning glory, though now half-hidden under her linen cap.

She felt him gazing at her and blushed slightly. 'I miss my dear Meredydd so much, John – but life must go on. I am so lucky to have you as a good friend.'

He gave her another of his lopsided grins. 'Then you can also have me as a customer, for I must find somewhere to live for a while, since my wife has barred her door to me!'

Nesta looked at him aghast, until he explained that there was no room for him in her cousin's house. 'Until she makes me spend a chestful of gold and silver on buying somewhere in the city, I will have to find lodgings. I hope you can find me a bag of straw up in your loft, dear lady?'

She stared at him wide-eyed. 'You would stay here, in a common alehouse?'

'Indeed I would, it's a palace compared to what I have endured these past few years. In fact, I would earnestly desire to collapse on to a mattress very shortly, for it's been a long and strenuous day!'

Nesta sprang to her feet, bustling to take care of her tall, dark benefactor. 'First you must eat, we'll see what this new girl can provide for you. Then you'll have no haybag upstairs, but a goose feather palliasse from my own room!'

Within minutes, a bowl of tasty rabbit stew was set before him, that Molly had been simmering in the cook shed, together with a wheaten loaf, cheese and a bowl of ripe plums. 'We'll do better than that tomorrow, when we have more notice,' promised Nesta, standing with arms akimbo to watch him eat.

When he had finished, though it was still day-

159

light, she led him up the wide ladder in the corner to the loft above. This extended right across the inn, a bare floor under the high roof, which was made of twisted hazel withies that supported the thatch. In one corner was a stout partition with a door, forming a small chamber for Nesta herself. Opposite were a few wattle screens forming open-ended cubicles for the better class of guest, who paid twopence a night for a blanket and a straw-filled sack to sleep on, plus food and drink. The common lodgers slept in the middle of the floor for a penny, with bread and ale.

Nesta fetched a blanket, a pillow and a soft mattress from her room, and settled John in one of the cubicles. 'There's no one else staying her tonight, so you'll not be disturbed,' she promised, as he sat gratefully on the edge of his bed to pull off his boots. 'God bless you, John, may he keep you safe this night!' she said fervently.

After sleeping like a log until dawn, de Wolfe had a breakfast of gruel, fried eggs, ham and coarse bread, before going up to the stables in St Martin's Lane to fetch his hired horse. He had thought to call at Fore Street to tell Matilda that he would be away for a few days, visiting his family. Then he used the excuse to himself that she was still likely to be snoring at that early hour, as except when attending early church services, she was as fond of her bed as she was of food and drink.

The rounsey was a decent little horse and John felt quite at home on her as he rode down the

160

steep approach to the West Gate. He waved to the porter on duty, who gave him a semi-military salute, another old soldier who recognized John de Wolfe. The news that Sir John was home from the Crusades had spread around Exeter within hours, and many people had acknowledged him as he rode through the streets, already bustling with townsfolk and merchants going about their daily business.

The marshy ground outside the walls, flooded when the river was in spate, looked much the same as he remembered it. The new stone bridge had been started in the year he left for Palestine, but the builder, Nicholas Gervase, had run out of money and only a few arches were completed. The old, shaky footbridge would not take a horse, so de Wolfe used the ford to cross the Exe, as the tide was low.

Once beyond the river, he carried on at a brisk trot, turning off a few miles further down the high road to Plymouth to take the southerly track that led to the coast, eight miles away. It was a pleasant summer morning, white clouds scudding high in a blue sky and he revelled in being back in a green country after years in the arid, dusty Levant. The road was narrow and rutted, but at least it was dry in this fine weather. The track ran down the western side of the Exe valley, past Powderham manor on the marshes of the estuary, with gentle hills to his right. He felt contented, but he missed the company of Gwyn jogging alongside him, as he had done for so many years. After a couple of hours' riding, he stopped before reaching the sea at Dawlish, to let his mare drink at a stream and crop the grass amongst the bushes at the side of the road. He sat on a fallen tree to eat some of the bread and cheese that Nesta had given him for the journey, as he looked ahead to where he could see the houses of Dawlish in the distance. Also visible were a few tilted masts, belonging to ships that were beached there and these reminded him that Thorgils, the master of the cog that had brought him home, was probably already with his wife in the village.

With a sigh, John knew that this destroyed any hope of his calling on the beautiful Hilda, his earliest love and one who still held a powerful attraction for him. Hilda was the daughter of the manor reeve at the de Wolfe's second manor at Holcombe and as teenagers, they had both lost their virginity together in a hayloft there. She was half a decade younger than John and it would have been impossible to contemplate a marriage between a Norman knight and the daughter of a servant, even though her father had been freed from his former bondage and made the reeve, responsible for organizing the daily work of the manor.

John had been fighting abroad for most of his adult life and, during his absence, Hilda had married Thorgils, a relatively rich mariner and owner of three ships. However, when John was home and her husband away, they had had many passionate reunions and were still very fond of each other – or so John hoped, as this three-year absence in the Holy Land was the longest period they had ever been apart. For all he knew, she might have had a couple of children by now, though Thorgils was getting old, almost twice her age.

He climbed back into the saddle and carried on, passing slowly through the village street in the hope that he might catch a glimpse of Hilda at the market stalls, but there was no sign of her.

John trotted on, the road now following the coast and he soon passed Holcombe, with its pleasant memories. He could have called there had time permitted, as Hilda's parents, though they guessed at the past relationship between the young people, were still both faithful manor servants to the de Wolfe family.

Soon he came to the River Teign, which flowed down from Dartmoor, the last few miles being a wide tidal channel. Though some hours earlier, it had been low at the Exeter crossing, the tide was now flooding into the sandy entrance to the estuary, so John took the ferry across to the other side. For a halfpenny, the boatman took him and the horse on to the flat-bottomed craft and poled it across, slanting against the strong current. On the other side, it was but a short distance to Stoke-in-Teignhead, a manor hidden away in a small valley amongst the trees beyond the western bank.

As he rode down the lane through the fringe of forest, he saw all the familiar sights of his youth, for he had been born and lived here until his father had sent him at ten years of age to be a page and then a squire to a nobleman in the north of the county. As the valley opened out into strip fields and cottages, the familiarity was almost overwhelming, even to an unimaginative man like John. There were a few people on the road and more working in the fields on either side – the children and younger lads staring curiously at this dark stranger, but older villagers soon began shouting and running towards him as they recognized him as their long-lost lord. His elder brother William was the actual lord of the manor and head of the family, a gentle fellow whose interests were in managing the estate, rather than John's dependence on the sword. However, John had always been very popular, especially amongst the younger villagers, who admired his reputation as a warrior.

After reunion with his family in the manor house, the next hour was a bewildering confusion of welcome, praise and thanksgiving for his safe return, the sexton ringing the church bell in an endless paroxysm of rejoicing. Many had given up any hope of seeing him again, thinking that like the majority of the men who had sailed from Dartmouth three years before, he would have died of wounds, illness or drowning at sea.

His mother Enyd was one who never contemplated his death, resolutely believing that he would come home. Her conviction supported the others, especially his plump sister Evelyn, who had spent much of the last three years praying for him, as she was as religious as Matilda, having wanted to enter a nunnery in her youth. William had secretly feared that he would never see his brother again, but had kept up a firm pretence for the sake of his mother and sister – and was now heartily pleased to have been proved wrong.

What remained of the day was spent in talking, eating and drinking, as the family, the steward, the bailiff and the reeves all clustered around John in the hall of the manor house to hear his tales of the Holy Land and especially of the journey home. None of them had known that he had been part of the Lionheart's bodyguard for the return from Acre and were prodigiously proud of him. When they heard that only John and Gwyn had been left with the king after all the others had been whittled away, they were astounded – and John's sombre confession of his remorse at not being able to prevent the capture was dismissed by them as God's will. Everyone in England knew that their king was in prison in Germany, but the details were scanty, except to the ministers and high officials.

'Does anyone in Winchester know that you are back?' asked William. 'Surely you should tell someone the true details of our king's capture?'

In the short time that John had been home, this had not occurred to him, but now that his brother had suggested it, he began to think that perhaps he had better report to someone. He had heard from Ralph Morin that Hubert Walter had been made Archbishop of Canterbury and Chief Justiciar of England, virtually a regent now that the king was in captivity. De Wolfe knew Hubert, who had been the Lionheart's right-hand man at the Crusade and had conducted most of the negotiations with Saladin. Morin had heard that the new archbishop was also in charge of parleying with Emperor Henry of Germany over the king's ransom and was the prime mover in raising the vast amount of money.

'Perhaps you are right, brother,' he said. 'As soon as my immediate problems are settled in Exeter, perhaps Gwyn and I should ride to London and tell our story.'

When the excitement had subsided and John was bursting with food and ale, his next desire was to be reunited with his old horse Bran and his dog Brutus. The big destrier, a warhorse he had won by defeating its previous owner in a tournament, was delighted to see him when John went to the stables, snickering his pleasure as John stroked his neck and fed him a few carrots.

His lanky brown hound was being looked after by the blacksmith, but as John walked towards the forge, just beyond the manor house, a frenzied barking and howling began as, almost by magic, Brutus could tell that his long-lost master was coming for him. The reunion was emotional for both of them and afterwards John pondered on the fact that he had had a far warmer welcome from four-legged beasts than from his own wife.

John stayed a few days at Stoke, his family and friends refusing to let him leave any sooner. Pleading that he had to return to Matilda and find them somewhere to live, as well as settle more business matters with Hugh de Relaga, they reluctantly let him go on the fifth day, after promises that he would soon return.

He left early on Bran, with the rounsey following quietly behind on a head rope. Brutus ran delightedly with them, dashing ahead and then

166

returning for some foray into the bushes on either side. At an easy pace, he crossed the Teign again and a few miles further on, decided to call at Holcombe, which was a short distance off the road. Though he came to pay his respects to the reeve and his wife, he had a sneaking hope that Hilda might be there, as he knew that she often visited her parents. He was again disappointed in this, though he enjoyed the welcome they gave him, assuring him that their daughter was well, though still without child.

When he reached Dawlish some miles further on, he saw that the *Mary and Child Jesus,* the ship that had brought him from Antwerp, was beached in the mouth of the small river, having repairs carried out on the planking. This told him that Thorgils was definitely at home, so with a sigh he plodded on through the village and took the track across the marshes towards the ferry to Topsham, where he could return the rounsey to its stables.

Beyond the village of Starcross on the edge of the wide estuary, John stopped to rest and water the horses. He sat on the bank of a small stream that ran in a culvert under the lane to eat the bread and meat that his mother had pressed on him for the journey, while the larger beasts drank and Brutus went off to sniff the new odours of otter, fox and badger that abounded amongst the scrub and rushes that covered this flat plain. The muddy shore was only a few yards away and the hound vanished in that direction. A moment later, he began barking and whining, then dashed back to his master to sit expectantly at his feet, his tongue hanging out in expectation. John knew the signs well enough and climbed to his feet.

'What are you trying to tell me, old fellow?' he said affectionately, rubbing the dog's domed head. For reply, Brutus dashed of once again, turning to make sure that John was following. They went along the edge of the stream to where it flowed into the Exe. The tide was ebbing and at once, de Wolfe saw what was arousing the dog's interest. Caught in a clump of reeds at the mouth of the stream was a man's body, left there by the retreating water.

John squelched through a few inches of brown ooze to reach it and saw that the corpse was already starting to putrefy in the warm weather, the face being swollen and discoloured, the tongue and eyes protruding. He grabbed the man's belt and hauled him out on to firmer ground, then dragged him up on to the bank where he could get a better look at the body. Brutus sat down a few yards away and looked at the process with interest, obviously proud of his part in discovering this novel event.

John bent over the dead man and saw that he was dressed in riding attire, a long tunic slit front and back for sitting a horse. It was of good quality and he wore a stout leather belt with a sheathed dagger at the back. The belt carried a bronze buckle with an unusual design, a dragon within a circle and John removed it in case it could help in identifying the victim. His boots were of good quality, over long woollen hose and there was also a baldric across one shoulder, but no sword or sheath, though if he had been riding, they may have been on his saddle bow. The man's face was unrecognizable due to the putrefaction, which was also swelling his belly, but what was easily recognizable was the massive wound across his neck, where his throat had been cut.

De Wolfe was so familiar with violent death after years on a score of battlefields, that the sight affected him not at all, apart from a professional interest in the nature of the wound. This was deep enough to reach the spine and had been made from right to left, as shown by its tailing-off under the left ear.

'So what have we got here, Brutus?' he asked his dog. 'He's a man of substance, by his clothing. Certainly no villein or serf.'

Brutus offered no comment and John bent to open the leather scrip on the front of the belt. There was no money in it, only a tin medallion of St Anthony.

'That didn't do him much good, I'm afraid,' John said to the hound. 'Maybe he was murdered for his money?'

He looked at the brown hair, cropped up level with the top of the ears in the usual Norman style, but that was no help in identifying the victim. There was no beard or moustache and the eyes were already flaccid and filmed, making it impossible to tell their original colour.

Then de Wolfe noticed a signet ring on the middle finger of the right hand. It was thin and made of some base metal, but John pulled it off the swollen finger for safe keeping, rubbing it on the grass to clean off a shred of slimy skin. After looking at it closely, he continued his monologue with his hound.

'Odd, there's no device engraved on it! What's the point of having a blank signet ring?' Then he tipped it in his fingers and looked at the inside surface. There he saw two lions *passant gardant* impressed into the metal and his thick black eyebrows rose.

'What's this, Brutus? The arms of our Lord King! I don't like the look of this, do you?'

The dog sat on his haunches, his head on one side, regarding his master attentively. John screwed up his eyes and scrutinized the ring even more closely, but there was nothing else to be seen except the two heraldic beasts, each in full face, the right paw raised and the head in profile, the combination that caused the French to name them leopards. It was the royal insignia of England, adopted by the Lionheart from his mother's arms of Aquitaine, a single golden lion on a red background. Richard had later added a second lion and no one else in England would dare to claim it for his own.

'So surely he has to be a man in the king's service, as I was myself,' he mused. 'And now he's died a very violent death.'

Always a man of action rather than word or thought, he went back to the rounsey and brought her to the body. Cutting a length from the long head-rope, he struggled to lift the corpse over the saddle, then roped the hands to the feet under the horse's belly, like an extra girth. Moments later, he was on his way again, the hired horse following on its shorter lead, carrying the sorry burden across its back.

On the ferry across to Topsham, he had some curious looks from the couple of other passengers, who shrank back as far as they could from the macabre load. No one was brave enough to question the tall, dark man who scowled at them as he defied anyone to ask why he was escorting a corpse. His intention to return the rounsey to the farrier in Topsham was abandoned, as he wanted to take the body back to the royal castle in Exeter, not dump it in an obscure seaport. He carried on up the road to the city, past St James's Priory and, deciding that parading it through the main streets was unwise, went around through Southernhay to the East Gate and then up the steep slope of Castle Street to the gatehouse.

When the duty man-at-arms called Gabriel from the guardroom, the sergeant came out with Gwyn, who had been playing dice inside. They both looked askance at the body on the mare, now dripping bloody fluid from the ravaged neck.

'You been a-killing someone, Sir John?' asked Gabriel.

John explained how he had come across this unfortunate man. 'Probably washed down the river – but God knows where he went in,' he said.

Gwyn, always ready with a contrary opinion, bent to look at the man's face. 'But he could have been thrown from a ship and washed up from the sea,' he suggested. 'He's been in the water a few days, in this warm weather.' Like

171

John, from long experience of fighting, he claimed a special expertise on the signs of death and corruption.

'Why did you trouble to bring him all this way to Exeter, sir,' asked Gabriel. 'You are First Finder now, you are supposed to have raised the Hue and Cry down in Starcross.'

Since Saxon times, anyone discovering a corpse, unless it died of illness in the bosom of its family, was supposed to knock up the four nearest households and raise a search for the killer, before getting the bailiff of the Hundred to notify the sheriff.

'What's the point?' objected Gwyn. 'This fellow may have been killed a dozen miles up river – and certainly at least a few days ago. And we don't even have a sheriff to report it to!'

De Wolfe shook his head. 'Those weren't the reasons, it was this.' He fished in the scrip on his belt and took out the ring to show them. 'That's the king's device! He must have been a royal officer of some sort.'

Gwyn took the ring and peered at closely. 'The lions are hidden on the inside, as if he didn't want who he was to be widely known unless he wished it.' He passed it to the sergeant of the garrison. 'Gabriel, have you ever seen one of these before?'

The sergeant shook his head. 'Never, but perhaps Ralph Morin knows, he's higher up the pecking order where royal matters are concerned.'

He summoned a couple of soldiers and they took the body to a cart shed against the inner wall of the inner ward. It was near the little chapel of St Mary and was sometimes used as a temporary mortuary. Here the unknown man was placed on a handcart and decently covered with a couple of empty sacks until some means of disposal could be arranged.

John left the two horses to be fed and watered and the three men went in search of the castle constable. He occupied one of the small chambers off the Great Hall in the keep, cluttered with spare armour, helmets and weapons, leaving enough room for a few stools and a table on which lay his clerk's lists of stores and duty rosters. Ralph was sitting alone with a pottery mug of cider before him, and brightened up when he saw John de Wolfe entering.

'Welcome back, how did you find your family?' He motioned them to the stools as Gabriel found some more mugs on a shelf and filled them with murky liquid from the previous year's vintage. After John had told Ralph of his visit to the manor at Stoke, he got around to the mysterious body on the edge of the Exe, describing how his hound had discovered it and the nature of the lethal wound in the neck.

'And here's the ring I took from the poor fellow,' he concluded, laying it on the table. 'That has a royal device, so who the hell is he?'

Morin needed only a quick glance inside the ring before handing it back to John. 'He's a royal courier, used to convey confidential documents for the *Curia Regis* and their officers. I think old King Henry set them up, though no doubt similar messengers have been used since time

173

immemorial.'

'I thought they used heralds on relays of fast horses,' objected Gwyn. 'Those uniformed fellows with a guard and a trumpet to clear the way on busy high roads.'

The castellan nodded. 'Indeed, they carry most of the routine dispatches from London and Winchester, like new laws and messages for the Justices of Eyre* when they are on circuit. But these others are supposed to be secret, fetching and carrying information that the Chancellor and Justiciars don't want bandied about the countryside.'

John picked up the ring and put it carefully back into his scrip. 'So having one murdered suggests that someone didn't want a message delivered – or wanted to know what the message was?'

Ralph tugged at the points of his beard. 'Quite likely – and it's a serious matter indeed. And one which I don't know how to handle. Devon does not even have a proper sheriff now, since the Prince took it all into his own hands.'

'What about de Revelle?' asked John. 'If he's not officially a sheriff, how can he deal with a murder?'

Morin gave a cynical laugh. 'Not so much how, as would he want to? His only interest is collecting the taxes for Prince John, though a fair slice of it goes into his own purse, I'll

*The king's judges who try serious cases; the Eyres became the Assizes, then the present Crown Courts

174

warrant. And he's a lazy bastard, as you know, John. He'll not put himself out to make any enquiries. He's back now and in his chamber, so you can ask him!'

'There's another aspect too,' said John slowly. 'If a king's courier is slain because of the message he carried, who would be the most likely to benefit from that? With all this unrest and rumours of treason, it's the Prince who is most suspect – and we know that Richard de Revelle is probably one of his creatures.'

The constable pondered this as he finished his cider and topped them all up once more. 'We're in a difficult position here, as though this is a royal castle and I'm a king's officer, the rest of the county belongs to Prince John. He can do what he likes, he's a Marcher lord in reality, head of a kingdom within a kingdom. But the Chief Justiciar should surely be told of the death of one of his couriers – the message he carried or the reply to it, might be vital to knowing how far John's insurrection has advanced.'

'Did you know that a secret courier was in the West Country?' asked Gwyn. 'Would you recognize him if you looked at the body, though he's going off fast.'

'I didn't know, but then I'm just a soldier, I'm not privy to much of the politics. I'll have a look at the cadaver, but doubt that will help.'

De Wolfe had been thinking hard, his forehead corrugated with the effort. He rasped a hand over his stubble as an aid to thought. 'I feel that I should ride to London and seek an audience with Hubert Walter. I know him well enough and I should show him that Gwyn and myself survived and give him what details we can about that journey, though I suppose he'll have already had those from the king, as I hear he's visited him in Germany. Then at the same time, I can return this ring and tell him what's happened to one of his spies.'

Ralph readily agreed with this plan and John promised that they would ride for the east within a few days.

'The dead man will have to be buried very soon, before he corrupts even more. Your garrison chaplain can no doubt arrange that with the cathedral. He deserves a decent burial as he doubtless died in the service of the Crown.' He rose to his feet and made for the door. 'Now I suppose I'll have to talk to my dear brother-in-law. No doubt he'll be as pleased to see me as a visitation of the plague.'

THIRTEEN

Sir Richard de Revelle was almost a decade older than John, a neat, slim man of average height, with a narrow, foxy face and a small pointed beard of the same light brown as his cropped hair. An elegant dresser, he sat behind his table dressed in a calf-length green tunic edged with gold embroidery around the collar and hem. He looked up from the scrolls he was studying as de Wolfe marched in, ignoring the efforts of the guard on the door to ask him his business.

'I see you have appointed yourself Sheriff of Devon – or at least, installed yourself in his room!' snapped John, sarcastically.

Richard looked up in annoyance at the interruption. As he saw who had entered, his face creased into a humourless smile. 'Ah, so it's you at last, John. I heard from Matilda that you were home.'

De Wolfe perched himself on the edge of the table, to add to the other man's irritation. 'Yes, after having done my best for three years for my God and my King!'

Richard sneered. 'I trust that God appreciated it, for you didn't serve the king very well, letting him fall into the hands of his enemies!'

John's scowl deepened at Richard's ability to always touch the most sensitive spot. 'At least I did my best, rather than sitting on my arse at home, making money,' he retorted.

'Yet I hear that you have made a lot of money even when you were thrashing about the Levant, thanks to our good Portreeve!' sneered Richard. Though he was no warrior, de Revelle always won in a battle of words with his brother-in-law.

'So why are you sitting in here?' demanded John.

'The Count of Mortain, who is the lord of Devonshire, graciously asked me to assist him in dealing with the administration,' said de Revelle, preening himself at the mention of his princely patron. He lifted a roll of parchment and waved it at John, emphasizing the fact that unlike his sister's husband, he could read and write. Richard had attended the abbey school in Tavistock when young and went on to study law for a few years, as he had a driving ambition to ascend the ladder of politics. He saw attaching himself to the rising star of Prince John the best way of fulfilling his aspirations, especially now that the king was under lock and key in Germany.

But de Wolfe was not impressed by manuscripts and account rolls. 'I need a proper sheriff, not a tax collector!' he growled. 'I have a murder to report to someone – the murder of a king's officer.'

Richard's pale eyebrows rose in mild surprise. 'A king's officer? What would he be doing in these parts? Prince John rules here.'

'Not in Rougemont nor Launceston, he doesn't! The king wisely kept them out of the hands of his untrustworthy brother,' snapped John, though he felt frustrated at being in territory where his own royal master seemed to have given away his powers.

The man behind the table shrugged indifferently. 'All I can suggest is that you allow the bailiff or serjeant of the Hundred where this body was found, to conduct an investigation. They have the ancient powers to assist the sheriff, so in his absence they can surely do it themselves.'

John's dark features coloured with indignation. 'Do you not even want to know the circumstances of this crime?' he demanded.

Richard turned up his hands in a gesture of helplessness. 'It is no concern of mine, John. I am not the sheriff, as he is the representative of the king, whose writ no longer runs in these counties. Perhaps you should tell the Royal Council in Winchester of your problem?'

Angrily, John slid from the table and strode to the door. 'That's exactly what I intend to do, Richard. And tell them a few other home truths about what's happening in Devon these days!'

He marched out and slammed the door behind him.

Back at the Bush, the place seemed cleaner, lighter and happier, even in the few days that he had been away. The number of patrons had increased significantly, intrigued by the new whitewash and thatch repairs. John also noticed several strange horses in the stables, belonging to travellers who were staying overnight. Nesta was delighted to see him back and proudly showed off the recent improvements. She then brought him a steaming pork knuckle on a trencher of yesterday's bread covered in fried onions, and sat down to watch him eat it, Edwin rallying around with a quart of ale.

'The next batch will be much better, John, now that Gwyn has brought in new barley,' she promised. As he ate, John told her about the dead body he had found and she was concerned to hear that he was probably a royal courier. John showed her the ring with the engraved lions and also the bronze buckle he had taken from the man's belt.

At once, she became excited. 'I've seen a buckle like that before, John,' she exclaimed. 'What did he look like?'

'A bit hard to tell, the state he was in!' he replied ruefully. 'A little shorter than average, stockily-built, good quality clothing. He had no beard or moustache and his dark brown hair was cropped in the old Norman style. Had you seen him before, then?'

She put a hand on his arm as he reached for his ale. 'It sounds like a man who stayed here for one night about three weeks ago. We've not had many lodgers lately, so I recalled this one, as we had but two staying that week. I'm sure that dragon buckle was his.'

In spite of the fall from fortune that the inn had suffered since Meredydd died, it still had a reputation for the best value for a night's lodging in

Exeter and it seemed quite feasible that a king's messenger might choose it on his long trek from London.

'Did he say who he was or where he was going?' he asked.

Nesta held a hand to her mouth in a typical feminine gesture as she thought for a moment. 'Cornwall! It was to Cornwall he said he was going, for he mentioned that it was a very long journey for him. He said he was glad that they had given him a good horse this time, whoever "they" were.'

'He made no mention of where he had come from?'

'No, but it must have been a long way from Exeter, as he said he was now well over half-way.'

John failed to squeeze any more from Nesta's memory, but was impressed with her recall and ready willingness to help. He was also becoming more aware of her physical charms and was pleased when she came to sit near him when he came in for a meal or a drink. The previous night, as he lay in his cubicle in the loft, he was also very aware of her proximity in her small bedchamber, only a few yards away, but he shrugged off the images that came unbidden into his mind, telling himself that this was the widow of an old comrade. Instead, he had made himself think of Hilda, but could not escape the fact that Dawlish was a dozen miles away, while Nesta was only a dozen paces.

John was jerked out of his reverie by Nesta being called away by Molly to attend to some

181

problem in the kitchen shed and her place was almost immediately taken by Gwyn, who had come down from his cottage to check on some of the jobs that he had ordered on the fabric of the tavern.

'It's looking a lot better, Sir John!' he declared proudly. 'Needs a man out the back when it can be afforded, someone to clean up, shift the barrels and look after the hens and pigs. That sort of work is too heavy for women – and old Edwin's foot limits him, though he tries hard enough.'

They talked for a time about the revival of the Bush, then Gwyn asked if they were really going to London and back.

'I must talk to someone, both about Vienna and about this dead man with the royal ring,' replied de Wolfe. 'The man I need to see is Hubert Walter, but now that he's been exalted to Chief Justiciar, perhaps he'll be above my reach.'

Gwyn shook his shaggy head, his ginger hair flailing about like loose straw from a wagon. 'He'll see you right enough! We were close in Palestine, he even used to talk to *me* – though he was only a bishop then, not an archbishop.'

'Hubert may be in Germany, I hear he'd been there with Queen Eleanor, as she is the driving spirit behind getting her son out of Emperor Henry's clutches. But I must tell someone in authority about this dead man – they may be expecting some answer or concerned that their own message may have fallen into the wrong hands.'

'You mean Prince John's,' growled Gwyn. 'I

wonder where this fellow had been in Cornwall?'

'You know the place better than I do,' said de
Wolfe. 'Any ideas?'

'The only place left belonging to the king is
Launceston Castle, so he may have been taking
messages there.'

Again there was nothing more to go on and
John said he would have to wait until they got to
London or Winchester to learn more.

'Which one are we aiming for?' asked Gwyn,
who had never set foot in either city.

'Winchester first, as it's on the way to London.
Ralph Morin said that they are gradually moving
the government to London – even the Exchequer
is shifting to Westminster Palace.'

Gwyn nodded and swallowed the better part of
a pint of ale. When he came up for air, he was
philosophical about the forthcoming journey.
'It's a long ride, they reckon it takes a good week
from here. But after us trekking from the bloody
Adriatic, it should seem like strolling around the
town.'

John had called to see Matilda earlier that day, a
duty visit to tell her that he had returned from
Stoke. He was surprised to learn that Hugh de
Relaga had left a message with her, inviting
them to a dinner at his house in Raden Lane that
evening. Hugh was one of the few of John's
acquaintances of whom she approved, as the
jolly little man was always attentive to her and
shared her love of expensive clothes and good
food. She also knew that he would probably

have several of the city's more prominent people there, as he was one of the two portreeves. She could boast there of her husband's royal connections by telling tales of his recent adventures abroad.

'At least I see you've bought new raiment,' she said, inspecting him critically. 'So you won't shame me with old rags as you've done in the past – though they are still that miserable grey and black.'

At about the fifth hour, after the cathedral bell had rung for Vespers, he escorted her to the area near the East Gate where, in a side street, Hugh had his house. It was a fine stone building, far too large for an unmarried man who lived with his elder sister, but as one of the leaders of the city council, a Warden of one of the Guilds and a prominent merchant, he had a position to uphold and often needed to entertain people of a similar social level.

Matilda, under a snowy wimple and resplendent in her best gown of plum-coloured velvet under a summer surcoat of green silk, enjoyed herself greatly. There were half a dozen others there, most of whom she knew, as she was an avid social climber and was for ever trying to prod John in becoming more active in the town's hierarchy – which was difficult, as he was absent most of the time.

He himself was not averse to good food, wine and some gossip, but she outshone him that evening, becoming vivacious to the point of being garrulous.

As he watched from across the long table, he

thought what a different woman she could be in company, compared to the spiteful and cold nature she displayed to him. He knew it was partly his fault, as he had no affection for her at all. Their parents had forced them into marriage years ago, as Matilda's father wanted to get his least attractive daughter married off before her scanty good looks faded even more. John's own father also wanted to settle his younger son with a family like the de Revelles, one far richer than his own.

The evening passed well enough, with no disturbances apart from his wife's voice becoming louder and more strident as she drank more of Hugh's excellent Loire red wine. For his part, he was glad to be sitting next to another old friend, his namesake John de Alencon, one of the senior canons of the cathedral and the Archdeacon of Exeter. A thin, almost gaunt man, this John had wiry grey hair around his tonsure and a pair of bright blue eyes in his bony face.

John related the now oft-told story of his return from Acre and the disaster of the Lionheart's capture.

De Alencon was also a staunch supporter of King Richard, unlike some of the other senior canons, who were keen to see Prince John on the throne of England. 'I pray for him every night, John,' he said sincerely. 'I'm sure that our new Archbishop of Canterbury will do all he can to secure Richard's release. Hubert Walter may not be a very enthusiastic churchman, but is the best negotiator we could hope to have.'

John had heard that there had been considerable resentment amongst senior clergy – especially in Canterbury itself – to the high-handed appointment of Hubert by the Lionheart from his foreign prison cell, but he made no comment and went on to tell the archdeacon about his discovery of the murdered royal agent.

'I'll see to it that he gets a decent burial, John, even if we don't know who he is,' promised de Alencon.

'I hope to give you his name within a few weeks, as I'm off to report to Hubert Walter on Wednesday. They must surely know who they sent to Cornwall.'

De Alencon sadly shook his head. 'I fear for this land if we have another civil war,' he said sombrely. 'I'm sure that the Count of Mortain is actively planning a rebellion and that a number of leading churchmen are supporting him. It's unfortunate – or perhaps even fortunate – that we have had no bishop here since John the Chanter died two years ago. It's rumoured that Henry Marshall, Dean of York, may be appointed before long, as he is the brother of William Marshal, your old Crusading comrade. But Henry is also a keen advocate of Prince John's ascent to the throne.'

De Wolfe was surprised to hear his friend being so outspoken about his prospective bishop, but they had kept their voices down so that they would not be overheard, though the level of chatter was now very high.

When the party was over, John escorted his wife back to Fore Street. She was in an uncommonly jovial mood and clung to his arm, though he knew this was more from needing a strong support after too much wine, than from any sense of affection. She even expressed her regret that he could not stay in her cousin's house, but after seeing her step unsteadily across the threshold, he hurried away down to the Bush with a light heart.

FOURTEEN

As Gwyn had said, compared with crossing half of Europe, the journey to Winchester was far from arduous and they reached it in five days. John had decided not to ride the older and heavier Bran and had rented another horse from Andrew's stables, though Gwyn was happy to use his own brown mare.

They stayed in inns on the way, a luxury after their rough living on the continent, but John was taking advantage of his recently increased wealth and saw no reason to stint themselves whilst on the king's business. When the walled city, for centuries the capital of England, came into sight, Gwyn was greatly impressed by the huge cathedral and the massive castle, but after a night's rest at an inn in the High Street, the morning brought disappointment.

Enquiries at the castle told them that the Chief Justiciar was in London, having just returned from another visit to Germany, where he was once again trying to negotiate the king's release. Within a couple of hours, the two men from Devon were on the road again, heading for the new capital on the Thames. After another night in Guildford and a second in Esher, the third day saw them across the Thames and into West-

188

minster. Having stabled their horses and rented a couple of beds at a hostelry in King Street, de Wolfe led Gwyn across to the palace, a group of rambling buildings attached to William Rufus's Great Hall on the river bank adjacent to Westminster Abbey. Inside the wide courtyard, the next problem was to gain admittance to the man they had come to visit. Hubert Walter was now the greatest in the land, being both head of the Church and the head of government, especially since the hated Chancellor, William Longchamp, had had to flee to Rouen.

John presented himself at the porch beyond the Great Hall and after telling a porter that he was Sir John de Wolfe, found a small room where a gruff clerk sat at a table shuffling parchments.

John identified himself again and said that he wanted to speak to someone who had access to the Justiciar, on a matter of importance.

The official, whose stiff hair surrounded a clerical tonsure, looked at him suspiciously. 'How do I know you are who you claim to be?' he muttered. 'What is this business that brings you here?'

De Wolfe glowered at the man. 'It's confidential, at least to such as you,' he retorted.

Nettled, the clerk glared back. 'You could be some French spy or an assassin wishing harm to the Justiciar.'

John felt like grabbing the fellow by the throat and shaking him, but Gwyn put a restraining hand on his shoulder, as he spoke to the obstructive clerk.

'My master and I fought alongside Hubert

Walter in the Holy Land – and we were part of the king's company on his journey back from there.'

The man behind the table looked suspiciously at them, but sensed trouble for himself if he got this wrong. 'Can you prove that?' he snapped.

For answer, John dipped his fingers into his scrip and produced the courier's ring. Holding it out, he pointed to the pair of royal lions engraved on the inside. 'Does this convince you?'

The man's attitude changed immediately. With a mumbled apology, he beckoned to the porter, who was hovering in the doorway. 'Escort these gentlemen to the Justiciar's chambers and find one of his officers to speak to them.'

With Gwyn grinning behind him at being called 'a gentleman', the man led de Wolfe into the gloomy passages of the palace and, after several turns then up some stairs, arrived at a busy room where many clerks and servants bustled about. The porter spoke to one of them and soon a fat priest appeared from another room, clutching lists of accounts.

John again explained who he was and why he needed to speak to the archbishop. When Brother Roland heard that this was the John de Wolfe that Hubert Walter had spoken of in connection with the king's capture, his eyes widened and he treated the knight with considerable respect.

'The Justiciar has heard from the king's own lips the sorry tale of his outrageous abduction in Vienna – and he spoke warmly of your faithful service,' he said obsequiously.

He led them through several more rooms and a passage to another antechamber where a chaplain was seated and after a whispered consultation, the chaplain vanished through an inner door.

A few moments later, he returned and ushered them into a large, but plainly furnished chamber where a lean man with a lined face and greying brown hair rose from his chair to greet them.

Hubert Walter did not assume the trappings that might be expected of such a powerful man. All that suggested that he was an archbishop was the plain red cassock with a small gold cross hanging around his neck.

'Sir John, old friend!' he said quietly, as he came across the room to grip de Wolfe's arms in greeting. 'And Gwyn of Polruan, too! It's good to see you safe and sound after all we went through in Palestine – though the king told me that you and he had suffered even more later on!'

Having been with the king's guards for much of the campaign, the two Exeter men had seen a lot of the Bishop of Salisbury, as Hubert had been then. Originally he was made the chaplain to the English crusading contingent after Archbishop Baldwin had died of disease – though Hubert did far more fighting and diplomacy than any priestly duties.

He went back his chair and motioned the others to bring up stools to the table. 'Now tell me of what happened after you sailed from Acre. I've heard it from Richard, but not in much detail.'

For half an hour John related the story of the eventful voyage and then the disastrous ride across country to Vienna. 'I feel shame at not being able to have prevented our lord king's capture,' he concluded sorrowfully. 'If we had not gone out searching for food, perhaps I could have saved him.'

Hubert shook his head. 'When I spoke to the king in Wurzburg, he was adamant that you did all you could for him. You had to buy provisions for the journey – and you could have done nothing to overcome a whole troop of soldiers, other than lose your own lives.'

John shook his head sadly. 'I would gladly have given my life for him, sir. This will plague me for the rest of my life.'

They spoke about it for a few more minutes, Gwyn respectfully asking the Justiciar how he found the Lionheart in body and spirit.

'He is now almost restored to his usual fiery self,' said Hubert with a smile. 'At first he was confined in a remote castle on a crag, at Durnstein on the Danube. Then he was dragged off by Count Leopold to Regensburg in Germany to meet the Emperor and your old enemy Count Meinhard of Gorz, but Leopold distrusted King Henry and took him back to Austria after two days. Then a month later, he sells him on to Henry and our king was taken to Wurzburg.'

John leaned forward with a question. 'There's been some tale going around that one of the king's troubadours, Blondel of Nesle, first discovered him by singing a song they composed together and heard the Lionheart respond with another verse from behind his prison bars at this Durnstein place!'

The Justiciar smiled. 'A picturesque fable, John! There was no mystery about where he was confined, right from the start. Emperor Henry even wrote a letter to Philip Augustus within days of his capture, giving the details. I have a copy in this very room, for they proudly bandied the news all over Europe.'

'So where is our lord now?' asked Gwyn.

'He's been shuttled about from Ochsenfurt to Speyer, where he was tried in March, though there he turned the tables on Henry and Philip by gaining the sympathy and support of many of the Emperor's rebellious princes and bishops. After that he was in Trifels Castle, then Hagenau, but is now at the royal court in Mainz. We are still trying to get a definite date for his release, but that bloody man Philip of France keeps trying to bribe Henry to hand him over to him.' His face darkened. 'And our Prince John is colluding with the French in that! Between them they offered the Emperor eighty thousand silver marks for our king.'

The mention of the prince gave John an opening for the second reason for his audience with the Chief Justiciar. Once more he pulled out the ring and gave it to Hubert Walter. 'I came across a murdered man last week, sire. His body was thrown into a river after his throat had been cut. This was the only identification upon him, he had been robbed of everything else including his money.'

With a puzzled expression, Hubert took the

ring and turned it in his fingers until he saw the engravings. He looked up quizzically at de Wolfe. 'Unless he had stolen this from someone, he must have been one of our court couriers. You say his body was found in Devonshire?'

As John confirmed this, Hubert rang a small bell that stood on his desk and immediately, the chaplain came in from the outer room. As he bent over the archbishop, Hubert murmured something in a low voice and the priest nodded and went out again.

'I've started some enquiries – we have a number of men who travel discreetly around the country, taking messages and collecting information. Our present concern is naturally Prince John and his supporters. After his rebellion was defeated earlier this year, he agreed to a truce, but he's not to be trusted.'

'Is this dead man one of yours, then?' asked John.

'I've sent to find out who was down in the West Country – and you say you think he had been as far as Cornwall, so possibly he has been seeking information about St Michael's Mount, which Henry de la Pomeroy holds on behalf of Prince John.' He rose from his chair again. 'It will take some time for my clerks to discover who this might be, so return here tomorrow when I hope to have some news for you. This unfortunate man deserves to have a name on his grave, if nothing else – and I might have a task for you as well.'

After their days in the saddle, John de Wolfe and

Gwyn were happy to have some rest and after returning to their inn, had a good meal of fried bacon, eggs and black pudding, washed down with a quart of ale. As they sat looking out of the unshuttered window at the crowded Royal Way outside, Gwyn wondered what 'task' the Chief Justiciar might give them.

'We are fortunate to be on such easy terms with the man who runs England,' he said. 'I still find it hard to believe that all this has happened to me in the past year or two, being just a rough soldier from Cornwall.'

John punched him on the arm, which had muscles like iron. 'Don't underestimate yourself, man! Hubert can see a trustworthy fellow when he sees one. I'll warrant he'll want us to find out why this courier died and who killed him. With no sheriff in the county, who else can do it? And if it was because he was poking about in John's affairs, then the last thing the prince will want is some investigation.'

The Cornishman grunted. 'That's probably why Richard de Revelle shows such a lack of interest, though being such a lazy swine, it's hard to pin any motive on what he does or doesn't do.'

They spent a couple of hours or so wandering around Westminster and along the river towards the city, then came back for more food, drink and an early bed.

'If Hubert finishes his business with us in the morning, we can be back on the road again later in the day – and home in Exeter within the week,' said John. He realized that he missed his lodgings in the Bush, especially the company of Nesta and he looked forward with foreboding to having to settle down in a house with Matilda.

Early next day, they were back at the palace to resume their meeting with the Justiciar. He was at an early Mass in St Stephen's Chapel, the palace's place of worship, but eventually arrived and they were ushered into his presence again by Brother Roland.

Hubert Walter was looking more haggard today, weighed down by the strain of both running a country and finding a vast sum of money to pay for the king's release. A hundred and fifty thousand marks was the equivalent of thirty tons of silver, two or three times the annual income of England. 'It's being collected by the special Ransom Exchequer and stored in the crypt of St Paul's Cathedral,' he had explained to them the previous day, but now he wanted to tell them about the corpse in the River Exe.

'He was Roger Smale, a former soldier working in the Chancery. As I suspected, he was sent down to Cornwall with messages for the constable of Launceston Castle, but also to spy out the situation at St Michael's Mount, fortified for the prince. Since the truce, he has not been attacked by us, but the *Curia* wanted to know if the stronghold was being further strengthened in preparation for future conflict.'

De Wolfe recalled the horrific wound to the man's throat which had half-severed his neck. 'He must have found out something, for them to dispatch him so brutally,' he said.

The Justiciar shrugged. 'There's nothing we

196

can do about it now, but I wonder why he was killed in Devon and not Cornwall.'

'Perhaps he found out other things as well. John's cause has sympathizers in Devon, as we know.' Some trace of family loyalty caused him to refrain from mentioning his brother-in-law, though he suspected that Hubert knew of all the potential adherents in that part of the country, especially as some of Exeter's twenty-four canons were known to side with Bishop Hugh of Coventry.

'We have lost one agent who seems have known his way around the West Country,' went on Hubert. 'So I am going to ask you to continue the faithful service that you have already given to our Lord King, by keeping your eyes and ears open for any other evidence of the prince's treachery. He had most of his castles taken from him back in February, when he kept claiming that the king was dead and that he was now on the throne, but he has refused to hand over Nottingham or Tickhill and is covertly provisioning them for a future battle. As I said before, we have a so-called truce, but that is really a waiting game to see what happens over the Lionheart's release.'

John and Gwyn readily agreed to his request, being happy to have some further way of serving the king, partly to assuage their consciences over their failure to prevent his capture. They arranged to forward any information via Ralph Morin, who had regular messengers going between the royal castle and Westminster. They took their leave of the archbishop, Gwyn still awed by their familiarity, which seemed far stranger here than in the common danger and discomfort of Palestine. Soon they were in the saddle again, riding west, with at least a name to give John de Alencon to read over the new grave in the cathedral precinct.

They arrived at the Bush, wet and weary, over a week later. The weather had turned bad and the roads were thick with mud, slowing them down and adding an extra day to their journey. The horses had been returned to their stables and the two travellers arrived on foot at the door of the inn, where Brutus was waiting to greet his master, having again used the mysterious powers of a dog to anticipate John's return. Nesta, equally delighted to see them safe and sound, rushed around to get them hot food and to take John's riding cloak to dry in the wash-shed outside. Gwyn had his usual leather jerkin and hood, which he threw carelessly over a stool to drip into the rushes.

Edwin plied them with ale and then, as they ate grilled trout, beans and leeks, Nesta sat with them at the table. She listened with awe to their tales of exotic places like Winchester and London and about exalted persons like the Archbishop of Canterbury.

'At least we know who the murdered fellow was,' said John. 'And we were right, he was a spy for the king's government. As we expected, the Prince is still up to his tricks and though there's supposed to be peace between him and the barons, no one in their right mind would trust him after his past record.'

He decided not to voice abroad their promised role as secret agents for the Chief Justiciar, as this might jeopardize any hope of learning things that they were not supposed to hear. However, John promised himself that he would tell Nesta when they were alone together, as he felt she could be trusted to keep it to herself. Also, with so many travellers passing through the Bush, she might overhear something useful. After eating, Gwyn decided to go home to his wife, who Nesta said had been down several times in the past two weeks to help clean up the inn and make sure that her protégée Molly was cooking satisfactorily. De Wolfe also thought he had better visit his wife, though less eagerly than his squire. The rain had stopped and the August evening was warm, so he left his damp cloak and walked up Smythen Street and across a side lane to come out in Fore Street, opposite the dwelling of Matilda's cousin.

The expected baby was getting near to appearing in the world and the women of the household were too preoccupied to bother much with a mere man. Even though the childless Matilda had never seemed over-endowed with maternal feelings, she was also caught up in the general enthusiasm and gave John a perfunctory welcome. He kept out of the way for a time, skulking in a room as far away as possible from the birthing stool and lying-in bed.

Eventually Matilda came in and he gave her an abbreviated account of his trip. Predictably, the fact that he had had two meetings with the Head of the English Church and seemed almost on gossiping terms with him, fuelled Matilda's fascination for anything ecclesiastical and gave her more ammunition to fire at her social rivals in the town.

'Have you thought any more about seeking a house for us?' he asked in a tone that would have better suited an enquiry about his own funeral arrangements.

'I have heard of several in the city,' she replied. 'But none would have been good enough for us. You are a knight of the realm and we can't live in some dreary dwelling more suited to a candle maker or apothecary.'

John decided to grasp the nettle and go along with her ambitions. Much as he liked staying in the Bush, especially with Nesta there, he knew that it could not be a long-term solution. 'Andrew the farrier, where I stable my horse, told me today that one of the houses in St Martin's Lane is vacant. The old lawyer who lived there has gone to Plympton to live with his daughter.'

Matilda's square face showed even more interest than when he was talking about the Archbishop of Canterbury. 'That was the house of Adam of Lyme,' she replied. 'It's in a good position, I could walk to the cathedral from there in two minutes!' The ease with which she could attend her endless devotions seemed a major criterion for her.

'The farrier says that it is old and has been neglected by the occupant since his wife died five years ago,' said John cautiously. 'It would need a lot of work done on it.'

They agreed to go and inspect it as soon as John could discover who held the lease.

Leaving an unusually placid Matilda behind him, he went wearily back to the Bush and after a pleasant hour talking to Nesta between her attending to her other patrons, climbed the steps and fell gratefully on to his bed and was asleep inside five minutes.

Next day, he walked with Gwyn and the hound up to the Cathedral Close, the large area around the huge church of St Peter and St Paul, whose two great towers dominated the whole of Exeter. Building work was still going on, though it was now nearing completion, as the original Norman cathedral, built on the site of a small Saxon abbey, had been almost totally rebuilt during the past sixty years. The Close, which was an ecclesiastical enclave independent of the city authorities, was also the burial ground for all Exeter and the surrounding area. Only in exceptional circumstances could burials take place anywhere else, as the cathedral jealously guarded the fees that came from disposing of the dead.

One of these graves was that of the courier John had found on the river bank. He enquired of a sexton and was shown a heap of fresh earth near the north tower. The whole Close was more like an excavation site than a peaceful cemetery, with newly dug graves mixed with old ones covered with weeds. The place was ill-kept, piles of rubbish abounding and beggars, drunks and noisy urchins competing for space with a few goats and even a rooting pig.

They stood over the lonely heap of red Devon soil and John took out the signet ring and looked at it. 'We know the poor fellow's name now, it's Roger Smale,' said John. 'I'll ask the archdeacon to come and offer a prayer over the grave and say a Mass for him at one of the cathedral shrines.'

Ignoring the yells of children racing around with their mangy dogs and kicking balls of tied-up rags, the two men stood there for a moment, one each side of the mound. John, in his long grey tunic clinched around his waist with his sword-belt, stared pensively down, his black hair blowing in the breeze above his dark, hawklike face. His squire looked as immovable as an oak tree, broad-shouldered in his scuffed jerkin, the ginger hair and moustaches framing his big, ruddy features.

'Are we going to seek his killers, Sir John?' he rumbled.

'He served the king as much as we did, in his way, Gwyn. So he deserves avenging, but where do we start looking?'

The Cornishman ran his hand through his tangled locks. 'We have a name now – and we think he must have come down the river. I can't really see him being washed up from the sea. So can we not ride up the Exe and the Yeo for a few miles and ask if anyone had seen him?'

They began walking slowly away before de Wolfe answered. 'No harm done in that. We have little else to occupy us at the moment. We'll try it tomorrow, though I have no great hope of success.'

John wanted to check on Bran in Andrew's stables, so they crossed the northern corner of the Close to the little church of St Martin, which stood at the end of the lane bearing the same name.

'I told my wife last night that this house was vacant – perhaps unwisely, for she seemed quite taken with the idea.'

He stopped outside a tall, narrow building, the first on the left side. Beyond it, set back a little, was a similar house, as there were only two in the alley. At each end were the backs of houses in either the Close or the High Street. Opposite was the farrier's establishment between the rear of a tavern in the main street and another house in a lane alongside the church.

Gwyn looked at it critically. 'A big old place for just two of you! Needs a lot of work done on it, too. Just look at that roof.'

Standing back, they looked up and saw that some of the thin wooden shingles of the steeply sloping roof were missing and others warped and cracked.

'Good front door, though,' said Gwyn, pointing at the stout boards of blackened oak, with rusty iron hinges and studded nails. Between the door and the farther end of the house, there was one window at chest level. It was firmly shuttered, and nothing else broke the high frontage of heavy oak frames which supported panels of cob, covered with discoloured whitewash.

'The price should be lower, given the state it's in,' muttered John.

When they crossed to the stables, John asked

the farrier if he knew who was offering the house for sale or rent.

'It's the old man's partner, a lawyer in Northgate Street,' replied Andrew. 'The place has been empty for more than a year, so maybe he'll be anxious to get rid of it.'

After reassuring his old stallion that he had not been forgotten, John told the stableman to get him ready for early next morning, when Gwyn and he would ride up the valley of the Exe seeking any clue as to the way in which Roger Smale met his death.

Their next stop was Rougemont, where de Wolfe sought out the constable, while Gwyn went in search of a few soldiers willing to start a game of dice. Gabriel was drilling some young recruits in the inner ward, avoiding the ox-carts that rumbled in with supplies and the chickens and pigs that rooted about in the muddy earth churned up by the incessant activity of a busy castle. Ralph Morin was in his chamber, checking the number and quality of newly delivered arrows from a local fletcher, but gladly took a break when John arrived. Broaching a skin of wine, they sat and drank while John told him of his visit to London and the information that the Justiciar had given him.

'So they don't trust Prince John, even after the so-called truce,' observed Ralph. 'It's a wonder that they don't deprive him of those six counties, but I suppose as the king gave them to him, only he can take them away.'

'And I'm appointed by Hubert Walter as a kind of unofficial watcher in the West Country, to warn of any signs that a new rebellion is fomenting,' added de Wolfe. 'In other words, a royal spy, not that I like the idea. I'd rather come out and confront the bastards, with sword and shield.'

'It may come to that, John. The barons took away many of his castles earlier in the year, but he still has Windsor, Tickhill and Nottingham. Also, some of his covert supporters have their own castles dotted around, which he could rely on if it came to civil war.'

John nodded gloomily. 'Unfortunately, there's a lot of people he could rely on. Thank God his mother, sensible woman, keeps her own stern eye on him while our king is locked up abroad.'

'We may be sharpening our swords again before long if King Richard doesn't come home soon,' said the castellan.

'Or even if he does!' added John. 'If the prince persists in defying his brother and starting an insurrection, Richard will have to crush him. The danger is that John is cultivating his alliance with Philip of France, who has greedy eyes not only on Normandy, but England itself.'

The talk turned to more immediate matters.

'What can be done to find the killers of this Roger Smale?' asked de Wolfe. 'With no effective sheriff, no one seems to care about the king's peace any longer.'

'I can see your brother-in-law eventually being elected as acting sheriff by the prince, in the absence of anyone else,' declared Ralph. 'God help us, he's only good for a tax-collector, I doubt his sword has been out of its scabbard these past ten years. You should be given the job, John, but the prince knows you are a staunch king's man.'

'No chance of that, Ralph. But Gwyn and I are going to try to learn something about Smale's last days, if only to satisfy ourselves.'

When he left the castle, he went down to find the lawyer in North Street and discuss the vacant house with him. The advocate, a middle-aged fellow who seemed quite sensible and cooperative, told him that the owner, now fragile in mind and body, was willing to dispose of the house on a ten-year lease for twenty-five pounds. He gave John a large key and said he was welcome to take his wife to inspect the dwelling at any time, so John's next stop was Fore Street, where he managed to attract Matilda's attention away from the heavily pregnant niece for long enough to tell her about the house in St Martin's Lane. She still seemed moderately interested and John arranged to walk up with her that evening to inspect it.

Back at the Bush, he ate a midday meal provided by Nesta and her new cook, a bowl of mutton potage followed by grilled sea bream with beans and cabbage. Fresh bread and cheese followed and after the privations of the past few months, John felt that he had entered a culinary heaven. Afterwards, Nesta came to sit with him and he told her about the house in St Martin's Lane.

'Why don't you walk up with me now and have a look?' he asked, when he saw how interested she was in seeing inside a town house.

'Won't your wife be annoyed at you taking a

strange woman there, even before she's seen it herself?' asked Nesta, anxiously.

He couldn't resist slipping an arm around her waist and briefly squeezing her. 'You're not a strange woman, you're my landlady! And she will never know, anyway, Matilda is too besotted with the prospect of soon having a new baby to croon over.'

Nesta pulled a light hooded cloak over her kirtle and walked with him to Southgate Street and across into one of the entrances to the cathedral precinct. As they crossed the rugged ground, he pointed out the new grave mound of Roger Smale.

'I'm going out with Gwyn tomorrow to see if we can find some trace of the poor fellow in the days before he was so foully killed. I promised the Justiciar that I would try to discover if any active plot was being hatched by Prince John down here in the west.'

The Welshwoman looked at him in concern. 'Be careful, John, I've heard that he and his men can be ruthless. We don't want you coming to any harm, after surviving all you've gone through these past few years.'

He warmed to her worrying about him, so different to Matilda's usual indifference. 'I'll manage, dear Nesta. Compared to Saladin's army, I doubt the Count of Mortain's rabble will prove much of a challenge.'

She still looked uneasy, but in a couple of minutes they were outside the heavy door of the house in St Martin's Lane. De Wolfe produced the key and with a squeak of rusty metal, turned it and shoved the door open. They found themselves in a narrow vestibule partitioned off from the main room. It was bare apart from a bench against the opposite wall, under which were a few old shoes. Above it was a row of wooden clothes pegs stuck into the wall. On the right was a door leading into the main hall and on the left, an opening leading to a covered passage that ran along the side of the house to reach the backyard.

'A bit grim, but nothing wrong so far,' observed Nesta. 'Let's see the hall.'

She went to the inner door and pushed it open to reveal panelled draught screens just inside. Beyond these was the only room in the house, apart from the vestibule. They stood by the screens and gazed around. It was very high but spacious, in spite of the narrow frontage.

'That roof must be twenty feet high!' said John, craning his neck to look up at the dusty beams far above, supporting the rafters that carried the wooden tiles. Here and there, they could see daylight where some were missing and a couple of small birds fluttered out, disturbed by these rare visitors.

At ground level, the floor was of beaten earth, rock hard from a century of treading feet. A thin scattering of mouldy rushes covered it, apart from the central firepit, which was ringed with stones. An iron trivet and a pair of roasting dogs sat forlornly over the long-dead ashes. The walls were all timber, the inner side of the frame-and-cob walls being planked for warmth A few faded tapestries hung on them in an effort to relieve the spartan appearance of the chamber.

'I've seen more cheerful barrack rooms than this,' grunted John. 'But it seems sound enough in its structure.'

Nesta had at first been disappointed by the bare, gloomy dwelling, but she could imagine what could be done to improve it. 'Given time and money, John, it could be made into a fine house. Of course, it will depend on what your wife thinks of it.' There was a tinge of jealousy in her voice as she felt herself excluded from the domesticity that she had lost with Meredydd's death.

'Let's have a look at the yard,' suggested John and led them back through the vestibule and down the side passage. Here there was a fairly large area, bounded by the back of the houses in the Cathedral Close on one side and a high fence between them and a similar yard next door.

'There are a lot of huts in here,' said Nesta. 'Looks like the back of the Bush. Best see what's in them.'

Exploration revealed a privy, a wash house, a wood store, a pigsty and a large kitchen shed, which still had a mouldering mattress in the corner, where obviously the cookmaid had slept. A well had been dug in the centre of the muddy plot, too near to the pigsty for Nesta's liking. They surveyed the scene and then looked back at the house, where a completely blank wall reached up to the roof.

'Well, it's all here, John, but needs a great deal of improvement.'

He readily agreed with her opinion. 'Depends

on how much the owner wants for it. The need for so much to be spent on the place should be a good lever to lower his price.'

They walked back to the Bush, John's mind half on the house and half on Nesta walking sedately alongside him. He wondered how long it would be before Matilda accused him of lusting after a common alewife, as no doubt one of her church cronies would eventually hear of it and revel in telling her.

When he went back to St Martin's Lane with his wife that evening, he took care to act as if he had never seen inside the place before. They paraded around for half an hour and almost reluctantly, Matilda agreed that, after a great deal of work, possibly it could be turned into a dwelling fit for the wife of a knight.

'But where did they sleep?' she demanded, when they were looking around the hall again.

John saw some discoloured lines in one corner, with old nails projecting. 'I think there was a partition there, cutting off a small room. Perhaps that was it.'

Matilda sneered. 'I'm not sleeping in some box, John! We would need a proper room for me to have a maid to help me dress and do my hair.'

De Wolfe looked at the dusty firepit and imagined the haze of smoke that would normally ascend from it to find its way out through the eaves high above.

'And I would like a fireplace with a chimney. I saw one in Brittany a few years ago, built in stone. We could combine that with a solar built on to the back of the house.' He became almost enthusiastic and wondered if he had now reach-ed an age where home comforts were more im-portant than the thrill of jousting or the bloodlust of battle.

Having seen all they needed, he locked up and walked her back to Fore Street. 'I'll be away tomorrow, on the Archbishop's business, but when I'm back I'll see about making a bargain with the owner.'

He was careful to mention Hubert Walter, as he knew that dropping the name of the highest clergyman in the land would keep his wife content – as would the thought of living in a house within a stone's throw of the cathedral.

The long day's ride up the Exe valley and one of its tributaries turned out to be fruitless. De Wolfe and Gwyn rode north from Exeter through all the small villages and manor up the river. They called to enquire at many alehouses and spoke to manor reeves and bailiffs, all of whom denied any sighting of a man answering the description of Roger Smale. True, their description was very vague and the only useful detail was the unusual buckle, which John wore on his own belt. He displayed it time and time again, without getting any flicker of recognition.

Several of the people they questioned, especi-ally the reeves and bailiffs, wanted to know what his interest was and what authority he had to ask such questions. John hedged his answers slight-ly, saying that he was on a commission from the King's Justices, which was not all that far from the truth, given that Hubert Walter was the head of England's legal system.

After riding as far as Crediton and Tiverton, the two men arrived back in Exeter as the sun was setting. As soon as they had stabled their horses, Gwyn went home to St Sidwells, while John walked down to the Bush, looking forward to some good ale, a good meal and Nesta's company.

When all three were set before him, he tackled Molly's boiled bacon, peas and leeks with appreciation and over a dish of plums and nuts, told the landlady about his disappointing expedition into the country.

'Never mind, John, you did all you could,' she said consolingly. 'It's three weeks since you found the body and from what you describe of him, he must have been dead for some time before that.'

Edwin, who had been hovering to listen to his tale, topped up his pot from a large jug. 'Can't win them all, cap'n,' he observed sympathetically. 'Maybe something will turn up one day to help you nail the swine who did it.'

John sat talking to Nesta for a long while, discussing the improvement in trade and income that was already apparent at the Bush.

'Just knowing that you are involved seems to have brought old customers back, John,' she said happily. 'Everyone admired you before, but since you came back from the Crusade and especially as you were so close to the king, you are a hero to every man in Exeter!'

De Wolfe grunted to cover up his embarrassment, though coming from the lips of such a pretty, amiable woman, he secretly revelled in her praise. 'There's one man who doesn't look on me with favour, and that's my damned brother-in-law. This rumour that he might be made sheriff one day is enough to make me want to go back to Acre!'

'But he can't be sheriff while Prince John holds the county in his grasp,' she objected. 'Surely when King Richard is released, he will kick out his wayward brother – then the Lionheart ought to make you sheriff!'

John grinned at the thought of such an unlikely event. 'Can you see me as a glorified tax-collector? Not that I'll ever get the offer.'

He spent another night in the loft, conscious again of Nesta's nearness in her little room until he fell asleep, oblivious to the snores of a fat merchant in the adjoining cubicle. Next morning was taken up with haggling with the lawyer over a price for a long lease on the house in St Martin's Lane. John emphasized the poor condition and dragged the man down to the house to have all the faults pointed out. 'It will cost me as much as I'm willing to give you, just to pay for the repairs and alterations!' he claimed.

With an offer of twenty pounds, which was about seven years' wages for a labourer, the lawyer promised to see if his old colleague would accept it and they parted amicably.

He called on Matilda to tell her what he had done and she seemed mildly interested, though immediately offering her own news that her niece's 'waters had broken', which caused John to flee from the house, which seemed even more full of women than ever.

Going up to the castle on its low hill, he called in on Ralph Morin to tell him of the complete failure of the expedition the previous day. 'I despair of seeing any justice done in this county now,' he said grimly. 'When William Brewer was sheriff, before the king gave Devon away four years ago, at least he made the effort to hunt down criminals. Now it seems that unless manor lords keep the peace in their own patches, no one cares about seeking miscreants, other than in the towns. And even in Exeter, the council has only two constables to try to keep order amongst four thousand people.'

The castellan agreed with him, but said he had no remit to intervene. 'I am only empowered to act against insurrection or invasion,' he said ruefully. 'I could contribute some of the garrison to a *posse comitatus*, should a hunt be mounted for marauding outlaws or highway robbers. But that could only be done at the behest of a sheriff – and we don't have one!'

John moved down a couple of doors and pushed into Richard de Revelle's chamber, bent on irritating his brother-in-law. 'I see you are still here, playing at being sheriff!' he said sarcastically, wanting to get his words in first.

'And what are you playing at, John?' retorted Richard, suavely. 'Practising to be an unemployed soldier, eh? God knows there are plenty of those about now, with no Crusade to offer an excuse for pillaging, drinking and whoring.'

John tried to ignore the jibe, but his unemployed state was too near the truth to prevent it from

214

rankling. 'I thought I would tell you that the Chief Justiciar has given me a commission to seek out and report any evidence of disaffection and treason against the king, until the Lionheart returns to this country – which now seems imminent.'

'Why are you telling me this, John? It is none of my business.' Richard tried to gloss over the matter with an air of indifference, but secretly he was concerned at the dangers of such a tenacious man as de Wolfe poking his big nose into the prince's intrigues. He was also piqued that his sister's husband was on such intimate terms with both the king and his chief minister, whilst he had make do with a more distant relationship with an errant prince.

They bandied words for a few more moments and then, given that Richard was Matilda's closest relative, John thought that he had better tell him about the house he was proposing to buy for her.

'I suppose it will be convenient for her devotions at the cathedral,' replied Richard, loftily. 'Of course, I have bought a large house in North Street, as my manors in Revelstoke, Tiverton and Somerset are sometimes too distant for convenience.'

John's patience with the arrogant, self-centred man soon ran out and he departed, leaving Richard to worry about whether he had sufficiently covered his own tracks in his own contribution to the prince's ambitions.

De Wolfe went back to the Bush for his noon dinner, where Molly brought him a large bread trencher carrying slices of roast mutton, with a platter of boiled onions, beans and carrots. Nesta came with a small loaf of maslin bread, made from both wheat and rye, and a slab of cheese, then sat with him as he ate and listened to his story about his offer for the house.

He followed this with a diatribe against Richard de Revelle for his sneering self-importance and total uninterest in the murder of a royal courier. As he was washing down the food with a pint of her new ale, he confessed his frustration at what seemed to be the prospect of endless inactivity in his life.

'How am I to spend my time, *cariad?*' he demanded in the Welsh they always used together. 'Am I grow old and soft, concerning myself with carpenters and stonemasons over this damned house? Is my sword going to rust in its scabbard – and will I and my horse grow fat from lack of exercise?'

Nesta frowned at his obvious anxiety and laid a hand gently on his arm. 'It's only natural for you to feel like this, John, after the strenuous life you have led recently. But things will settle down – you could become more active in this wool enterprise that you have with the portreeve.'

De Wolfe shook his head. 'Can you really see me sitting in the Guildhall, poring over bills and receipts?' he growled. 'Anyway, first I'd have to learn to read and write! I'd rather become a shipman and help Thorgils take our bloody wool to Flanders!'

She smiled at the thought of him doing either

216

of these tasks. 'I suppose you're right, John. You belong in a saddle, with a lance under your arm. If it were not that I would fear for your life and limb, I'd say go back to competing in tournaments, as you used to. Though you no longer seem to need the prize money nor the ransoms.'

It was true that five or ten years ago, he was a successful contestant in the jousting that paid high rewards for the winners, as well as ruin or death for the losers. Though made illegal in England by the old King Henry, there were plenty of tourneys held outside the law – and many knights travelled abroad to compete in large-scale contests.

'An attractive idea, Nesta – but I'm getting too old at almost forty. The risks of defeat increase greatly with age, for we get too slow and less agile than these young bloods!'

Looking at the attractive redhead sitting next to him, he was conscious of another defect in his life. Over the years, he had had a number of mistresses, both in Devon and elsewhere. There was a certain widow in Sidmouth whom he used to visit and, of course, the delightful Hilda of Dawlish. She was now out of bounds for at least another month, as he had learned from Hugh de Relaga that her husband Thorgils had decided to have a break from voyaging while his ship underwent extensive repairs. On the weary six-month journey across the continent, John had occasionally bedded a buxom serving wench, but lately his sensual appetite had been unsatisfied. Relations of that kind with Matilda had ceased long ago, as like his sister Evelyn, her desires were mainly in the direction of becoming a nun. Several times, during some of their shouting matches, she had bitterly expressed her regret at her father's refusal to allow her to take the veil. But when his thoughts turned to Nesta, he told himself that this was forbidden territory. The memory of Meredydd was still too fresh in her mind and he had a strong sense of obligation to the archer to take advantage of his wife.

Old Edwin limped up to console him with his ale jug and to lighten his mood. John complimented Nesta on the improvement of the brew.

'I learned this recipe from my mother in Gwent,' she replied. 'But the good grain that Gwyn found for me is the main reason for the fine taste.'

John rasped at the dark bristles on his face – it was time for his weekly shave, but Nesta's mention of Gwyn reminded him that he should pay another visit to his family down near the coast.

'Gwyn was always a favourite of theirs, with his amiable nature and his easy wit,' he said. 'I promised them that I would bring him with me next time. Perhaps after the next Sabbath, we'll take a ride down there.'

The days went by and his offer for the lease was accepted, so John needed to seek out workmen to begin renovating the neglected old dwelling. One of the regulars at the Bush was a master mason and another a carpenter, so he had long talks with them about what could be done to improve the place. Several times Matilda was weaned away from her cousin's house to visit St

Martin's Lane with him, as the new baby was delivered at last and the fever of expectation replaced by the sober reality of endless feeding and washing soiled swaddling clothes.

He found her less scornful and abrasive as the novelty of a new house possessed her and they disagreed less than usual. Matilda wanted the earth floor covered with flagstones, a feature of the best houses – and he had his way with the chimneyed fireplace, mainly because it could be incorporated in the building of a solar for Matilda. The mason sketched out a rough plan with a piece of chalk on a slab of slate, showing how the panels of cob and the inner bracing beams could be removed from the back wall up to the level of the eaves and replaced with mortared stone.

'It will take us a couple of months, Sir John,' advised the artisan. 'We will have to order and cart the stone from the quarries at Beer, as well as having the timber cut for the solar and the roof gable.'

Much of this was beyond John's comprehension, but he trusted the man to get on with the job, though the proposed cost made him wince a little. It was a fortnight before he could carry out his promise to go down to Stoke-in-Teignhead with Gwyn and September had arrived before they set out one morning.

As John knew it was pointless hoping to see Hilda with her husband at home, they avoided Dawlish and took the inland route through Kennford, Haldon Forest and Chudleigh to cross the river at King's Teignton and ride down the western bank to his family's manor.

Haldon Forest was an area of particularly dense woodland, a few miles in extent, near the south-eastern edge of Dartmoor. As they rode the narrow road through it, both men kept sharp eyes and ears open for unwelcome company, as this stretch of road was notorious for armed robbers, both predatory outlaws and the more organized gangs of trail bastons. Though John kept a hand near his broadsword and Gwyn fondled the shaft of the ball mace that hung from his saddlebow, they traversed the mile of road without seeing anything move, other than a fox slinking into the undergrowth.

They had the usual warm welcome at Stoke and after eating their fill, sat in the hall of the manor house to hear John's latest news of buying a house.

'You're settling down at last, John,' beamed his sprightly mother. 'A pity it has to be with that surly woman Matilda, but perhaps she will mellow with time.'

Enyd made no pretence at liking her son's wife and secretly wished that he could have married Hilda of Holcombe. Her husband, shortly before he was killed, had given Hilda's father his freedom from serfdom, which also made Hilda a free woman. But at that time, the social gap between them would still have been too wide – though now that she had married a wealthy shipmaster who owned three vessels, she would easily be eligible, had she been available.

The talk turned to the increasing dangers on the highways of England, sparked by Gwyn's mention of their wariness coming through Haldon Forest.

'That place and many others are becoming dangerous,' complained John's brother. 'A week ago, they robbed and half-killed a corn merchant riding from Brixham to Exeter. His servant was also badly beaten and they still fear for his life.'

John told them of the body of the king's courier that he had found on his way back from his last visit to Stoke. 'God knows where he was put into the river, we can find no trace of him on his journey back from Cornwall.'

No one at Stoke had any memory of such a man in that area and John remained convinced that Roger Smale was killed upstream of where he was found.

He and Gwyn were persuaded to stay two nights and spent much of the next day inspecting the manor, of which William de Wolfe was inordinately proud. He was an excellent estate manager and his steward, bailiff and reeve were sensible, reliable men. They made the manor a profitable and happy place, unlike many where the manor lord was a harsh and often cruel tyrant. Orderly fields, plump sheep and barns now being filled with an early harvest ensured that the community would not go hungry over the coming winter.

'We have a good surplus of oats and barley, which I am selling on, so your share of the profits will be even better this year, John,' confided William. 'By the sound of what you are doing to this house of yours, you'll need it!'

They left early next morning and took the

same route home.

When they reached Haldon Forest, they were even more alert than on the outward journey, after William's account of the recent attacks on travellers. All seemed quiet and when they were almost within sight of more open scrubland beyond the trees, they relaxed a little. A moment later, Gwyn's big mare whinnied and jerked, her acute hearing picking up the whine of an arrow in flight. Almost simultaneously, the missile thwacked into the thick leather of Gwyn's saddle pommel, missing his leg by inches. With a roar of anger, he instantly swung the mare's head around and galloped off the track into the undergrowth, where he estimated the shot had come from. As he went, he grabbed the shaft of his mace from the saddlebow and plunged under the trees, where he almost ran down the archer, who was just about to loose another arrow at him. Swinging the heavy spiked ball on the end of its chain, he smashed the bow from the man's hands and following through, the mace ball caught the ruffian across the temple, pulping the skin and bones.

Simultaneously, John de Wolfe had been attacked by two men who rushed from the bushes, one wielding a rusty sword, the other a short spear. The three bandits had picked the wrong pair to attack, as the seasoned Crusaders, each with twenty years' experience of fighting behind them, reacted with almost automatic precision.

Bran, virtually without orders, reared up and his front hoofs came down on top of the man with a spear. With a force of almost half a ton, the assailant was flattened into the hard-packed earth of the track. At the same time, John's long sword had slithered out of its scabbard and as the big destrier came back down, it whistled through the air and almost completely severed the other outlaw's arm at the elbow.

With a scream of pain and terror, he fell to the ground and watched his life's blood pumping out into the dust of the high road. The two horsemen, wary of further attacks, closed together side-by-side in the middle of the track and scanned both sides of the road for further assailants.

'There seem to be no more, Gwyn,' called John after a moment. 'But keep your eyes open while I see if these bastards are going to live.' He slid from his saddle and, with his sword half raised, warily approached the two he had routed. The one that Bran had crushed was obviously dead, his neck bent back at an impossible angle.

The other lay in a spreading pool of blood, which had run into the ruts of the dried mud in the road. He was already barely conscious, his face having a deathly pallor, but he had enough wits left to spit weakly at de Wolfe as he bent over him.

'You are dying, man!' snapped John. 'Are there more of you here?' But the fellow's eyes rolled up and he fell back, still just alive, but totally unresponsive.

'Is your man able to speak?' he called to Gwyn, who was looking down from his steed at the bowman he had struck.

'No, and he's not going to live long, Sir John.

223

His brains are leaking from his ear!'

The forest was silent, apart from the twitter of uncaring birds and the distant howl of one of the few surviving wolves.

'These three must have been trying their luck alone,' observed John. He wiped the blood from his sword in the long grass and slid it back into its sheath. 'They don't seem to be part of a bigger gang.'

Gwyn dismounted and they looked at the three unsuccessful robbers, who were now either dead or on the point of expiring. Though they had just slain three men, they had no false sense of sorrow or guilt. These fellows had tried to murder them in an ambush solely for the contents of their purses; it was a matter of 'kill or be killed' and they felt no remorse for the outcome of their vigorous defence.

'These seem to be low-class villains,' grunted John. 'Tattered clothes and home-made weapons, so they are presumably outlaws trying their luck on passers-by.'

Gwyn stood with his huge hands on his hips, staring at the scattered corpses. 'What the hell are we going to do with them?' he asked.

De Wolfe shrugged. 'Drag them off the highway and leave them to rot. With no sheriff to report to, no one cares what happens to them. The local manor might bury them if they can be bothered, but I expect the local animals will see them off come darkness.'

As they pulled two off the track on to the weedy verge, Gwyn complained about the state of the country under Prince John. 'We're descending into barbarism, I reckon! I keep hearing that these attacks are now so common that many folk will only use the roads in company with at least a dozen others.'

When they got back to Exeter and made the same point to Ralph Morin, he not only agreed, but pointed out that even large groups of travellers had been attacked by bands of marauding outlaws. 'You were lucky only to have a trio of lousy fighters against you,' he said. 'Even tough Crusaders like you would have a hard time if you were jumped on by Willem the Fleming or Harald de Marisco. They can each muster a score or more men, so it's said. Even a squad of my men-at-arms would have their work cut out to defeat an ambush by them.'

They were sitting in the Bush, as Ralph had come down to see what changes had been made at the inn since John returned home.

'Is there nothing that can be done to clear these vermin out of the forest?' asked Nesta, who was sitting with them. 'It's got worse these past few years.'

The big constable shrugged. 'There are a lot more vagrant soldiers about now, since the Irish wars cooled down and the Crusade is over. Knights without land and mercenaries without masters abound in the countryside. The forest is often the only place they have to lurk and highway robbery their only occupation.'

'In some places, large gangs have actually sacked small towns, so I've heard,' contributed Gwyn.

'Not having a sheriff with any guts is another

cause,' grated John. 'Six counties being bled dry by that useless prince, but no effort made to enforce law and order. The bailiffs and sergeants of the Hundreds are in the pocket of the manor lords and are only concerned with piddling local disputes.'

Gwyn scratched his tangled hair to annihilate a few wild beasts lurking there. 'Sir Ralph, why not lend us a few of your garrison men to hunt down some of these bastards?' he suggested. 'Sergeant Gabriel would relish the chance of giving his idle soldiers some real fighting. Most of the youngsters I've seen lounging about Rougement can never have seen a weapon wielded in anger.'

The castellan's bushy eyebrows came together as he considered this. 'You mean a sort of *posse*?' he asked. 'But as we said before, you need a sheriff's warrant to do that.'

Gwyn shook his head. 'I meant more like the Templars, who were founded to protect pilgrims travelling to the holy places in Palestine. In fact, many of our travellers here must be pilgrims going to Canterbury or St David's – or even to take ship to Santiago de Compostella.'

Morin looked at de Wolfe. 'What do you feel about that, John?'

'It's a novel idea, certainly. The Chief Justiciar has commissioned me to root around for evidence that the Count of Mortain is still planning a revolt, so maybe we could make the excuse that these bands of armed robbers might also be offering themselves as mercenaries for him.'

Ralph took a huge swallow of ale before answering. 'I don't think we need an excuse to give it a trial, John. The King's Peace is being broken on the king's highways. I'm now the only royal representative in Devon, so I reckon I'm entitled to do what I think necessary to keep order.'

They fell to deciding on how to organize their vigilante operations, already keen to clear certain areas of the 'forest', a term which was not confined to dense woodland, but any wild land not under cultivation. Nesta became uneasy about John's obvious eagerness to take part in anything that involved the use of sword and mace.

'Don't go getting yourself maimed or killed, Sir John!' she admonished sternly. 'God and all his saints saw fit to preserve you for three years when you were on their business in the Holy Land, but you can't expect their benevolence to extend to chasing armed robbers!'

FIFTEEN

September slid into October and the days shortened, but the transformation of John's new
house in St Martin's Lane was still going on. It
was near completion, however, and he took
advantage of Matilda's absence for a week to
take Nesta to look at what had been done. His
wife had been invited to her brother's manor
in Tiverton for a family gathering to celebrate
his fiftieth birthday – and pointedly, de Wolfe
was not included in the guest list, much to his
relief.

The front of the house was quite unchanged,
apart from new limewash on the panels of cob.
Nesta wondered what had taken so long and cost
so much, until John took her inside. As they
entered the hall, she gave a gasp of wonder at the
farther wall, which had been completely replaced by new stonework. A large fireplace occupied
the centre, with an arched stone mantle over a
deep recess, in which was placed a large iron
basket to hold the logs. Above the arch, a conical
stone funnel stood proud of the wall, tapering to
a narrow flue that vanished through the roof, to
take all the smoke away from the hall. A wide
stone hearth had a raised rim to prevent burning
wood from falling out on to the floor.

High up at one side of the chimney, was a narrow opening, like a small arrow-slit from a castle wall.

'What's that for?' Nesta asked.

'It goes through into the solar, which as you'll see, is built on the outside of the wall,' answered John. 'It's for Matilda to spy on me, when I'm trying to seduce young women down here!'

Nesta giggled and gave him a look that he could only describe as roguish.

He hastily changed the subject. 'What do you think of the floor? She only let me have my fireplace if she could have flagstones!'

The old earth had been covered by massive slabs of a slatey stone, shipped from Cornwall. On them sat a long oak table, with a bench on each side and a heavy chair at either end. In front of the hearth, were a pair of 'monk's settles', wooden chairs hooded up the sides over the top, to keep out draughts. The solitary glassless window facing the lane was firmly shuttered and the other walls carried sombre tapestries depicting biblical scenes, which Nesta guessed were Matilda's choice, as John would have preferred pictures of battle.

'Come around to the yard,' he commanded and when they came out of the side passage, she saw that a room had been built on massive legs, so that it projected under a gable from the top half of the house. A flight of stairs led up to its door and at ground level, another small room had been inserted between the supports.

'That box is for her lady's maid!' he explained, scornfully. 'She insists on having some poor wench to help with her gowns and frizzle her hair!'

'Has she found one yet?'

'No, nor do we have a cookmaid, which is a damned sight more important. She'll have to live in the kitchen shed there, but at least I've had it made a bit larger and more comfortable than the old one.'

Nesta declined to go up and look inside the solar, as this would be where John slept with his wife and somehow, she preferred not to see such an intimate place. They left the house in a rather subdued mood, each wondering what the other was thinking, but Nesta's cheerful spirit soon revived and by the time they got back to the Bush, she was offering to look out for a reliable cookmaid for the new house.

That evening turned into something of a celebration, as Gwyn came down with Agnes to check on Molly's progress as a cook. The master mason and carpenter came in later with their senior journeymen, to announce that they would be clearing up and removing their tools from St Martin's Lane that week, so John decided to invite them all to eat at his expense to mark the end of their labours and the rebirth of the Bush's fortunes.

After they had all eaten and approved Molly's fresh salmon and roast pork, followed by frumenty,* the best ale in Exeter flowed freely and an impromptu party developed. Old Edwin

*Wheat boiled in milk with spices, cinnamon and sugar

revealed a hidden talent in playing merry country tunes on the three-holed pipe and Gwyn, with a gallon of ale and cider inside him, used his deep bass voice to bellow the words of many songs picked up over campfires across Europe.

The regular patrons of the Bush readily joined in the fun, as since his return, their hero Sir John de Wolfe was the city's most popular man. Soon, the few women present were hauled to their feet as they danced the jigging steps of rural England, laughing and chattering as those at the tables banged out the rhythm with empty ale jugs. With autumn logs crackling in the firepit, the scene in the dark taproom began to look like some scene from Celtic mythology.

John looked on with amiable approval and even ventured a couple of ballads of his own, carefully censored because of the respectable women there – the Bush was rarely used by whores, as Nesta discouraged that trade, leaving it to disreputable inns like the Saracen, two streets away.

Then Agnes dragged him to his feet and they laughingly attempted the simple steps of the dance, mostly hand-holding, advancing, retreating and turning. John was no dancer and only the loosening of inhibitions caused by the ale persuaded him to take part. Then Agnes, who had a very shrewd head on her plump shoulders, waited until one of the masons had released Nesta, then steered John into the landlady's path. Smiling happily, she cavorted with him around the firepit and even his saturnine features creased into an almost foolish grin as they stamped and pranced to the obvious approval of the others, who clapped in time to Edwin's piping and the thump of a small drum that someone had produced.

When they finally flopped down on to their bench, Agnes noted with satisfaction that John's arm remained draped around Nesta's shoulders. She knew, through Gwyn, of de Wolfe's frustrating marriage and also of his past affairs with Hilda of Dawlish and other women, but also knew that he was a lonely man at heart. It was about time, she decided, that he enjoyed some female company.

When the party broke up, Gwyn took Agnes up to her sister's in Gandy Lane, as it was far too late to get out of the city, the gates being firmly closed at dusk. The others faded away and John, slightly unsteady on his feet, offered to help Nesta clear up, with Edwin and the two other servants. But the Welshwoman, having herself drunk a little more than her usual moderate amount, declared that it should be left until morning and told the others to go to their homes.

'Off to bed with you, Sir John, Great Crusader!' she said with an unusual lack of inhibition. She climbed the ladder to the loft, and missed her grip on the top step, falling back into his ready arms.

John pushed her up to safety and they stood swaying slightly outside her small room. There were several lodgers on the other side of the loft, but their lusty snores told that they were oblivious to what was going on. Her cheerful mood suddenly melted into tears and she laid her head on his chest.

'John, thank you for everything. What would I do without you?'

His arms went around her and he drew her tightly to him. She raised her face and kissed him on the lips, long and earnestly. Then with a sudden movement, she twisted away and opened the door to her bedchamber. 'Good night, sweet man, sleep well and may God watch over you this night!'

She slipped inside and the door closed with a click as the wooden latch dropped into place.

John stood there stupidly, touching his lips where they had kissed. His rapid arousal faded almost as quickly as it had arisen and he stumbled across to his cubicle and sat heavily on the edge of his mattress.

'I think I'm in love again, blast it!' he muttered.

For the next few days, John went around in an abstracted frame of mind, behaving perfectly normally, but in a distant mood that Gwyn detected only too well. Agnes, who had almost a wise woman's sixth sense, had told him what was going on and received a rebuke from her husband for meddling in matters that didn't concern her. John still had his reservations about becoming emotionally involved with a friend's widow, but he found Nesta increasingly attractive and desirable. At intervals, he chastised himself for his juvenile qualms – for God's sake, he was a Norman knight, a member of a class who thought no more of seducing or even ravishing an alehouse keeper than kicking a stray dog! Why should he be different with this particular woman?

Yet Nesta affected him in a way similar to the feelings he had for Hilda, who was now out of his reach – and strangely, he felt more remote from her now that Nesta had come into his life. Not an introspective man, he usually dealt with such situations by demanding some robust action. One morning, he marched up to Rougemont and pulled Gwyn out of a game of cards in the gatehouse.

'We need to start our campaign against these bastards who are infesting the roads,' he proclaimed. 'Let's see what Ralph Morin has to say about it.'

They found the castellan in his chamber, haranguing Gabriel and another sergeant about the lacklustre appearance and performance of the last batch of recruits to the garrison.

'Maybe we can offer something that will put some steel into their backs,' suggested de Wolfe. 'It's about time we took some action against these scum who are attacking travellers and thieving from villages with little to discourage them.'

After an hour's discussion and plotting, they decided to comb the forest area where John and Gwyn had been attacked.

'Those three we dispatched seemed lone wolves, but there have been many more organized raids on passing traffic, so there must be a more substantial gang in there somewhere,' he said.

They set a day the following week, giving the sergeant time to pick a score of men and get them fit and well equipped.

'Are we going to tell de Revelle?' asked Morin, dubiously.

'I'll tell him, just to let him know how idle we think he is, but it's really none of his business. We are doing this on behalf of the *Curia* and Hubert Walter. In fact, when we talked in London not long ago, he hinted that he was thinking of setting up some unemployed knights in every county, as "keepers of the peace", so we're just anticipating his wishes.'

John was as good as his word and loped into his brother-in-law's chamber, ostensibly to offer him congratulations on his recent birthday. 'I trust you had a good celebration, Richard – Matilda told me that it was a festive occasion.'

De Revelle showed no embarrassment at the implied rebuke for the lack of invitation to John and merely asked if his sister's house was fit for habitation yet, again with the implication that it was hardly suitable for a woman of her status.

'We hope to move ourselves in there very soon,' said John, omitting to say that he looked on the occasion with gloomy foreboding. He would a thousand times prefer to stay in his little cubicle in the Bush, almost within arm's reach of Nesta.

'You have engaged servants, I hope?' enquired Richard, loftily.

'A customer of Hugh de Relaga has recommended a young woman who used to cook for him before he moved to Dartmouth. And a church friend of Matilda's has palmed off a French girl on her to act as her personal maid.'

Richard sorted parchments on his table with an impatient gesture, implying that John's presence was delaying important work. 'I hear that you are contemplating some vigilante activities against trail bastons,' he said loftily. 'Are you setting yourself up as an unofficial sheriff?'

De Wolfe glowered at him. 'We've already got one of those, by the looks of it, except that he seems to have no interest in keeping the king's peace!'

Richard shrugged indifferently. 'It's none of my business, John. I am merely doing a service for the prince – who at least is in England and not absenting himself for three years, probably never to return.'

He always knew how to rile his sister's husband, as any criticism of the Lionheart was anathema to John.

'I'm just doing what any honest knight should do, trying to clear our roads of the murderous villains that infest them!' he roared. 'When you have personally found a king's servant with his throat cut and then been attacked on the highway by a couple of thugs intent on killing you, it's a great incentive to do something about it!'

Richard pulled some documents towards him is a gesture of dismissal. 'Then I wish you luck, John. I always travel with a strong bodyguard, so the matter is of no consequence to me.'

John gave up trying to hold a reasonable conversation with him and marched out, giving the heavy door a satisfying slam behind him.

SIXTEEN

The first expedition of the posse from Rougemont was an anticlimax, after the excited young men-at-arms had worked themselves up into a lather of expectation at defeating a band of murderous outlaws. Ralph and John had chosen Haldon Forest as their target, as this was where de Wolfe had been attacked. Twenty men, together with the two knights, Gwyn and Sergeant Gabriel marched the five miles out of Exeter, being seen off by rather mystified townsfolk as they stamped their way out of the West Gate, as if leaving from some distant battle.

They all wore short chain mail hauberks, breeches and round helmets, their weapons being a mixture of pikes and swords, with half a dozen archers amongst them. It would have taken twenty-score men to thoroughly comb that area of woodland, but a start had to be made somewhere, if only to leave a message that the authorities were not going to let lawlessness go unchecked.

They stopped on the road at the point where the three would-be assassins had been killed. There was no sign of the bodies and as the castle constable had already questioned the bailiff of the Exminster Hundred, who told him that no one had recovered or even told him about corpses in that area, it was assumed that the local wildlife had dealt with their disposal.

The soldiers fanned out in pairs and began advancing into the forest, keeping within shouting distance. They had no hope of coming upon any outlaws by stealth but on this preliminary foray, wanted to make their presence known and to discover any camps that may have been set up.

After a couple of hours, they had passed beyond the halfway mark in the direction of Trusham village, when a cry from men on the left of the line brought the three leaders to the place. In a clearing, there were the remains of a fire, with a wisp of smoke still rising from logs which had been hastily kicked apart. Nearby were some crude shelters of woven branches built against the trunks of trees, in which were a few scattered articles of tattered clothing.

'They've made a run for it, no doubt they heard us coming from a furlong away,' declared Ralph Morin.

De Wolfe kicked at a half-eaten carcass of a chicken, lying near the fire. 'A hell of a way to live, especially with winter coming on. Still, I expect they think it's better than having their necks stretched on the gallows in Exeter.' From the appearance of the rough shelters, he thought that about six men had been camping out there.

'We'll not catch them today, I fear,' said Gabriel, hefting his long pike in frustration. 'They can circle round us and vanish in any direction without us getting a sight of them.'

'Still, we've made it clear that they can't have their own way any longer,' said Ralph resignedly. 'If I had five hundred men, we could encircle the place and drive them to the centre, like rabbits in a harvest field.'

The men relit the fire and sat around it to eat the bread, meat and cheese they had brought with them, washing it down with water from a nearby stream.

Afterwards, they carried on until they emerged from the trees in sight of the strip fields of Trusham and began marching back home through smaller lanes.

'At least it's given these lads some exercise and a taste of discipline,' said Gabriel. 'Maybe next time, they can get some proper action.'

'I can't see any other way of trying to deal with these criminals,' growled John. 'We can't escort travellers like the Templars and the Hospitallers did in Palestine. But if we catch, kill or hang a few outlaws, then it may help to discourage the rest.'

Life at the Bush went on almost as normal, as during the following week Nesta and John made no mention of the intimate moment outside her room. It was by no means ignored, however, as the frequent smiles she gave him seemed warmer and on his part, John lost no opportunity of getting her to sit close to him on the bench when he was having a meal or a jug of ale. When it was time to sleep, however, they seemed to have an unspoken agreement that they would not ascend the ladder at the same time, as if to avoid the temptation to repeat the brinkmanship that had occurred on the night of the impromptu party.

The house in St Martin's Lane was almost ready for occupation now. John had met Mary, the cookmaid recommended by Hugh de Relaga, and was favourably impressed. A well-built girl in the mid-twenties, her Saxon mother was the cook to a leather merchant in Goldsmith Street. She frankly admitted that she was the illegitimate daughter of a soldier who had not waited in Exeter for her birth. Handsome rather than pretty, she had an air of competence and independence that he liked. Mary readily accepted the offer of the job and was happy to live in the cook shed and even look after Brutus, as she was a dog lover like Gwyn.

Matilda had also engaged the maid that she was offered, though John kept well clear of that transaction. He saw the girl once with his wife before they moved in, a thin rabbit-toothed creature with a permanently frightened manner. This Lucille spoke not a word of English, as she had come from the Vexin, a part of Normandy north of the Seine, which Philip of France was trying to seize. Her speaking only French suited Matilda, who had an obsession with wishing to appear totally Norman.

On Gwyn's advice, John also took on an old man, who lived on Stepcote Hill, who could come to do the rough outside work, like chopping wood, drawing water from the well, emptying the privy and feeding the pig and chickens. All this domesticity was new to John and as he knew that Matilda would never deign to soil her own hands with work, he was determined to get sufficient servants to keep the place running.

In spite of his fears that time would hang heavy without a war to attend, it passed quickly. He visited Hugh de Relaga a number of times to see if there was anything he could do to help him and twice he went off with Gwyn to take written orders for wool to Buckfast Abbey, some twenty miles away towards Plymouth. Buckfast was a Cistercian foundation, famous for its sheep breeding and wool production, so their exporting business sent a lot of their produce to Flanders and the Rhine, using Thorgils' ships to transport it.

John also spent a lot of time in the Bush and was pleased to see the trade growing rapidly after the new improvements that he had funded. Molly turned out to be an excellent cook and he hoped that Mary would prove as expert in St Martin's Lane. Now having the best ingredients, Nesta also improved the quality of her ale to such an extent that it was soon acknowledged to be the best in the city. All this, including an increase in the number of travellers who came to lodge overnight, meant that the income rose appreciably. Though like himself, Nesta could not read or write, she was very proficient at counting coins! They sat every week at a table and added up the profits for the past seven days. The silver pennies, the only coins in circulation, were locked away in a stout chest in her bedroom, after recording the results on tally sticks, lengths of hazel twig with spaced notches indicating the amounts. Nesta insisted on passing on to John any excess over running expenses, as repayment for the money he had lent her. Though initially reluctant to accept it so soon, he decided that it would offend her if he refused, but he made it plain that his funds were always there if the need arose.

About a week before he was due to make his reluctant move out of the Bush into the new house, the inevitable happened. He made a daily call on Matilda in Fore Street to see that all was well – but on this occasion, when she came to the door, her usually impassive features were twisted into a malignant scowl.

'I wonder you have the gall to show your face here!' she rasped. 'Up to your old tricks as soon as you come back to these shores.'

He knew without asking what she was referring to, but she continued to rant at him. 'You can fornicate all you like when you are cavorting abroad, John de Wolfe – but to start all over again under my very nose is too much! And with a common alehouse keeper, to add insult to injury! As if that wasn't bad enough, the whore is *Welsh*!'

Her sneering tone was like a poker stirring a dull fire into leaping flames, as John had a ready temper, easily provoked into activity. 'I suppose one of those frustrated old baggages you call your friends has been peddling tittle-tattle about me!' he snarled. 'Third-hand tales with about as much truth in them as you have charity in that cold heart of yours!'

His sudden anger was made all the stronger by

the fact that he felt unjustly accused, as not only had he not made it into Nesta's bedchamber, but had even forbidden himself that pleasure because of noble feelings about her late husband.

Matilda was unmoved, as she stood in the doorway with her fists on her wide hips, glaring pugnaciously at him. 'A barefaced liar, too! Do you really think I don't know about that common serf's daughter in Dawlish – or that brazen widow in Sidmouth? God alone knows how many other trollops you have scattered around the countryside!'

Before he could vent his indignation any further, she slammed the door in his face.

Ignoring the stares of several curious passers-by, he stamped away back up to Carfoix and went into the nearest alehouse, which was perhaps appropriately called 'The Hanged Man' with a crude depiction of a gallows over the door. It was a tavern that he had never patronized before and its sordid interior made it unlikely that he would do so again. The nearest drinking-place for the slaughterers in The Shambles, it was nothing but a bare room with a few rough benches and a row of casks against one wall. There were no tables and the filthy straw on the floor was soiled with bloodstains that had dripped off the leather aprons of the customers. However, in his state of foul temper, he wanted a drink and did not trust himself to go straight to the Bush where he might upset Nesta by blurting out Matilda's taunts.

A potman who was so thin that he must have been suffering from some wasting disease, brought him a misshapen pot with a quart of poor ale, all of which slightly cheered him by adding to the contrast between this seedy place and Nesta's trim establishment.

A dozen burly butchers and slaughterers stood around, drinking and gossiping noisily, some giving John sidelong glances as they wondered why such a well-known knight and Crusader was drinking in such a miserable place.

He found an empty bench in a corner and sat in solitude with his quart, his anger slowly cooling into gloom. Though his wife's taunts about his other infidelities were true, she had known about them for years – it was the unfounded accusations about Nesta, combined with her usual loathing for anyone with Celtic blood, that had riled him most. He was not particularly concerned about them falling out and hurling insults at each other – that was commonplace whenever they had been together for any length of time. It was the complication that the house in St Martin's Lane was almost ready for them to move in and having spent a considerable part of his ready cash on it, he wondered whether she would now refuse to live there, just to spite him. However, as he slowly drank the sour ale, his temper subsided and he could look more calmly on the situation. Firstly, he was stuck with Matilda as a wife – much as they disliked each other, there was no way in which their marriage could be ended – unless he strangled her! Divorce was virtually unknown and after some sixteen years, he could hardly plead for an annulment on the grounds of consanguinity, which did not exist, except for the devious nobility who might have the ear of the Pope. Neither after all this time, could he claim that the marriage was void because of lack of consummation – though that particular activity had been notably absent for a dozen years.

So what about this damned house, he wondered? On reflection, he thought that there was little chance of her declining the opportunity to live in such a prestigious spot, right next to her beloved cathedral, especially as it now had a unique hearth and chimney, flagged floors and a new solar. Matilda could flaunt these, together with a lady's maid and two other servants, before her snobbish friends who made up the upper middle-class in the city, mostly wives of the richer merchants and few priests and canons. One such was Julian Fulk, the fat, oily parish priest of St Olave's, who Matilda seemed to think was on a par with St Peter himself. If he had not known of her frigidity, he would have suspected her of being his lover, from the simpering deference she showed Fulk and her endless attendance at his miserable church.

De Wolfe finished his ale and, feeling somewhat better for his cogitation, he marched out into the crisp autumn air. Some kind of religious procession was winding its way down the High Street, choristers singing and others playing instruments. It reminded him that this was celebrating the Feast of St Cecilia, the patron saint of music, so it must be the twenty-second day of November already.

As he walked down towards the Bush, he

wondered where the Lionheart was now, doubtless somewhere in Germany fretting about his
release. Ralph Morin had had news from a
herald passing through from London, that
though much of the huge ransom had now been
collected, there was still a long way to go and
there were worries that Emperor Henry and
Duke Leopold would become impatient and sell
the king to Philip, to cut their losses.

This train of thought brought him to Hubert
Walter, the man who was so desperately trying to
wring the money from an already impoverished
England. John felt guilty that he had been unable
to advance the task that Hubert had given him, to
find any evidence of Prince John's treachery, but
he could not see any way of seeking such
information. The killing of Roger Smale was the
only possible clue, but it also seemed a dead end.

With a sigh, he strode across Southgate Street
and down Priest Street, heading for the Bush and
a decent pot of ale. As he neared Idle Lane, he
decided not to mention Matilda's accusations to
Nesta – though knowing how fast gossip spread
within Exeter, it was only staving off the inevitable for a time.

SEVENTEEN

The following week, now almost into December, Ralph Morin and his fellow vigilantes took a patrol of six mounted soldiers up the main road eastwards, along the highway that went via Honiton towards Ilminster and thence to Bristol and London. Though there was no continuous forest very near Exeter, there were substantial patches where the road passed through dense woods for several miles. Although the trees were supposed to be cut back for a distance of a bow shot each side, this was rarely done and in places, the track almost ran through tunnels, where the large trees arched overhead.

With Morin and de Wolfe at their head and Gwyn and Gabriel bringing up the rear, they trotted along, intent on showing themselves to any prying eyes that might be lurking in the fringes of the forest. As they came around a bend in one of the narrower sections, a violent scene suddenly presented itself.

Ahead of them, a number of horses and people were jostling in the road, shouts and screams being mixed with the clash of weapons. Spurring Bran forward, with the castellan alongside him, John galloped down the few hundred paces that separated them from the melee, closely followed by the other men. As John hammered along, already drawing his sword in readiness, he saw that a pair of horses had fallen, overturning the litter that had been carried between them. Two women were crouched in the road, screaming at the tops of their voices. Half a dozen attackers were obviously gaining the upper hand over the same number of men trying to defend themselves and the ladies. Two of the travelling party were lying in the road, one ominously still and the other writhing in agony.

The battle was short and vicious, as the military contingent thundered up to the scene of the ambush. At the first sight of the soldiers, the outlaws abandoned their attack and fled for the cover of the trees, but one who was still fighting a member of the escort, was felled by a blow from the man's sword as he turned away.

'Archers, dismount and get after them!' bellowed Ralph Morin, as the attackers began vanishing into the undergrowth at the side of the road. With John and Gwyn alongside him, they hauled their horses around and charged off the track as two soldiers were stringing their bows and firing off a volley after the retreating ruffians. Within a few yards, the mounted men had to slide off their steeds, as dense saplings and brambles made it impossible to ride any deeper into the forest at anything other than a walking pace. Scrambling after the assailants, Gwyn tripped over one, who lay groaning with an arrow shaft sticking from his back. Within a couple of minutes, Ralph and John realized that it was fruitless to continue the chase, as the remaining fugitives had already gained too great a distance on them and had faded into the trees.

'Back to the road, they may need our help!' yelled the constable and when they had recovered their horses, they walked out on to the road, Gwyn dragging the wounded man by his arms, to dump him at the side of the track.

There was confusion at the scene of the ambush, as the men-at-arms were pacifying the frightened horses and trying to attend to the wounded travellers. John now saw that the two females were nuns and that the immobile figure in the road, who appeared to be dead, was a priest. The tall man who had struck one of the attackers – who now lay whining in the dust, clutching his bleeding shoulder – stumbled across to Ralph.

'Thank God you came in time, sir!' he panted. 'I am Justin, one of the proctor's men from the cathedral. I must attend to those poor ladies!'

John and Ralph went with him to assist the pair of nuns, who were clutching each other as they sat in the dirt. One was elderly and was muttering prayers with her eyes firmly shut, while her companion was a much younger woman, doing her best to console her sister-in-God.

'Are you hurt, ladies?' asked John gently, looking at their torn habits and the dirt on their white wimples.

The younger one smiled bravely and shook her head. 'Thank you, sir, not wounded, but bruised and shaken from being pitched from that litter.'

The soldiers had now managed to force the fallen horses to their feet and as they struggled up, the covered litter, supported by long poles slung between the harnesses, righted itself. Leaving Justin and two of the other servants to get the two nuns back aboard, John and Ralph went to assess the damage to the ecclesiastical party.

'The priest is stone dead, I fear,' growled Gwyn, who was standing over the inert shape of a fat, middle-aged cleric. 'He's had a blow on the head that's stove in his skull.'

The other injured man was one of the cathedral servants, who had suffered a severe blow from a mace to his shoulder and chest. 'His arm's broken and I think some ribs are stove in,' announced Gabriel. 'But he should live, if we get him back to the cathedral infirmary.'

Gwyn had appointed himself gaoler to the two injured robbers, as he had grabbed the one with the broken shoulder and dragged him across to lie in the weeds of the verge, alongside the man with the arrow still projecting from his chest. This one was already *in extremis,* being semi-conscious and gasping for breath as blood began bubbling from his mouth. The other one was bleeding from a wound across the top of his shoulder. He was moaning with pain, but Gwyn felt that his shifty eyes were looking for a chance to leap up and make a run for the trees.

Meanwhile, John went across to the litter to see how the two nuns were faring. They had been helped back into the long, hammock-like device which had a tent-like roof and side curtains. The younger one, who sat behind the one with the thin, lined face, again thanked their rescuers, but was herself crying at the death of their priestly colleague.

'Father Edward was escorting us to Glastonbury, where we are to join the community of sisters at the abbey,' she sniffed. 'We have come from Tavistock, stopping at Buckfast Abbey and Polsloe Priory in Exeter. We left there several hours ago, with a new escort kindly arranged by the Archdeacon.'

Justin, the man from the cathedral, told John that Father Edward was a canon of Tavistock Abbey and had been killed when he tried to stop one of the outlaws seizing the purse of silver he carried for expenses on the journey.

Within a quarter of an hour, order had been restored and Ralph Morin announced that he would take the travellers back to Exeter, escorted by his men. 'We can take the ladies to Polsloe, where the injured fellow can be treated.'

Polsloe was a small convent a mile outside the city, run by a few sisters whose main function was medical care, especially of women's ailments. John said that he would stay with Gwyn and deal with the two remnants of the robber band, one dead, one alive. After the cavalcade had gone, they went to stand over the survivor, a skinny fellow of about thirty, dressed in a dirty red tunic with gold embroidery, obviously stolen from a previous victim. He had a few blackened teeth in his mouth, visible when he cursed both of them, using some of the foulest language that even the campaign-hardened de Wolfe had ever heard.

Gwyn gave him a hefty kick in the ribs as he

lay in the grass. 'Keep that filthy tongue in your head, you murdering bastard!' he growled. 'Or use it to say your last prayers for killing a priest and attacking nuns!'

'Are you going to kill me here and now?' snarled the man.

John looked down at him with distaste. 'You are going to die, that's for sure – either at the end of a rope or having your head taken off.'

'That's the best way,' said Gwyn. 'We can get five shillings bounty for it if we take it to the sheriff.' In an undertone, he added: 'If we had a sheriff.'

John knew he could not bring himself to kill the man in cold blood. Since Acre, where he had seen several thousand Saracen prisoners beheaded in a mass execution, he could not contemplate the act, even though it was perfectly legal for anyone to kill an outlaw on sight. 'There's some rope on my saddlebow, Gwyn. Tie his hands and he can walk back to Rougemont behind your horse. If he can't keep up, just drag him along, it's far less than he deserves.'

'What about the corpsed one?' asked Gwyn, as the arrowed victim was now well and truly dead.

'Leave him, like the ones in Haldon Forest. Our furry friends will soon get rid of him.'

In spite of their threats, the two horsemen went at a sedate pace back to Exeter, so that the prisoner could keep up with them without falling down and being dragged. Exhausted, he toiled up the slope to the castle and was hauled over to the keep, where the prison was situated in the undercroft. This was the basement, partly under-ground and completely separated from the upper levels. The only entrance to the keep itself was up the wooden stairs to the main door on the first floor, a safety measure in case of siege.

The warder was an evil, obese Saxon called Stigand, a sadistic man of low mentality who was both gaoler, torturer and storeman. The undercroft, a gloomy vault bounded by the slimy stone arches that supported the upper storeys, was divided in half by a rusty iron fence into an area which held the stinking cells, the rest being storage. Stigand lived here, in a foul nest under one of the arches, where a mattress accompanied a brazier that both cooked his food and heated the branding irons and ploughshares for Ordeals.

Gwyn untied his prisoner, who claimed to be Arnulf of Devizes, and prodded him down the few steps that led from the inner ward into the semi-darkness of the undercroft.

Stigand appeared from his den, his waxy face and piggy eyes gloating with anticipation. 'I heard from the others who came back just now, that you were bringing an outlaw. Is he to hang straight away or do you want me to first make him suffer a little?'

'Just put him in a cell until we know what's to happen to him,' snapped de Wolfe, who could not stand the sight of the foul custodian.

Before Arnulf was pulled away towards a gate in the iron stockade, he pointed a finger of his uninjured arm at John's belt. 'How did you get hold of that, then?' he croaked. 'I've only seen one like that before, a dragon in a circle.'

253

Surprised, John held up a hand to stop Stigand tugging at the prisoner. 'Where did you see it?' he demanded, putting a thumb behind his belt to push Roger Smale's buckle forwards.

Arnulf shrugged indifferently, with the desperate bravado of a man already marked for execution. 'I'm going to be hanged whatever happens, so I may as well tell you. It was on the belt of a man we slew, up Crediton way. Never seen a design like that before.'

'When was this? Another highway robbery?'

Arnulf shook his head wearily. 'No, it was a bit unusual, that killing. A month or two back, our leader, Walter Hamelin, was paid to ambush a certain man, kill him and steal any parchments he might be carrying.'

Gwyn gave the man a hefty push in the chest, which made him howl, as his arm was dangling uselessly by his side. 'Are you spinning us some bloody yarn?' growled the Cornishman. 'It sounds like a pack of lies. Who would pay for such a killing?'

Arnulf cringed as Gwyn raised his fist again. 'It's the truth, I tell you. On my dear mother's grave, I swear it! Walter was told a few days before that this man would be travelling alone down from Crediton and we were to lie in wait for him and slay him. He described him as a fair-headed fellow, riding a big strawberry roan.'

'So who ordered it and what happened to any documents you found?' demanded John. 'How did he know how to meet your leader, this bastard Walter you speak of?'

'I don't know, it was privy to Walter and this

254

young man who ordered it. Walter got a bag of silver, that I do recollect, for he gave the rest of us each five pence as our share, though it was Walter himself as cut his throat. We just grabbed him off his horse and threw his body into the river.'

'So who was this young man you speak of, you cold-blooded swine?' persisted John, glowering at the self-confessed murderer's accomplice.

Arnulf sagged, seeing any hope of earning himself a reprieve fading. 'Some smart fellow, looked like a knight's squire. He met Walter at some arranged place on the road, but I know that Walter had seen him before in Crediton. Though an outlaw like the rest of us, he was always sloping off into town.'

'Do you know this squire's name or where he was from?' shouted Gwyn, thrusting his ferocious face towards the man.

'Never heard his name, but I did catch that he had to take these bits of written parchment back to Berry when he came again to see if Walter had carried out his task.'

'Berry? You mean Pomeroy's castle near Totnes?' snapped John, alert now that names were being named.

Arnulf tried to shrug, but his shoulder was too painful. 'I don't know, it was no concern of mine. I got my few pence, that's all I cared about.'

More questions drew nothing useful and the doomed man was dragged off by Stigand to spend the short remainder of his miserable life in a rat-infested cell with a slate slab as a bed and leather bucket for his ablutions.

John and Gwyn went up to the floor above and sought out Ralph Morin, who was eating and drinking to fortify himself after their escapade at the forest's edge. John told him of what Arnulf had said and the castellan whistled through his beard at its significance.

'So now you've got something you can tell Hubert Walter! If that squire was from Berry, then it incriminates Henry de la Pomeroy, which is no great surprise.'

The de la Pomeroys were a widespread dynasty named after their apple orchards in Normandy, whose early members had come over to fight with William of Falaise at the Battle of Hastings and as a reward, had vast tracts of land given them in several parts of England. The present lord in the south-west was Henry, whose main residence was at Berry Pomeroy Castle, twenty miles south-west of Exeter. He was known to be a keen supporter of the Count of Mortain and had fortified the island of St Michael's Mount at the extreme end of Cornwall, to act as one of the prince's strongholds.

'The Justiciar will already be well aware of Henry's partiality to John,' observed de Wolfe. 'But for him to slay a king's servant and steal his dispatches must surely be a new development, suggesting that the prince is contemplating open revolt again.'

The constable agreed and said that he would get an urgent report drafted by his clerk and send it to Hubert Walter by a herald who was due to return to Winchester in the next few days.

'What about this Walter Hamelin, who was the actual killer, according to that piece of scum down below?' asked Gwyn.

John rasped a finger over his black stubble. 'Yes, he deserves a rope around his neck, too. That Arnulf says he visits Crediton openly, so maybe one of these days we can spare a few hours to flush him out!'

The murder of Roger Smale preyed on John's mind, especially now that they knew the name of his killer, as well as a strong suspicion that it was done at the behest of Prince John.

He thought about it during that night as he lay in bed, with Matilda snoring a few feet away under the heavy coverlet. What was the point of hanging little rogues, when those higher in the chain went unpunished? Hubert Walter had asked him to keep his ear to the ground in the West Country, but when something happened, there was no one in authority to take any action. John turned over restlessly and decided that Roger Smale must not rot away unavenged under his mound of damp earth outside the cathedral.

Next morning, he went back to the undercroft at Rougemont and ordered Stigand to let him into the cells. Grumbling at being interrupted while frying his breakfast of eggs and bread on a skillet over the branding brazier, the gaoler opened the outer gate for him and went back to his crude cooking. The half-dozen rusty cages inside the prison area were empty apart from Arnulf's and John strode down to glare in at the

solitary occupant. The outlaw was sitting deject-
edly on the slate slab that served as his bed, his
feet in the sodden, filthy straw that covered the
floor, watching a pair of rats squabbling over
some refuse in the corner. It was dark, cold and
stinking and although John was hardened to
misery, he felt that a man's last days in a con-
demned cell need not be as cruel as this.

The man looked up listlessly as he became
aware of someone outside his cell. 'What do you
want now?' he rasped. 'Have you come to gloat
over me?'

De Wolfe folded his arms and stared at the
prisoner. 'I need some more information about
this man you spoke of, this Walter Hamelin.'

This seemed to spur Arnulf out of his apathy
and he scowled angrily at the tall man in the long
grey tunic, a broadsword slung at his waist.
'Why should I? What's in it for me? You're going to gibbet me whatever happens.'

'Listen to me! Only God knows when the
justices will come to try you, it may be months
yet,' growled John. 'Do you want to stay as
filthy as this for all that time?' He gestured at the
dirty pan of drinking water, in which floated
soiled straw and rat droppings – and at the slop
bucket, overturned under the slate slab.

'What choice do I have?' snarled Arnulf. 'I'd
like to kill myself, but there's no way of managing that in here.'

'Tell me what I want to know and I'll get that
evil bastard out there to give you clean straw and
a blanket. I'll even bribe the swine to get you
some food that would at least be fit for dogs.'

The outlaw looked suspiciously at his visitor, then decided that he had nothing to lose and possibly something to gain. 'What do you want to know?' he muttered.

'Where can I find this Walter? I need to talk to him, to discover who wanted Roger Smale killed – and why?' snapped de Wolfe.

'Talk to him? You mean kill him, I suppose,' sneered Arnulf.

'That would be up to the justices – unless he tried to kill me first, when I would certainly slay him!' said John calmly.

'You'd have your work cut out! Walter's never been bested by anyone yet.'

John became impatient with this verbal fencing. 'You said that though outlawed, he sometimes went back into town. D'you mean Crediton?'

'Yes, most often. Though he has been into Moretonhampstead and Tiverton, even came once here to Exeter.' The man was almost boastful about his former leader's boldness.

'Why does his risk that?' demanded John.

The man leered up at him. 'Walter's fond of a tavern – and even fonder of a woman now and then. And he does a bit of business, selling venison and other game we poached from the forest. There's little risk, with no sheriff's men to bother him. If the town bailiff or the forest officers get too nosy, he either bribes them or makes a run for it.'

John thought about this for a moment. 'How often does he go there? Does he have a favourite tavern in Crediton?'

Arnulf shrugged. 'Depends which part of the forest we were in. It was rare for him to go a week without wanting to ride some doxy. And as for an inn, the Bell was his usual haunt, for he had some arrangement with the landlord. Walter took me there once to help him take a deer we'd killed.'

John tried the man with a few more questions, but there was nothing useful that he could squeeze from him. On the way out of the under-croft, he grabbed Stigand by the throat and threatened him with violence if he failed to clean up the prisoner's cell and treat him more humanely. Thrusting a few pence at him, he promised to send Gwyn in regularly to check that Arnulf received some edible food at least once a day.

As he walked across the muddy inner ward, he wondered why he had suddenly been struck by this attack of compassion for a murderous outlaw, when he had seen scores of other men die in equally foul circumstances. Perhaps age was turning him soft, but then he decided it was just an honest bargain, exchanging a favour for information, scanty though it was.

In the guardroom of the gatehouse, he found Gwyn at his usual game of dice and after waiting to see him win a ha'penny from Sergeant Gabriel, told them of his visit to Stigand's captive.

'Are you thinking of laying an ambush for this Walter fellow?' asked Gabriel. 'He must be a pretty slippery chap to come and go into Crediton as he pleases.'

'Half these towns turn a blind eye to outlaws,'

declared Gwyn, as he dropped his winnings into his scrip. 'They buy illegal game from them and then sell them food and drink to keep them happy in the forest. It all helps to keep the wheels of trade turning – and why should the townsfolk put themselves out to get them arrested?'

Gabriel nodded his agreement. 'I have heard tell of outlaws slipping back to live full-time in towns well away from where they came from. Some have started businesses and even become respectable burgesses!'

'Well this bastard isn't respectable and I'm going to do my damnedest to catch him!' declared de Wolfe. 'We need to get some idea of his habits up around Crediton. I'm too well known to go snooping, so I think it's a job for you, Gwyn. Investigating alehouses should suit you well!'

His henchman agreed, as the prospect of legitimately drinking a great deal appealed to him, especially as John gave him four pence to fund the investigation, enough to buy sufficient ale to float a rowing boat.

The Cornishman went to collect his mare from the castle stables and, within the hour, had set off on the few miles to Crediton.

'That rogue in the cells was right. Walter Hamelin does patronize the Bell quite often.' Late that evening, Gwyn was reporting to John on his spying mission, as they sat in the Bush enjoying mutton pasties and a jug of Nesta's best ale.

'How did you come to discover that?' asked de

Wolfe, wondering if his friend had threatened some hapless patron of the alehouse in Crediton.

Gwyn grinned through his ginger moustache. 'Easy! I claimed that I was looking to buy some illegal venison for my master and had heard that Walter Hamelin sometimes had a haunch or two for sale.'

'Who told you? The landlord himself?'

'Indeed it was! It looks as if he acts as a middleman for Walter. A risky business, poaching deer from the forest – a capital offence, but I suppose if you're already an outlaw, you can't be hanged twice.'

John was distracted for a moment, as Nesta came across from talking to other customers and slid on to the bench alongside him. He told her what Gwyn had been up to that day and she was intrigued to know what they were going to do next.

Gwyn swallowed almost a pint of ale before answering her. 'I've already done it,' he said. 'The landlord told me that Hamelin was due in on Friday with two brace of pheasants and a couple of hares that another customer had ordered. If I wanted to talk to him about venison, he said I should come and bargain a price with him.'

Nesta's arched eyebrows rose in surprise. 'They seem very casual about outlawry in Crediton. Have they no fear of the law there?'

John scowled, his bushy black brows meeting in the middle. 'That's the problem, there *is* no law worth speaking of! That scab in the castle gaol said that the local officers can easily be bought off, with no proper sheriff to police the county.'

'So what are you going to do about this Hamelin fellow?' persisted Nesta.

Gwyn looked at de Wolfe for approval. 'I suppose I'll have to go and talk to him on Friday, see if I can lure him outside where we can seize him?'

John ran his fingers through his hair, pulling the thick dark locks back towards the nape of his neck. 'He'll be wary, meeting a complete stranger. You told the landlord that you wanted the venison for your master – did he ask who that was?'

Gwyn nodded. 'He did, but I told him my master wanted to keep his name well away from any illegal dealings, which seemed to satisfy him.'

John pondered this for a moment. 'We need to ambush him, but no doubt he'll be cautious, for all that Crediton seems a safe haven for rogues. If we gallop into the town with a posse, he'll vanish through the back door, that's for sure.'

Gwyn nodded, as he slurped some more ale. 'We don't even know what he looks like, so I'll have to keep that meeting, just to clap eyes on the man. I'll make a date to collect the haunch of meat, then somehow we can nab him when he leaves, for he has to go back into the forest afterwards.'

But Nesta, always mindful of their safety, had thought of a danger they had not mentioned. 'What if he recognizes you, Gwyn? He was the leader of that gang that attacked the nuns. You

were there too and you're not exactly inconspicuous!'

The Cornishman was unconcerned. 'They
vanished into the trees like greased lightning as
soon as they saw us coming. Only Arnulf was
left in the road, fending off one of the escort –
and he's locked in the cells.'

Nesta was not totally convinced, but the two
men seemed set on this escapade and John partly
mollified her by promising to take Gabriel and a
few men-at-arms with them.

When Friday afternoon came, six men set off on
the eight miles to Crediton, which they reached
at twilight. All except Gwyn took cover in a
wood just outside the town, the others tethering
their horses there and waiting for half an hour to
allow Gwyn to reach the Bell tavern. They had
brought an extra horse from the castle stables, in
the hope of having a captive to take back with
them.

Leaving the youngest soldier to look after their
mounts, the remaining four set off separately to
follow Gwyn into the town. All wore nonde-
script clothing, John covering his long black hair
under a pilgrim's hat, the wide brim shadowing
his face in the approaching dusk. Though he was
well known in Exeter, having been abroad for
three years made it unlikely that he would be
easily recognized in Crediton, but to add to the
image of a pilgrim, he had a long cloak to con-
ceal his sword and carried a staff in his hand.
Pilgrims were often seen in the town, as its main
claim to fame was as the birthplace of the great

St Boniface, who centuries earlier had taken Christianity to Germany and become its patron saint.

There were several small alehouses in the town, apart from the Bell, and John sent the two men-at-arms into one with a penny for their ale. They could hardly linger in the street for any length of time and there was no way of telling when Walter Hamelin would appear, if at all.

John walked on up the High Street with Gabriel, who had entered into the spirit of the adventure and disguised himself as a tanner, even to the extent of borrowing a leather apron from a friend in Exeter, which stank of the noxious animal substances that were used in treating hides. They passed the Bell on the other side of the main street, but there was no sign of the Cornishman outside the low thatched building.

'We'd best go into the churchyard and wait,' muttered John, as they came level with the large parish church. Slipping through the lychgate, the two men lurked behind the stone wall, trying to look unobtrusive, while still keeping an eye on the door of the Bell. John was afraid that they might waste a whole evening waiting for Walter, the deepening darkness making it more difficult to see who was coming and going.

But almost immediately, Gabriel hissed a warning. 'There's Gwyn on the doorstep, looking up and down the street. There's no one with him.'

Going back into the roadway, they waved at him and he came across.

'He's been and gone again,' he reported. 'The

landlord says he'll be back later, but God alone knows when.'

'Does he know where the bloody man has gone?' demanded de Wolfe.

'He's gone to visit a doxy, so it depends on his stamina as to when he'll be back,' replied Gwyn, with a broad grin.

'Maybe a good time to nab him, with his breeches down – if we knew where he was,' suggested Gabriel.

'He's gone to see his regular whore, according to the landlord,' said Gwyn. 'A hussy called Alys, who plies her trade from a cottage next to the slaughterhouse at the end of the road.' He pointed in the opposite direction to that which they had come and immediately, John began striding off, already loosening his cloak so that he could get at his sword.

The High Street soon petered out and beyond the last straggle of cottages the position of the slaughterhouse was easily apparent by the stench of rotten entrails piled outside. Beyond it, a dim light flickered behind the shutters of a solitary window in a cob-and-thatch hovel, too small to be called a cottage.

'That must be the place,' growled Gabriel. 'It's got a lighted candle, perhaps he likes to see what he's doing!'

There was no gate or fence around the hut and John stepped quietly up to the window and put an eye to a crack in the ill-fitting shutter. Then backing away, he went back to the other two and spoke in a whisper. 'It's him all right – unless someone else is enjoying the delights of Alys.'

'Shall I go back and fetch the other two lads?' suggested Gabriel.

'No, if three of us old warriors can't grab one man, we ought to go home and sit by the fire for the rest of our days!'

Gwyn nodded in the gloom. 'Yes, let's jump him now, but we'll need the others to drag him safely back to Exeter.'

They moved quietly up to the door, a rickety collection of planks with leather hinges, but no handle or latch. John opened it by simply raising his foot and smashing it against the flimsy barrier, which flew back with a crash. With his sword drawn, he charged inside, closely followed by his two companions. The light from the candle was dim, but he had no difficulty in seeing a man straddling a woman on a grubby mattress placed on the floor in one corner. His roar of challenge was matched by a strident bellow from the man, who leapt up dressed only in an undershirt, the pandemonium being added to by piercing shrieks from the woman who lay naked on the palliasse. She had good reason to be frightened, as three large men appeared around her bed, all brandishing large swords.

'Who the hell are you?' yelled the man, staring wildly at these apparitions, as he pulled his shirt down to cover his pubes. He was a tall, well-built man, fair-haired with coarsely handsome features.

'Are you Walter Hamelin?' roared de Wolfe. 'If you are, then we're arresting you!'

'Arresting me? God's teeth, what are you talking about, damn you?' He sounded indignant, as

267

well as shocked.

'We are king's officers!' shouted John, stretching the truth a little. At least Gabriel was part of Exeter's royal garrison and John's warrant from the Justiciar effectively made him a king's agent. 'We are seizing you as an outlaw and also as a murderer,' he added.

Walter virtually danced on the bed in desperation as he looked wildly around to see if he could reach his clothes piled on the floor, where his long dagger sat on his belt. It was a futile gesture, with three long sword-blades pointing steadily at him. Alys had given up screaming and had grabbed a woollen blanket and pulled it over herself, covering her head.

'We are entitled to kill you now!' boomed John. 'But we're taking you back to Exeter to question you, so get your breeches on. This is the last time you'll ever soil a woman, whore though she may be!'

Gabriel bent to remove the dagger from Walter's clothing and threw the serge trousers at him.

Still standing on the bed, the outlaw sullenly pulled them on as he snarled at John. 'Who are you and how did you find me?'

'I'm Sir John de Wolfe, a knight and a servant of King Richard. These men are my squire and the sergeant of the garrison at Rougemont. We were the ones who broke up your murderous attack on a priest and those nuns on the road to Honiton. That's all you need to know, so get these on!' He kicked a pair of boots towards the mattress, where the harlot still cowered under her blanket.

As soon as Walter had dragged them on, Gabriel sheathed his sword and stepped forward with a length of thin rope, which he had brought wrapped around his waist. As his two companions held their swords at the ready, he lashed Hamelin's wrists together behind his back. With the outlaw's own dagger in his hand, he used it to prod the captive in the back and urge him towards the door, keeping hold of the loose end of the rope.

As they left the miserable shack, Gwyn cackled at Walter. 'At least you didn't have to pay her this time, you've had your fun for free!'

In return, the outlaw spat a string of foul blasphemies at the Cornishman and received a clout across the ear for his trouble.

Hamelin continued to curse as they marched him back down the High Street, the moon giving them light enough from a clear sky.

Before they reached the alehouse where they had left the other soldiers, Walter ran out of abuse and managed to speak rationally again. 'What are these bloody questions you want to ask me? You're not sheriff's men. Why don't you just kill me and get it over with?'

De Wolfe stopped their progress in the middle of the street and held the tip of his sword to the man's throat. 'Maybe I will, just as you callously slashed the throat of Roger Smale and threw him into the river!' he growled.

Walter shrugged, causing the tip of the blade to scratch his neck. 'So that's what this is all about!' he sneered. 'I usually slay people for free, but that time I got paid for it!'

'And who was it who paid you?' demanded John, angry at the man's offhanded admission of murder.

'Some dandy of a squire from Berry Pomeroy. I seemed to recollect he called himself Justin something-or-other.'

John dropped his sword from the man's throat, but kept it ready at his side as they began to walk on again. 'And how did he know how to find you?' persisted de Wolfe.

Walter leered at him in the pale moonlight. 'You'd be surprised at some of the folk who depend on me, some of them high and mighty.'

'Depend? What do you mean – "depend"?' growled Gwyn, who obviously detested this brigand.

'A burgess wants a nice bit of venison or a vicar fancies a couple of brace of pheasant,' boasted Walter. 'And sometimes, an upright man wants his wife or his mistress done away with, while he's conveniently miles away in Dorchester!'

They reached the other alehouse and stopped in the road outside. While Gabriel went in to fetch the two men-at-arms, John continued his questioning. 'So this Justin wanted a particular man dead, is that it?'

'Yes, but he mainly wanted some parchments he was carrying. He paid me ten shillings for the deed, half in advance, the rest when I handed over the stuff from the man's pouch.'

'You did better than Judas Iscariot, then!' growled Gwyn. 'He only got thirty pieces of 'silver, you managed a hundred and twenty.'

'Did this Justin say who had ordered him to employ you?' snapped de Wolfe.

'He didn't say and I didn't ask. It was none of my concern. We met both times in the Bell. It was arranged as usual by the landlord.'

'Was Henry de la Pomeroy mentioned at all? Or Prince John?' persisted John. He wanted to know how deeply the Lord of Berry could be tied into this murderous conspiracy, but Walter Hamelin was too far down the chain of conspirators to be of much use.

'All he let slip was that he was a squire and lived in Berry Pomeroy castle,' growled their prisoner. 'He stayed at the inn the second night, as he said it was too far to ride back almost to Totnes that late in the day.'

By now, the two soldiers had come out of the alehouse and added themselves to the guard around the captive. They marched on to where they had left the horses, where the youngest soldier reported that he had seen no one since they left.

Walter was hoisted on to the spare horse, his hands tied in front of him so that he could still grip the pommel of the saddle, as the reins were held by Gabriel, who rode on one side with Gwyn on the other. John de Wolfe led the small procession through the moonlight, the other men-at-arms bringing up the rear. Their prisoner had given up his barrage of cursing and blasphemy and sat in sullen silence as they jogged along the deserted road.

'The North Gate will have closed long since,'

said Gwyn. 'How will we get this fellow to the castle?'

'Don't worry about that, I know all the night porters,' Gabriel assured him. 'They'll open if I tell them it's king's business.'

All city gates were closed at dusk, but like the curfew that was supposed to keep people off the streets at night, the regulations were often broken, either for important people or for a bribe.

John had suspected that Walter might have made some desperate break for freedom, knowing that he was inevitably headed for the gallows, but after a couple of miles had passed without incident, he felt more confident that they would deliver the outlaw to Stigand's tender care.

The track generally followed the little River Yeo, which joined the much larger Exe halfway to the city. It crossed the Yeo at one densely wooded point over an old humpback stone bridge a few yards long, which had a low parapet on each side. Halfway across, without the slightest warning, Walter Hamelin suddenly threw himself sideways from his saddle and fell to the ground virtually between the legs of Gabriel's horse. The animal shied in alarm and caught unawares, the rider had difficulty in staying on its back. There was instant confusion in the gloom, now all the deeper because of the high trees all around the bridge. Amid the shouting and yells of alarm from the escort, the prisoner, who had caught a hefty blow from one hoof of Gabriel's mount, managed to scrabble his way the few feet to the parapet and throw himself across it. Everyone else was sliding from their saddles to intercept him, but John and Gwyn were blocked by the horses on the narrow trackway. Gabriel almost fell from his own frightened mare, but managed to catch Walter by the ankle as he squirmed across the rough stones bordering the bridge

'I've got the bastard!' he yelled, but it was a premature claim, as with a frantic kick, the outlaw freed his leg and vanished head first over the wall. By now, the others had struggled to the spot and leaned over to look down into the river. Though only a dozen feet wide, it was in full spate, the water splashing over large stones in the gleam from the moon.

'Can you see him?' roared de Wolfe.

'Not a sign, he's washed down under the bridge,' hollered one of the soldiers.

'I heard a hell of crack as he went down,' shouted Gabriel. 'I reckon he landed on his head on those rocks.'

John stood up and began running across the bridge in the direction they had been going. 'Quickly, follow the river down, he can't have got far!'

Three of the men rushed across the bridge after him, but Gwyn and Gabriel went back over the bridge and clambered down to the bank, following the boisterous torrent downstream. The other party was opposite and in the poor light, they all began to comb the water's edge as they stumbled along in the direction of the flow, shouting and cursing as they went.

After a hundred yards, Gwyn let out a thunderous bellow. 'Here he is, caught up against a tree stump!'

As the others strained to see from the opposite bank, Gabriel helped him to haul out the sodden shape of Walter Hamelin and dump him on the grass at the base of a tree.

'He looks dead to me!' called out the sergeant.

John fumed on the other side. 'He can't have drowned in that time, he's not been in the water five minutes!' he yelled.

Gwyn, after a moment's examination, mainly using his fingers in the dark, called back across the turbulent water. 'No, but he can crack his head open! And I think he may have a broken neck.'

'I said I heard him hit something,' declared Gabriel. 'Well, it saves having to hang the murderous swine!'

EIGHTEEN

De Wolfe was in two minds whether to tell Nesta of Matilda's unjust accusations about them and eventually decided that for the time being, he would say nothing. After her first outburst, Matilda followed her usual habit of glowering in a sullen mood for a few days, but she made no more open reference to the matter. John had gone through this before, when she had discovered his other infidelities over the years. As he had been absent so often, she stored up her justifiable complaints for when he was home between campaigns, using his sins as fodder for the martyrdom she affected. In truth, her main complaint was the fear that his indiscretions might be used to belittle her in the eyes of her women cronies, though this rarely happened. She suspected that most of them were in the same situation, as it seemed that almost every man in Exeter had similar illicit liaisons – and many were quite open about it. So the pair endured their meaningless marriage as before and now at least, there was the novelty of the new house to divert them from open hostility.

The adventure in Crediton a few days earlier was already half forgotten, though Ralph Morin had made sure that the next messenger to

Westminster would take a message confirming Henry de la Pomeroy's involvement in Roger Smale's murder – and emphasizing to the Chief Justiciar John de Wolfe's role in trying to establish some law enforcement in Devonshire.

In the first week of December, John hired some porters and a cart to bring Matilda's belongings from Fore Street to St Martin's Lane, consisting mostly of her two trunks of clothing and some smaller articles. Before he had gone to Palestine, they had rented a small house near St Pancras Church, but as that had been furnished, everything for the new place had to be bought new and was already in place.

Lucille staggered behind the cart with an armful of gowns that could not be squeezed into the boxes and Mary carried two wooden pails filled with oddments that Matilda had used in her cousin's house. As Mary had been Hugh de Relaga's contribution, Matilda grudgingly accepted her, though she looked upon the woman's shapely figure and rather bold eye as yet another temptation for her wayward husband.

Though there was no snow, there was a bitter east wind and John was glad that he told the old yardman to get a good fire going in his new hearth.

Matilda immediately retired to her solar above, where the endless nagging and scolding of Lucille began. When the porters had lugged the heavy trunks up the steps, Matilda set to, sorting her beloved gowns, surcoats, cloaks and headgear and harrying her new maid into laying them reverently back into the boxes and on to shelves on one wall. The solar, which was a wife's territory, was sparsely furnished, with a single high-backed wooden chair, a couple of stools and a single trunk for John's clothes. The bed was on the floor, a thick mattress slightly raised on a plinth, covered in blankets and a heavy coverlet of sewn sheepskins.

While Matilda was snapping her orders at the already tearful Lucille, John went out to the kitchen shed to see how Mary was settling in. She had already spent a few nights there and had made her quarters as comfortable as she could, claiming that she was quite happy with her accommodation.

'This is a lot better than the last place, Sir John,' she said in her broad local accent. Though she had a fair grasp of Norman-French, they always spoke in English together, except when Matilda was present, who insisted upon using her allegedly native French.

Mary had a palliasse in one corner, a table and a couple of stools near the small central fire-pit where she did her cooking.

Brutus was already comfortably installed on an old sack and John could see that both the dog and himself were more likely to have a homely welcome here than in the gloomy hall inside the house.

He sat on one of the stools and Mary poured him a mug of ale from a pitcher. She then took a couple of flat cakes from the bakestone that sat on the edge of the fire and slid them on to the scrubbed boards of the table.

'Here's butter and some honey – see if you

approve of my cooking,' she said firmly, with the implication that she would brain him with the ladle that hung nearby, if he failed to appreciate them. They were delicious and he rolled his eyes at her, his mouth being full.

'A word of advice, Sir John,' she said softly. 'Beware of what you say before that Lucille, for I've heard servant's gossip that she is too ready to carry tales and tittle-tattle.'

When he left the shed after finishing all the drop cakes, his spirits had been lifted a little, as he had found both a good cook and a friendly ally. Reluctantly, he went back to the Bush to collect his few possessions to take to St Martin's Lane. A large cloth bag was sufficient to carry his spare undershirts, hose and two grey tunics, together with the wolfskin cloak that he had won from a Bohemian mercenary in a jousting match in Germany.

For a few minutes he sat with Nesta, who was sad to see him leave. He even fancied there were tears glistening her eyes as he left, but he promised that, whenever possible, he would be back there each day.

'I've got to exercise that big dog, haven't I?' he said with false jollity. 'Most times Brutus will probably want to come in this direction – in fact, I can guarantee it!'

Back at St Martin's Lane that evening, he felt a sense of depressing anticlimax. It was very cold and the wind was whistling through the roof shingles and penetrating the shutters. There was oiled silk stretched over the inside of the window, attempting to keep out some of the draughts, but the lofty hall was still chilly, the tapestries shifting slightly in the breeze.

Most of the light came from the fire, where a pile of chopped logs lay at the side of the chimney to replenish the blaze. He sat in a cowled seat at one side of the hearth, Matilda in the opposite one. She was wrapped in a heavy woollen cloak, her feet wrapped in a shawl, resting on a low stool.

After some desultory words about the house, they fell silent, she dozing and he scowling into the fire. In the flickering flames from the oak logs, he imagined he saw pictures, including some of the bleak roads through the Alps that he had travelled a year ago and others conjuring up images of King Richard still in captivity. He thought of Prince John, waiting to displace his king from the throne, aided by scoundrels like the bishops and greedy men such as Henry de la Pomeroy and Richard de Revelle. He looked across at his wife, her jaw drooping as she breathed noisily during her slumber. Was this how the rest of his life would be, slumped in boredom night and day?

John almost envied the peasant and the artisan, who at least had honest toil to occupy them between the cradle and grave. But he was a knight, brought up since a child as page and squire, to have no skills except with lance and sword. He had no other talents except fighting and no need to seek more money, as he had sufficient for all his needs.

What was he to do with his life, stuck in a

loveless marriage and without even the solace of religious belief to offer Heaven at the end? Though it was obligatory to believe in God, he never gave it any thought, it was just part of the fabric of life, drummed into everyone since infancy. He had no interest in the ostentatious panoply of the Church and though he was sometimes dragged to Mass by Matilda on special occasions, he felt it was just a meaningless ritual.

After a while, he shook off his dismal thoughts and bent to put a couple more logs on the fire, resting them across the curled iron supports of the firedogs. This was the first time he had seen it lit and he was glad to see that there was sufficient draught up his new chimney to take the smoke and sparks up and away from the interior of the hall. As he settled back, he fondled the soft ears of Brutus who lay at his feet, swooning with the new luxury of lying near a fire.

'We'll go for a walk as soon as the mistress takes herself to bed,' he murmured to the old hound. He knew that Matilda loved her sleep, almost as much as eating, drinking, new raiment and grovelling on her knees before a priest. She went to her bed early and got up late, so he should have plenty of opportunity to take a stroll down to Idle Lane.

An hour later, he walked down to the Bush and enjoyed Nesta's company, though the inn was busy and she was bobbing up and down from his table to help her serving girls and make amiable conversation with her regular patrons. He watched her admiringly, as she laughed with some, scolded others and fended off wandering hands without giving offence. A very popular landlady, many of the customers appreciated her good looks and her shapely figure, but she had the gift of being friendly without encouraging their lechery. Even the drunks, who often caused a nuisance, were usually placated or evaded without provoking a fight. When they became too obstreperous, some of her loyal customers would always help Edwin to push them out into the street.

Nesta wanted to ply John with more food, but Mary had served them an excellent spit-roasted duck at the noon dinner and then cold meats, bread and cheese for an early evening supper, so he settled only for a mutton pasty in the Bush.

Gwyn came in later, as he had brought his wife and boys down to spend the night with Agnes's sister. His only news was that the two nuns who had been involved in the attack had now been sent off to Glastonbury, with a much larger escort of men hired by the cathedral chapter. 'I hear that all the canons are buzzing with anger at the death of their brother from Tavistock,' he said.

'Though they seem grateful to you for saving the Huns and for dealing with both Arnulf and Walter Hamelin, they are calling for some official action to combat the rising lawlessness.'

De Wolfe grunted. 'Some hope, with no proper sheriff! I presume that the royal judges still come on their circuit to the Eyres of Assize?'

Gwyn turned up his huge hands in doubt. 'I

suppose so, someone has to try the cases and send men to the gallows. Though the Eyres were always so irregular that half the prisoners either died of goal fever or escaped before they could stand before a court.'

Eventually, with Nesta being so busy, John decided to make his way home again, leaving Gwyn continuing to drink the vast quantities of ale that he was able to swallow without any obvious effects.

Whistling to Brutus to leave the bone that Nesta had given him, they went out into the cold night air. The sky was clear and the stars bright as he walked across to Priest Street, named after the large number of lodgings used by vicars choral, secondaries and lay brothers from the cathedral. A half moon was rising in the east and he could see his hound zig-zagging ahead of him, as he explored the ever-changing smells of the sewage in the central drain and the piles of rubbish in the side alleys.

Priest Street rose to become Sun Lane before meeting Southgate Street and it was here that he saw Brutus stop dead and point with his out-stretched head towards a house on the right, in a row of moderate-sized burgages belonging to local merchants. As John came up to the dog, he was aware of a disturbance inside the house, a crash followed by a yell of pain, then a woman's scream.

'What's going on in there, Brutus?' he asked, assuming that it was some domestic dispute that was none of his concern. Then the screams be-came louder before they subsided into a sobbing that could still be heard through the slatted shutters on an upper room. He heard a noise behind him and turning, saw a man in the doorway of the house opposite, with a woman peering fearfully over his shoulder.

'Is it murder?' quavered the neighbour. 'Shall we send for the constables?'

As he spoke, another door opened in the house next to that from which the moans were coming and another man appeared, grasping a stout stick. 'What's going on?' he shouted.

'Who lives in there?' demanded John.

'Richard de Beltona and his wife,' called the first neighbour. 'He is a cloth merchant and a most respectable man!'

Suddenly the screams began again and de Wolfe hesitated no longer, but launched himself at the front door, beating on it with his fist. 'Open the door! Are you in trouble?' There was no response and he went to the lower shutters to try to pull them open.

'Try around the back,' advised the next-door neighbour, coming into the road. He recognized John as someone with authority and was content to see him take the initiative.

John wore no sword whilst in the city, but pulled his dagger from his belt as he loped around the corner of the house. With Brutus at his heels, he went down the narrow gap between it and the next building. By now, half a dozen locals were gathering in the pale moonlight, one shouting that he had sent his son for the city watch. At the rear, John found himself in a yard with the usual outbuildings in a patch of rutted mud enclosed by a high fence. As he approached the back door, it was suddenly wrenched open and he was confronted by the figure of a man, swathed in a hooded cloak that shadowed his face. Before he could react, the man struck him a heavy blow on the forehead with a short cudgel, which sent de Wolfe staggering, blood pouring down into one eye. He tripped over a boot scraper set alongside the door and fell back full length on to the ground.

Dazed, but conscious, he crawled to his hands and knees in time to see the man racing across the yard to a lane behind, with Brutus snarling after him. As the fugitive reached the gate in the fence, the dog sank his teeth into his leg and with a howl of pain and rage, aimed a kick at his tormentor. Brutus dodged away with a howl, having ripped a piece from the man's breeches, but swearing viciously, the intruder slipped through the gate and slammed it behind him.

By now, John had staggered to his feet, holding on to the wall of the house until his head cleared, though he could only see through one eye because of the blood. However it was enough to see his dog dancing around excitedly by the gate, barking furiously. It was too high for him to jump and by the time John reached him, the man had vanished into Rack Lane, which ran parallel to Sun Lane.

He thought of letting the enthusiastic hound pursue the fellow, but then decided that it was not worth the risk of having his beloved Brutus clubbed to death for the sake of some family fight. As he patted the dog's head, he took a piece of cloth from his jaws and stowed in a pocket in his cloak.

By now, several of the timorous neighbours had congregated in the yard and John stalked back to them. 'Is there still a commotion in the house?' he demanded.

'Just some sobbing, Sir John,' said one, who recognized him. 'Had we better see what's wrong?'

De Wolfe, telling the dog to stay where he was, pushed past the nervous burghers and, still feeling hazy from the blow he had taken, went through a kitchen to a storeroom filled with bales of cloth. In the corner was a flight of open steps, dimly lit by a rush light on a shelf. Following the feeble moans from above, he climbed up and went into a room which occupied half of the upper floor. There was a large bed raised just off the floor, covered with tumbled pelts and blankets. Amongst these on one side of the mattress was the inert shape of a man – and on the other, the huddled shape of a woman, from whom came the heartbreaking sobs.

He went a little nearer, until in the semi-darkness he could see what was amiss. Going back to the head of the steps, he called down to the upturned faces below.

'Two of you, fetch your wives here at once! And get lights and some stretchers on which to carry these poor folk.'

Half an hour later, the house in Sun Lane was buzzing with activity like a wasp's nest that had been stirred with a stick. Two goodwives from across the road were attending to Clarice, wife of Richard de Beltona, whose husband still lay comatose on the bed, a spreading blue bruise covering one side of his head.

Clarice, a small woman of about thirty-five, was slumped on the floor with her back against the bed, alternately sobbing and groaning. The two neighbourly women were kneeling each side of her, making soothing noises as one wiped her forehead with a perfumed kerchief and the other gave her sips of brandy wine from a cup. Her night shift had been decorously pulled across her legs and a blanket draped around her, but John knew from his first sight of her, that the nether garments had been ripped and that an ominous leakage of blood stained them over the thighs.

'She needs Dame Madge, as soon as possible!' declared another wife, the one from next door.

'Who's Dame Madge?' growled John, totally lost in matters of women's problems.

'The old nun from Polsloe Priory,' answered her husband. 'She is a miracle worker when it comes to treating ladies.'

'How would we get this poor woman there?' demanded the wife. 'She can't be taken on a horse! It must be near midnight and the city gates are shut until dawn.'

'Then this nun must be brought down here,' said John, decisively. 'The gate will open for me, I assure you.'

'You need that head attended to, Sir John, if only for you to see where you are going!' said a voice from behind him. 'I'll send to Polsloe straight away.'

The speaker was Osric, a very tall, thin man with a shock of fair hair. Dressed in a short tunic and breeches, he carried a long brass-topped staff, the insignia of a town constable. A Saxon, he was one of the two men employed by the city council to keep the peace in the city – a hopeless task, but it was the only token of law and order in Exeter.

'Are men coming to take her husband up to St John's Infirmary?' demanded de Wolfe, rubbing at the dried blood on his forehead.

Osric nodded in the improved light of three horn lanterns and a couple of candles. 'They are fetching the bier that hangs in Holy Trinity near the South Gate.'

Having done all he could at the scene of the crime, John collected Brutus from outside and trudged through the chill night back down to the inn, still feeling dizzy and sick after the bang on the head. It was very late when he arrived and Nesta had taken herself to bed, but Gwyn and couple of men were still gambling downstairs.

Gwyn leaped up in alarm when he saw John's bloodied head and guided him to a bench and brought him ale, while one of his cronies went out to the wash-shed for a cloth and water to clean up the dried blood and clot, so that they could look at the wound.

'It's not so bad,' said Gwyn judicially, staring at the one-inch cut just inside the hairline. 'What's the other fellow look like?'

'The bastard got away, but not before Brutus sank his teeth into his leg. I hope the swine dies of gangrene!'

As he was telling them the story, Nesta appeared on the steps from the loft, her night shift covered with a blanket. Wide-eyed, she saw Gwyn cleaning up his master with a bloodied cloth and with a squeal of concern she hurried across and took the rag from the Cornishman to finish the job with a woman's gentler touch. More explanations followed for Nesta's benefit and she joined in the general condemnation of lawlessness in the city.

'That poor woman, to see her husband struck down before her very eyes, then be ravished by that monster!' she exclaimed, then bustled away to get clean linen to bind around his injured scalp. She held this in place with a close-fitting coif laced under the chin, then sat close to him and chafed his icy hands with her own.

It was cold in the taproom, as the fire had died down to glowing embers. Gwyn was concerned about John's condition after such a violent knock on the head, as he began shivering as he sat on the bench, leaning on the table.

'He should be lying down, *cariad,* and kept warmer for few hours,' he murmured to her. 'I don't see how we can get him all the way back to St Martin's Lane like this.'

'Get him to his bed upstairs, then,' she said in a worried voice, afraid that he might have sustained some serious injury inside his skull.

'I should be going back up to that house to see how things have gone,' muttered John.

Nesta scolded him gently. 'You're in no fit state for that, it's not your responsibility, anyway. You've already done more than anyone else.'

De Wolfe was too cold and tired to argue and when Gwyn and one of his carpenter friends hoisted him to his feet and carefully eased him up the stairs, he made no protest. No one else was lodging in the loft that night and they took him across to his cubicle and laid him down, Nesta fussing over them like a hen with chicks. She brought a blanket and a large sheepskin from her own room and laid it over him, then told Gwyn to revive the fire and put more logs on it, to try to waft some warmth up to the dormitory.

'I'll sit with him for a while until he sleeps,' she told Gwyn, who had decided to go up to Sun Lane. He wanted to make sure that a 'hue and cry' had been started, before going up to the castle to alert Ralph Morin that the violence had spread into the town itself. Though drunken fights and some deaths occurred within the city walls, an outright assault and rape in a dwelling was out of the usual run of crimes.

When he left, the other men went with him and Nesta was left alone in the loft, though Molly and the serving girl were not far away, sleeping in the kitchen shed and the wash house as usual. Sitting on a small milking stool near his bed, she could see that he was still awake, huddled under the covers.

'This is a fine affair, John,' she said softly. 'Your first night in your new house and you spend it elsewhere, alone with a young lady!'

'I expect that Matilda will have something to say about it,' he murmured.

'In fact I'm bloody sure she will!'

A few minutes later, she could tell from his breathing that he was asleep and after a while, she went quietly back to her box-like room and got into bed, pulling extra blankets from a chest to cover her. She lay for a while looking up into the darkness, thinking of what might have been that night.

NINETEEN

When John awoke soon after dawn, he felt virtually back to normal, apart from a burning itch around his wound. He had suffered far worse many times before and now no longer sick and giddy, he got up and went down the steps, where he found Gwyn eating at a table. Nesta bustled in with oat gruel, bread and cheese, to enquire solicitously after his condition.

'I'm fine, good lady! I just need to track down the swine that gave me this cut and pull his head off!'

Gwyn, who had slept on the floor near the fire, poured some honey over his porridge and passed the jug to John. 'I went back up to the house after we put you to bed. The injured man had been taken up to St John's and Brother Saulf said that he was showing signs of recovering his wits, so it looks as if he'll live.'

'What about the wife?' asked de Wolfe.

'That old nun from Polsloe was brought down by the other town constable, the fat one they call Theobald. She examined the lady and said she had certainly been sorely ravished, but was in no danger, except to her mind. She is sending a litter down this morning, to take her up to the priory.'

John attacked the gruel with a wooden spoon with a ferocity that suggested he wished it were the assailant's guts. 'So all we have to do now is find him! No luck with the hue and cry last night?'

Gwyn shook his hairy head. 'No, Osric and a few men-at-arms joined the neighbours in scouring the streets, but it was the middle of the night, with no hope of finding anyone.'

'We'll get the bastard somehow,' growled John. 'But first I'd better go home and face my wife.'

Though not usually an early riser, the unfamiliarity of a new bed had woken Matilda early and the realization that her husband had not slept in it, got her up and dressed before he arrived. She had brusquely demanded her breakfast and Mary was serving it to her in the hall when John walked in.

Ignoring the unusual padded coif on his head, she glared at him. 'And where did you spend the night, might I ask?' she snapped. 'The first one in our new dwelling and you spurn my company, probably for a drunken revel or the arms of some strumpet!'

His face darkened, as although he expected some complaint, he did not relish yet another unfair accusation even before he had the chance to open his mouth. 'I spent it much of it in the Bush Inn, if you must know!' he snarled. 'That was after fighting with a rapist and being treated for this injury!' He pointed at the bulge under his linen helmet.

'The Bush!' she yelled. 'I might have guessed

it was that Welsh whore again! How far will you go to shame me, husband?' She began a tirade, but he brought her up short by kicking a stool across her new flagstones, making a clatter that stopped even Matilda in mid-speech.

'Quiet, woman! Do you know a lady called Clarice, wife to a merchant, Richard de Beltona?' he demanded stridently.

She gaped at him open-mouthed at this sudden twist in their dispute. Deflated, she answered in a flat tone of voice. 'Of course, she is a friend of mine. I see her often at the cathedral.'

'Then I regret to tell you that she has been raped in her own bed – and her husband beaten senseless alongside her!'

Matilda's pug face rapidly changed from anger to genuine concern. She hauled herself to her feet, leaving half her meal left untouched, a sure sign of her agitation. 'I must go to her at once, poor woman!'

'You can't, she's on her way to Polsloe, to be cared for by Dame Madge and her nuns. The husband is lying unconscious in St John's, up near the East Gate.'

Matilda sank back in to her chair. 'And you have been involved in this, John?'

'I went to their aid, yes. And got a hole knocked in my head by the assailant as he escaped. So keep the door locked when I'm not here!'

He doubted that any sane man would want to ravish Matilda, but he felt he should pay her the compliment.

Her anger evaporated, though she did not go so far as enquire about his injury. 'Richard de

Beltona is a cloth merchant in a good way of business, though Clarice complains that he is mean, as he could afford a better house than the one in Sun Lane.'

Again, her interest seemed more about affluence and social status than about the actual outrage.

They were interrupted by Mary putting her head around the screens near the door. 'A servant just came from the house of the Archdeacon, Sir John. He brought a message from his master to say that he would be obliged if you would call upon him as soon as is convenient.'

Mary's head vanished and Matilda looked at her husband with a tinge of respect, as any mention of a senior churchman wishing to consult him went some way to rehabilitate him in her eyes. 'What can he want? De Alencon is the most senior of the canons.'

'I expect it's to talk about a priest getting murdered and two nuns being frightened out of their wits!' replied John gruffly.

He was quite right in his forecast, as he discovered as soon as he arrived at John de Alencon's house. Many of the canons lived in the houses that lined the north side of the Cathedral Close. Exeter was a secular cathedral in that it was not part of a monastic establishment, such as an abbey and had no monks. It was governed by a Chapter of twenty-four canons, who derived their incomes from the livings of various churches. Some of them were independently affluent and lived in luxury in large houses, both in the cathedral precinct and in estates else-where. John de Alencon was not one of those who indulged in ostentatious comfort, but pre-ferred a modest, ascetic life. His house in Canon's Row was plainly, almost sparsely furnished and he had the minimum number of servants to keep his household functioning.

John de Wolfe was no great admirer of the senior clergy, who he considered generally to be a lazy, avaricious lot who farmed out many of their duties to their subservient vicars. But he admired his namesake for his simple lifestyle and his devotion to King Richard, especially as many of the other canons leaned towards Prince John.

Though generally spartan in his tastes, de Alencon had a weakness for fine wines, so even at that early time of day, a cup of good Anjou red was set before de Wolfe when he called upon his friend. They sat in the study, a bare room with only a table, a few hard chairs and a large wood-en cross on the wall. The archdeacon, his lined face looking even more worried than usual, got straight to the point.

'This lawlessness is getting too much to bear, John. I know you have no official standing in the matter, but you seem the only man in Exeter who seems to be involved in combating it! The city is full of praise for you in finding the killer of that unfortunate king's messenger that I put to rest in the cathedral yard not long ago.'

'Pure chance, I'm afraid,' said John. 'I just seem to have the knack of being around when there is some violence!'

De Alencon raised a hand in deprecation. 'You are too modest, as always. You also saved the lives of those two nuns on the road, where our brother priest was so foully murdered. Now today I hear of your involvement in these dreadful crimes last night, not a few hundred paces from the cathedral itself.'

John took a sip of the wine and shrugged. 'I hate seeing evil go unpunished – and these days, it seems to be not only unpunished, but ignored!'

The priest nodded his agreement. 'Exactly, which is why I wanted your advice. We have discussed this in Chapter several times, especially since the killing of the priest from Tavistock and the disgraceful treatment of the nuns. At our Chapter meeting early today it was resolved that something must be done.'

'Easy to say, but much harder to achieve,' observed John.

'Chapter wants a proper sheriff appointed, one who would enforce law and order.'

'That's rich! A sheriff is the *king*'s representative in every county, yet Devon was given to the Count of Mortain to rule outwith the royal authority. As you don't need telling, many of your canons favour Prince John, so they can't have it both ways.'

'But that's exactly what they do want,' said the archdeacon gently. 'They are going to ask Prince John to install a sheriff – and are suggesting Richard de Revelle as the appointee.'

De Wolfe looked aghast at this proposition. 'That would be a disaster! He'd never stir himself from his chamber, where he counts the taxes and takes his own tithes from them. I had heard such a suggestion, as the prince has already got him counting his coins. But as a fearless law officer, he would be worse than useless.'

'I tend to agree, John. But they are set upon it and as you know, some have the ear of the prince. I thought I would warn you what is afoot.'

'But appointing a sheriff is not within his gift!' objected de Wolfe. 'I tell you now, the Chief Justiciar will not agree and I doubt the king would either, except that he is far away in captivity.'

De Alencon shrugged. 'I suspect that the prince will just go ahead without such approval. After all, he is virtually the absolute ruler of six counties and has appointed his own chancellor, exchequer and other officers, independent of Winchester or London.'

De Wolfe shook his head in despair. 'It will be a fiasco, John. Mark my words, when Hubert Walter gets to hear of this, he will forbid it. He has already spoken to me about his concerns that the prince is once again planning to challenge the Lionheart's right to the throne. Look how places are covertly being fortified and garrisoned, places like St Michael's Mount and Berry Peverel.'

They spoke further about the ominous signs of revolt and de Alencon told him that when a new bishop was installed in a few months time, the likely incumbent would be Henry Marshal, the Dean of York, who was another keen supporter of the prince.

John came away from Canon's Row with an even stronger presentiment of trouble, but the prospect of his brother-in-law becoming sheriff was the worst part. His arrogant pomposity would be intolerable – and no doubt Matilda's pride in becoming sister of a sheriff would be even more insufferable.

He collected his horse from the stables opposite his house and rode first to the tiny hospital at St John's Priory, just inside the East Gate. This had but six monks offering the only medical care in the city, apart from a few apothecaries who dispensed medicines. Outside the city, there was nothing at all and the villagers depended on 'wise women' and helpful neighbours for their only hope of treatment.

At St John's, the small infirmary was run by Brother Saulf, a tall, gaunt man who had once attended the famous medical school of Montpellier in southern France. He told John that Richard de Beltona was still in a bad state, but his deep unconsciousness had lightened in the last few hours.

'I trust in God that he will not die, but it may be days before he has recovered enough of his wits to speak, if he ever does,' said Saulf, in his deep, sonorous voice. 'And even if he does, he probably will not remember the events that caused his injury.'

John went into the single ward of the little hospital, a high chamber with a row of pallets down each side and a huge wooden crucifix on the end wall, indicating that most of the healing here was done by God. The hall was full of sick

298

and injured and Beltona was lying immobile in one of those nearest to the door. He lay breathing heavily, his eyes closed, one swollen with blood that had seeped down into his eyelids from the swelling above, reminding John of the ache in his own cranium.

There was nothing to be done except to thank Saulf and hand him a few coins towards the hospital funds. Then John mounted Bran again and went the mile or so to Polsloe Priory, to enquire after the well-being of Mistress Clarice. The small Benedictine house was surrounded by a high wall and the gatekeeper was not disposed to admit an unknown man, even though he called himself Sir John de Wolfe. Evidently his reputation had not percolated to this outpost in the woods outside the city.

However, after he had firmly closed the gate on John, he went across to the modest buildings of the priory and soon returned with the forbidding figure of Dame Madge. She was almost as tall as John, though slightly stooped. A long face, with a large hairy mole on one cheek, was usually set in a grim expression, except when dealing with her sick and often frightened patients, who she treated with a gentleness that contrasted markedly with her usual manner.

They stood in the open gateway until John had explained who he was and that he had only called to enquire after the stricken lady's condition. The old nun thawed immediately and invited John to the refectory for a meal, which he gracefully declined.

'I'm sure your time can be better spent healing

the sick, than in talking to an old soldier like me,' he said with a grin. 'I have a score to settle with whoever did these evil deeds.' He pointed a finger at his coif, still bulging over Nesta's bandage.

'I wondered if the lady had said anything about who might have assaulted her so grievously?'

Dame Madge shook her head, her veil swaying over the white linen wimple around her craggy face. 'It is a difficult and sensitive business, asking questions so soon after a woman has been ravished,' she said gravely. 'All I have learned from her is that the man was large and strong, which I'm sure applies to most of the men in Devon!'

De Wolfe thanked her and told her of the husband's condition in St John's before taking his leave, but just as he was putting his foot in Bran's stirrup, she called after him.

'Sir John, I've just recalled that the lady did murmur that he smelt of tar, but again that is probably not of much use to you.'

But it gave him something to ponder over on his short ride back to the city.

Mary had served up an excellent dinner in the house in St Martin's Lane, which even the grumbling Matilda could not fault. At noon, they sated themselves on fried eels with onions, followed by roast pork, cabbage and carrots, then crystallized ginger, bread and cheese. Later that afternoon, John was digesting this with the aid of ale and cider, sitting in the hall of Rougemont with his usual companions. Gwyn, Gabriel and Ralph Morin were discussing the events of the previous night and John's news about the bishop's bid for a sheriff.

'We need a sensible man to enforce law and order in the county, but not that crafty bastard de Revelle,' said Gwyn.

'I don't see how he can be made sheriff,' growled Ralph. 'The post is nominated by the king, then the county court has to formerly elect him. John Lackland can't do that.'

De Wolfe nodded his agreement. 'The problem is that the prince's old nickname no longer applies, as he certainly lacks no land these days. But I agree, as a sheriff is the king's man in each county, only the king or his representative like the Chief Justiciar, can put one in place.'

'And who's going to tell Prince John that?' asked Morin.

De Wolfe shrugged. 'When Hubert Walter finds out, he'll tell the king, wherever he is. We'll see some action then, I'll warrant!'

Gwyn took a gargantuan swallow of his ale, then rubbed a hand over his damped moustaches. 'I wish the king would get back home and sort out his kingdom,' he said mournfully. 'We hear these rumours of the ransom being paid and of him being released, but nothing ever happens.'

It was true that there had been several false reports of the Lionheart's return, just as there had been claims that Philip of France had succeeded in buying the king from Emperor Henry.

'The latest I heard from the last herald that came through from Winchester was that there was still a way to go to collect the full one hundred and fifty thousand marks,' reported Morin, who was in the best position to get the latest news, albeit usually several weeks old. 'The old queen is poised to go over to the Rhine herself to fetch her son, when the moment comes,' he added.

The talk then turned to the brutal assault in Sun Lane the previous night. After John had told them about the state of the two victims – no one seemed to be bothered about his own injury – the problem of catching the villain was discussed.

'He's probably miles away by now, as there was nothing to stop him walking out through one of the city gates today,' said Gabriel. 'No one knows what he looks like.'

'All we know is that he's big and strong and that he smelled of tar!' said John. This reminded him of the piece of cloth and he fished in his scrip to bring out the piece of breeches-leg that Brutus has ripped off the man in the backyard. It was an unremarkable scrap of coarse cloth about the size of his hand, brownish in colour, with a bluish thread in the weft of the weave.

'Looks foreign to me', said Gabriel. 'But then, so much cloth is brought in from the Low Countries, much of it in your ships, Sir John.'

'Your partner, Hugh de Relaga, must know a lot about foreign fabrics, John,' suggested Ralph. 'Why not show it to him? He might recognize where it came from.'

John nodded, but was not excited about the possible clue. 'I'll do that, but of course where it was made has little to do with who now owns it. My cloak is from Bavaria and my belt from

Spain!' Another thought occurred to him and he held the rag to his long nose and sniffed. 'That poor woman was right, it does smell of tar.'

He handed it round and they all agreed that there was a faint stink of the black residue that came from burning coals, though Gwyn, with his nautical pretensions, said he thought it more like pitch or bitumen.

'Does it tell us anything about this swine?' growled Morin.

'They sometimes use it on shingle roofs to stop them leaking,' ventured Gabriel. 'Perhaps he's a builder?'

'Or a seaman,' contradicted Gwyn. 'Stuff like that is used for caulking the seams in ship's planks.'

John tossed the piece of cloth on to the table and they all stared at it for a long moment, as if waiting for it to speak to them.

'What about that old hound of yours, John?' asked Ralph. 'He tore that cloth off and you say he bit him in the leg.'

'Yes, but it can't have been a deep injury, for the fellow ran away like the wind.'

The castellan shook his head. 'No, I meant he must have got a good scent of the fellow – and you've still got that bit of cloth to show the dog. Maybe he can track a scent, just as the lymers do in hunting.'

Lymers were hounds who tracked by smell, as opposed to those like the greyhound who chased by sight.

'I could try him, I suppose,' said John, dubiously.

303

'Best do it before the trail gets any colder,' suggested Gwyn. 'I'll come with you now, before it gets dark.'

They went back to St Martin's Lane and collected an enthusiastic Brutus and took him down to the back of the now-silent house in Sun Lane. In the yard at the back, John held the piece of torn fabric to the dog's nose, then opened the gate at the back through which the assailant had escaped.

'Go on, boy, find him!' encouraged Gwyn and sure enough, Brutus went off with his nose to the ground, zigzagging back and forth, then moving off rapidly into the alley and then into a wider lane that angled up towards Southgate Street. They followed the dog down the street towards the gate, ignoring the curious stares of stall-holders and their customers as they jogged behind. Brutus turned off again to the right and went down Rock Lane towards the Watergate that stood at the lowest point of the city walls. This had been built in recent years to allow direct access to the wharf along the river, as Exeter became much more active in trading. Though the larger seagoing vessels had to moor down at Topsham, smaller ones could berth at the quayside, which dried out at low tide.

'He's going out on to the wharf!' shouted Gwyn triumphantly, as they approached the gate. 'I said that pitch was used to caulk ship's planking!'

They went through the arch of the Watergate and out on to the flat expanse of dockside. There was a length of stone wharf along the river bank, beyond which it lapsed into bushes and grass.

Brutus ran on to the wharf and began circling around. For the first time, he seemed uncertain of himself, as the trail was confused by various odours from the coils of tarry rope and bales of merchandise awaiting shipment.

Two small cogs were moored at the quayside, riding high and upright, as it was the peak of the flood tide. In fact, one was just preparing to leave, its single sail hoisted and the bow hawser about to be cast off by a man standing at a bollard on the edge of the wharf.

'Hey there, hold it!' yelled Gwyn in a voice that could be heard half a mile away. He began running to the bemused fellow, John close behind him, with an excited Brutus adding his loud barks to the sudden confusion. The shipmaster, standing at the stern of the cog alongside the steersman, also began yelling at this interference with his vessel's departure.

John left Gwyn to stop them casting off and went to the edge of the wharf nearest the shipmaster, who was almost level with him at this state of the tide. 'I need to look at your crew before you sail,' he shouted.

The captain of the ship, a hard-faced man with a black beard, swore a few choice oaths at him and told him to clear off, but John was in no mood to be intimidated.

'I am a king's officer,' he yelled, stretching the terms of Hubert Walter's commission a little. 'Are these all your crew?' He waved an arm to encompass the four other men scattered around the deck of the little ship.

Before he could get a reply, the problem was solved as Brutus went right to the edge of the wharf and began barking and snarling furiously at a man standing within a couple of arm's lengths of him. Though now in a short brown tunic and breeches, he was tall and heavily built. John had no way of recognizing him as the man who had cut his head last night, but the man's actions now put it beyond doubt. Pulling a long knife from his belt, he ran to the shipmaster and grabbed him from behind, holding the dagger to his neck.

'Cast off, I say!' he shouted. 'Throw off the ropes, or I'll cut his throat.'

The other sailors looked bemused, but as the villain repeated his threat, one began moving towards the stern mooring rope, intending to unlash it. John drew his sword, which he had picked up when he had collected Brutus from his house. Though the gangplank had been pulled inboard, he made a running jump and landed on the deck, followed by Gwyn, who had his dagger ready in his hand. Not to be outdone, Brutus also made a flying leap up on to the deck and made straight for the man who had given him a kick the previous night.

John was instantly afraid that his dog would be stabbed, but the canny animal ran around behind the man and jumped up, sinking his teeth into his back, out of reach of the blade. In seconds it was all over, as with a yell, the attacker had to release the shipmaster, who promptly gave him a vicious elbowing in the belly, by which time John had smashed the knife from his hand with

306

a blow from the flat of his sword. Gwyn now floored the rapist with a blow from his ham-sized fist and kept him down on the deck by standing on the back of his neck.

John called Brutus away and slowly order was restored. The shipmaster, grateful for their intervention, even though it was their presence that started it all, said the man's name was Joel of Calais, a ruffian who was a good shipman, but an evil man to cross. As the shipmaster was anxious to catch the flood tide, John did not delay them any longer and after lashing Joel's wrists with rope, he was pushed ashore and jostled through the city with Gwyn leading him like a cow to slaughter – which was what would happen to him eventually. The inhabitants rapidly learned who he was and by the time they had dragged him up Southgate Street as far as the Carfoix crossing, a jeering crowd was fol-lowing, some spitting at him, gesturing angrily and soon throwing missiles of all sorts at this black-hearted ruffian who broke into decent folk's houses at night to beat and ravish them. They delivered him to Stigand's care in the castle undercroft and went to report to Ralph Morin that he now had yet another guest in his castle gaol.

'That must be the quickest investigation and arrest in Exeter's history!' said the castellan. 'What with catching Arnulf of Devizes and then letting Walter Hamelin break his neck, you're single-handedly clearing Devon of all its vil-lains!'

'The credit for catching this shipman is all

down to the hound,' admitted John, feeling rightly proud of his old dog.

'But what do we do with the swine now?' demanded Ralph. 'Just hang him and be done with it?'

John shook his head. 'He should be either tried before the sheriff's court or committed to the next Eyre of Assize or when the Commissioners come ... but we don't have a bloody sheriff!'

'Let the bastard rot downstairs then,' decided Ralph. 'With a bit of luck, he'll die of dog-bite fever, thanks to Brutus!'

Even Matilda was mildly impressed by the acclaim that her husband and his hound had generated by that evening. She had been to St Olave's for one of her twice daily conversations with the Almighty, where her women friends, all wives of affluent merchants, had been enthusing about the capture of the evil ravisher, as well as her husband's success in his other recent exploits.

After their early supper of cold meat, bread and cheese, she was almost civil to John as he recounted the events of the afternoon. She even desisted from complaining about Brutus lying near the hearth, a change from her usual caustic remarks about 'that stinking dog'.

The same accolades were voiced far more robustly when he took 'the stinking dog' down to the Bush, after Matilda had retired to the solar for Lucille to help her to bed. At the inn, a larger crowd than usual had gathered to congratulate de Wolfe and Gwyn – and Brutus had a large and meaty bone given him by Nesta and Molly.

Another convivial evening followed, though this time they stopped short of music and dancing. After it was over, John made his way back home without being diverted by rape and robbery with violence. After a final cup of cider with Mary in her warm cook shed, he climbed the stairs to the solar and for the first time, slid into bed in his own house, oblivious to the heavy breathing and occasional grunts from the other side of the mattress.

As he lay staring at the new rafters just visible in the glow from a tiny rushlight set on a shelf, his mind went back to a year ago, when he would have been somewhere on a small ship, being tossed about in the Adriatic. So much had happened since then, yet twelve months had passed and his sovereign lord was still a prisoner of his enemies.

John never prayed, as since his youth he had felt that it was talking to an empty void, but if he had even a remnant of belief, he would petition God to release Richard Coeur de Lion from his incarceration – and certainly prevent him falling into the hands of Philip Augustus of France, who would find some excuse to have him killed. With the memory of the Balkan *bora* whistling in his ears, he turned over and slid into blessed sleep.

TWENTY

The second week of December brought the first snow. John rose from his cold conjugal bed soon after dawn and fancied that the light coming between the cracks in the shutters was brighter than usual. When he peered out of the door, he looked out on a white world, the yard and the roofs running down the back of High Street being coated in a couple of inches of pristine snow.

He was due to call on Hugh de Relaga at the Guildhall after the cathedral bells had rung for Sext and None. By then, the High Street was already grey slush churned by the feet of hundreds of traders, porters and goodwives doing their shopping at the stalls that lined the main streets of the city. Hugh greeted him with his invariable good humour and a cup of hot posset, welcome on such a cold day.

He reported that trade was doing well, even though no exports could be dispatched out of the deep-sea sailing season – and also in spite of the greatly increased taxes to pay for the king's ransom. The previous king Henry had imposed a 'Saracen tithe' to help pay for the coming Crusade and now Hubert Walter had introduced a new ransom tax on both income and movable

310

goods.

'Still, there's still plenty left for us, John' said Hugh cheerfully, as he pushed a heavy bag across his table towards his partner.

'Any news of the king?' asked John in a sombre voice. 'It will soon be exactly a year since he was taken in Vienna.'

'I had a trader in here only yesterday, who had come from Dover on a coastal vessel in only five days,' replied Hugh. 'He said that the second instalment of fifty thousand marks was due to be taken to the Emperor by Queen Eleanor herself. It will be taken by wagon down to Queenhithe and put aboard a ship a few days before Christ Mass*.'

John knew that a similar payment had been safely delivered early in November. 'Let's hope that this will secure his release after all these delays,' he grunted. 'I'd not trust Henry of Germany an inch – and neither does the old queen, by the sound of it.'

After an hour's talk about their business and the need for a new contract with Buckfast Abbey for next season's wool, he took his money back to the house. Matilda had gone to the cathedral and he hid the fat purse under the clothes in his trunk. This time he turned the key and put it in his scrip, mindful of the ease with which Joel the Ravisher had broken into the house in Sun Lane.

The rest of the short day was spent in aimless activities, which brought home to him the

*First recorded use of the words in Old English was 'Christis Maesse' in 1028

311

problem of what to do with the rest of his life. He took Bran for a trot down on Bull Mead, the open ground below Southernhay, where the fairs and tournaments were held, then came back for his dinner of poached salmon and mutton stew. Matilda announced that her brother had sent a message to ask her to visit him that afternoon at his town house in North Street.

'Richard is staying there a night on his way down to Revelstoke,' she said haughtily. 'He is returning from Gloucester, where he has been on important business.'

John guessed that his business was with the Count of Mortain, whose prime residence was at that city on the Severn, as he had married Isabel, Countess of Gloucester at the time that his brother Richard had gained the throne and given him his six counties. What Richard de Revelle was doing at Gloucester was a matter for speculation, but John suspected that he was angling for further advancement.

When his wife had left in her best finery, trailed by the dismal Lucille, who always seemed to have a head cold and running nose, John took himself to the castle to pass the time. As usual, Gwyn was there playing dice with the gatehouse guards and they went to the keep together to find Ralph Morin. At the bottom of the steps, they heard a commotion from the undercroft and saw Stigand hauling himself up the steps in a state of agitation.

'He's killed the other fellow!' he wheezed as he came nearer. 'Strangled him with his bare hands!'

Gwyn pushed the obnoxious gaoler out of the way and hurried down the steps, de Wolfe close behind. In the gloom of the undercroft, they could see that the outer gate in the iron fence was open and once inside, they could see the large figure of Joel sitting on the sleeping slab of the largest cell at the end of the row. The gate to this was padlocked and they peered in to see what had happened, gagging at the stink that came from inside.

'He's dead, the bastard!' snarled Joel, raising his head. 'He had it coming, trying to steal my piece of bread.'

Lying on the filthy straw of the sodden floor, they could see an inert shape, the body of Arnulf of Devizes, the man they had captured after the attack on the priest and nuns.

'Did you kill him?' barked John, though the question was unnecessary, as no one else was in the cell with him.

'I did indeed – and saved you the trouble of a hanging,' grunted Joel, with brazen indifference. 'And you can't string me up twice, so why should I care?'

Stigand had waddled up to them by now, puffing with exertion.

'Why did you shut these two in the same cell, you fool?' demanded John.

The fat man shrugged. 'Saved me emptying two buckets of their ordure ... What did it matter, anyway? They were both going to die.'

John shook his head despairingly at the man's inhumanity. 'I'll tell Sergeant Gabriel to get a couple of men down here to shift the body out.

313

For God's sake, clean that place out, put fresh straw down. I told you before, even if a man is going to the gallows, there's no need to treat him far worse than any pig in a sty!'

Upstairs, they found Ralph Morin in his chamber and told him of the death below his feet. The castellan sent a soldier to find Gabriel and then went out with them into the hall, to sit near the firepit and share a jug of cider. The talk soon turned to Richard de Revelle and John told them of his recent trip to Gloucester.

'It's not time for him to take the tax money there, so he's up to something else,' he concluded.

'So that's where he's been, the crafty devil!' said Ralph. 'He's not been in his chamber for more than a week.'

John had previously told Ralph about the cathedral's desire to have a sheriff appointed and the castellan agreed with John that this may have been the reason for de Revelle's trip.

'Hubert Walter won't stand for a sheriff being put in by Prince John!' he declared. 'We all know that we need one, but pray God it's not de Revelle!'

But later, that was exactly the news that John received. Matilda came home well after dusk fell, escorted by a couple of her brother's servants. As soon as she came into the hall, he could tell that she was almost bursting to tell him her good tidings.

'My brother is to be the new sheriff!' she exclaimed, even before she shed her heavy cloak into Lucille's waiting arms. 'Prince John himself has given him the post, on the recommendation of the bishop.'

Matilda was almost visibly swollen with pride, as her brother was her idol, a paragon of success in the world. The main beneficiary of their rich father's will, Richard had estates in several counties. He was well educated and literate, and she compared him very favourably to her own husband, whose only talents she perceived were wielding a sword, drinking and wenching. She conveniently ignored the money he had brought to them from campaigning and tournaments and the present very profitable partnership with Hugh de Relaga.

'He takes office straight away, after the appointment is confirmed by the county court,' she crowed. 'As I am his sister, we will be invited to more feasts and events, which will give you a chance to better yourself amongst the important people in the county!'

She was so benign and happy that John could not bring himself to deflate her and start another quarrel by pointing out that the prince had no authority to appoint a senior officer of the king. He mumbled some non-committal sounds and her euphoria glossed over his obvious lack of enthusiasm.

Matilda had not yet finished her good news. 'My brother has invited me to spend the Feast of Christ Mass with them at their manor in Tiverton,' she gushed.

'He is returning to Revelstoke tomorrow to fetch Eleanor, then they will collect me in a week's time and we shall all go to Tiverton. I will be away a week, but no doubt you will find plenty to occupy you, John.'

A barbed undercurrent of sarcasm had crept into her voice, but her mood was too buoyant to pursue it. There was no mention of him being included in the invitation, for which he was truly thankful.

Dragging Lucille behind her, she went straight to her solar, as she had had supper with her brother – not enquiring whether John had eaten. No doubt she was checking all her gowns and cloaks, he thought cynically, to see what further finery would be needed to befit a sheriff's sister. John leaned down from his seat by the fire to stroke the head of his now-famous old dog.

'We're in for some tempests in the next few weeks, Brutus,' he murmured. 'When her brother gets kicked out by Westminster, I suppose she'll shift the blame on to me, as usual!'

TWENTY-ONE

It was now two months since they had occupied the house in St Martin's Lane and during that time, John's enforced celibacy had become irksome. Hugh de Relaga had told him that Thorgils had decided to give up even coastal voyages for the rest of the winter, so seeing Hilda was out of the question. He had no desire to resort to brothels, as he had done occasionally in his younger days – and which he knew Richard de Revelle still patronized, as there was no lack of them in Exeter.

Relief came easily and from an unexpected quarter.

From the first, his relations with Mary were cordial, as there was an immediate rapport between them, but one free of any emotional ties. She rapidly learned of the smouldering antagonism between John and Matilda and an unspoken conspiracy developed between them to improve his lot. It was Mary who fed him, supplied him with clean clothes and gave him refuge and companionship in her kitchen shed. It was Mary who got him hot water to shave and wash once a week and the sight of him naked when he sometimes discarded his nether garments to be washed, never gave rise to any embarrassment.

Though the master-servant relationship persisted, they were friends in every sense of the word. She had a roguish eye and, at her age, was by no means a virgin, so rapidly the occasional touch and gesture developed into a hug and kiss. Before long, they were enjoying a quick tumble on her mattress in the kitchen shed, when Matilda was either at church or fast asleep.

The only problem was Lucille, who lived in her box under the solar steps. It was only a few yards away and Mary soon realized that the French girl was well aware of what was going on. As the two were not particularly friendly, she did not trust Lucille to keep her mouth shut, especially to her mistress. Mary fed her and was civil to the girl, but partly because of language problems, Lucille never unbent towards the cook.

By late December, Mary had reluctantly decided to stop bedding her employer, confessing to him that she could not afford to risk losing such a good job and a home for the sake of an occasional tumble. John accepted with good grace and confined his activities to a quick hug and a kiss.

A few days before the celebration of Christ's birth, Richard de Revelle reappeared, whilst journeying between his Devon manors. John avoided him, as he knew that a sneering or shouting match would be inevitable if he tackled him about his invalid appointment as sheriff. He preferred to leave it to the men in London and Winchester to react as they thought fit. Richard's acidulous wife, Lady Eleanor, who as the daughter of an earl, looked down on Matilda in the same way that the latter sneered at John's less affluent family, was travelling to Tiverton in a litter. John felt a little admiration for his own wife, who refused to join Eleanor in her swaying conveyance and insisted on riding a horse to Tiverton. For all her other many faults, she had been a competent horsewoman since her youth and John now hired a good rounsey for her from Andrew's stable, fitted with a side saddle.

He saw the cavalcade off when Matilda joined it at the corner of the lane with the High Street and as they made their ponderous way towards the East Gate, he breathed a sigh of relief at the prospect of a whole week to himself. Lucille, who was too timid to approach a horse, let alone try to ride one, was left behind, which ruined any chance of reviving his activities with Mary.

It was four days before Christ Mass, the exact anniversary of the Lionheart's capture in Vienna and later he and Gwyn sat rather despondently in the Bush, drinking ale and going over that fateful day in their minds.

'We did all we could, Sir John,' said the Cornishman quietly. 'The two of us couldn't have saved him against those odds.'

John had to agree. 'I suppose not, it was a hopeless venture once we had turned around after Sicily. Looking back, I suppose we should have pressed on to the Spanish coast, it would have been a better prospect than trying to creep through central Europe.'

Eventually they left this overworked topic and went on to the other matter that had Exeter's gossips in full spate. Nesta had joined them, looking pert and pretty in a green kirtle, with a white apron tied around her slim waist, a lock of her auburn hair peeping from beneath her linen coif. John had abandoned his headgear, now that the wound had healed to a reddened scar, buried under his own black thatch.

'When does de Revelle think he's taking over as sheriff?' she asked. 'I've only met the man once, but disliked him on sight when he came here trying to buy the inn, taking advantage of a newly bereaved widow.'

'It's supposed to be directly after Christ Mass, according to Matilda,' said John. 'The actual appointment will be confirmed by the Shire Court, but will be a formality, as half those freemen, bailiffs and serjeants are in Prince John's pocket already.'

'Gabriel told me this morning that Ralph Morin has sent a message by the courier about it to the Justiciar,' announced Gwyn. 'Let's hope he gets there safely, not like that poor fellow Smale.'

Nesta hurried away to settle some argument between Molly and Edwin over where to put the decorations for the coming festival.

A pile of freshly cut ivy and holly was lying on the floor and Gwyn and John joined in the task of wreathing them around the walls and hanging them from the rafters.

'I'll be down here every night, now that I've been deserted by my wife!' exclaimed John. 'I'll have to eat at home sometimes to please Mary, but I'll be down here often for more of Molly's

320

good food!' he promised.

He could have spent the festival in Stoke-in-Teignhead, but he had been down there for a few days the previous week, doing his duty as a faithful son. He felt he would enjoy himself more amongst his friends in Exeter, as Hugh de Relaga had invited him to early dinner on the eve of the festival.

When that day came, he went along with Hugh's family to the cathedral and discharged his infrequent spiritual obligations at an early special Mass. After a lavish meal in his house at noon, which included a roast swan, they watched a Miracle Play put on by the Guilds. This was performed at Carfoix, the junction of the four main streets and was staged on the back of a large wagon draped in cloth and carrying wooden scenery. A large crowd watched as enthusiastic apprentices re-enacted the traditional stories of Adam and Eve, Noah's Flood, and the Nativity. Dressed as angels, devils and all the well-known characters, the lads (including those dressed as women) went through the exaggerated gestures demanded of them, while a priest stood at one side, loudly reading an explanatory commentary, in both Latin and vernacular English.

That evening, John was back at the Bush, with Brutus lying with a bone in his usual comfortable spot under the table. Gwyn had for once stayed at home with his family, but the place was crowded with regular patrons, all intent in eating and drinking to welcome in Christ Mass day.

'I've made a special brew for the occasion,'

declared Nesta, banging a quart pot in front of him. 'And if you don't eat all the food we put before you, Molly says she'll never speak to you again!'

Instead of her usual tight-fitting coif, Nesta tonight wore a snow-white veil and wimple.

'You look more like a nun, or better, an angel, than an innkeeper!' said John, in a rare moment of admiration.

She bent to give him a quick peck on the cheek and whispered in his ear, 'I may be an angel, John, but I'm certainly no nun!' Then she glided off to attend to her other customers, leaving him to ponder her words.

As the evening wore on, a group of townsfolk came around the streets, singing and dancing. Holding hands in a wide circle, these were 'carollers', as they sang both religious, secular and sometimes bawdy ballads. Carols had been banned from churches as being sacrilegious, so they had to be celebrated in the streets. When they had moved on, some of the patrons of the Bush began to copy them in the taproom and a smaller circle formed where men and women, now loosened-up by Nesta's special brew, sang and stamped lustily below the holly and the ivy hanging from the beams. John joined in willingly, grasping Nesta's warm fingers on one side and Molly's on the other, until fatigue and the need for food sent him back to his table. Here half a goose was put before him, followed by an oblong mince pie, shaped to mimic the cradle of Jesus. Made of minced mutton, currants and spices, it was followed by a special frumenty, a sweet porridge flavoured with fruit, cinnamon and nutmeg.

By midnight, many of the more sober customers had left to attend Mass at either the cathedral or at one of the twenty-seven churches in the city and John was left sitting with Nesta as they shared a flask of red wine as a change from ale.

'What a difference half a year has made, John,' she said softly. 'You have changed my life, from the depths of despair to real happiness. Though I miss Meredydd, I feel as if my life has begun all over again.'

He nodded, his long dark face somehow looking younger as he looked down at the woman sitting close beside him. 'I too am content, *cariad*. I wish I could spend all my time in the Bush, instead of only half of it!'

'I'm glad your wife has gone to Tiverton this week. Without you around, I would have been so alone, just left with sad memories of former years.'

Their eyes met, his dark ones lurking under heavy brows, her large hazel orbs set in a smooth rounded face. Something new passed between them, so that he stood up and raised her by the hand, then wordlessly took her to the wide steps to the loft. At the top, he pushed open the door of her little cell and then shut it firmly behind them.

Nesta sank to the edge of her thick pallet and held out her arms to him. As he knelt to kiss her, she whispered again, 'John, I told you, I'd never make a nun!'

* * *

323

The next week was a foretaste of heaven for both man and beast. Brutus had a bone every day and John had Nesta. He spent every night there, only going back to St Martin's Lane at dawn, in time for Mary to give him a good breakfast. The cook knew perfectly well what was happening – as did much of Exeter – and not being in the market for him, bore no jealous feelings at all. In fact she was both pleased and amused at the change in her master, who with Matilda absent and having found Paradise down in Idle Lane, was amiable and cheerful in a way she'd not seen before.

Nothing lasts for ever and in this case, it was only a week before Nemesis arrived on a dappled palfrey. Matilda was home and after a flurry of unpacking and harassing Lucille, she sat in her usual place near the hearth, waiting for Mary to hurriedly prepare a meal. She was still too full of pride about her brother's elevation to sheriff to bother much with John, but he knew it would only be a matter of time before some gossiping friend would tell her of her husband's new interest in the Bush Inn. He felt he should begin to broach the subject of de Revelle's appointment, to prepare her for what must surely be a great disappointment. As soon as he could get her attention after her eulogy about the grandeur of the festivities at the Tiverton manor, he described the problem about Richard de Revelle's proposed shrievalty.

'As the king's representative in Devon, only the king can appoint him,' he said cautiously.

She immediately dismissed the notion. 'You

are only trying to stir up trouble again, John!' she snapped. 'Prince John was given the county after the king's coronation, to rule as he thinks fit. He already has a chancellor, justiciar and exchequer of his own, so of course he can appoint his own sheriff!'

'So why did the king keep Rougemont and Launceston castles in his own hand – and why are many of Prince John's fortifications now being pulled down?' retorted her husband.

Matilda glared at him around the corner of her chair. 'As ever, you are only trying to make trouble for my brother! Is it pure dislike or jealousy of a man who is achieving something in his life?' she cried. 'Unlike you, he's not shiftless and aimless unless he has a war to fight or a harlot to straddle!'

So within an hour of her return, they were squabbling again – and he knew that when she found out about the time he had spent in the Bush, the battle would be endless. They ate in sullen silence, then Matilda took herself off to her solar, shouting for Lucille as if she were calling to a dog.

It was another few days before the expected challenge to her brother came about. The time moved on to the New Year, still celebrated by most on the first day of January, even though the Church had long ago moved its date to the twenty-fifth of March, on the grounds that the one set in early Roman times was a pagan festival.*

*1st January was not legally New Year's Day in England until 1752.

Richard de Revelle had again installed himself in the sheriff's chamber, but rapidly made it known that he was now there in a different capacity as the true sheriff. He called his senior clerks to him and had proclamations written to the two portreeves of Exeter, the Masters of the various Guilds and to the burgers who made up the city council as well as sending them to the other major towns like Totnes and Plymouth. These informed them that Sir Richard de Revelle was now Sheriff of Devon, appointed by their lord, the Count of Mortain and that all important business and the conduct of the courts now operated through him.

De Revelle also tried to impress upon Ralph Morin his superiority in the hierarchy of the county, but that pugnacious soldier told him bluntly that he was an officer of the king and took no orders from someone who held his dubious post at the behest of a mere Count.

On Epiphany, the sixth day of the new month that celebrated the Magi's visit to the infant Jesus, a small procession entered Exeter from the London road. Half of the dozen men were a guard of men-at-arms under a sergeant, escorting a tall, grizzled man in his sixties, accompanied by another heavily built man with a large white moustache, both of whom had a squire and a body-servant.

They made straight for Rougemont and surprised the constable, who had no idea that they were coming. A flurry of activity settled their horses and escort, then Ralph Morin had food and drink organized for them in his chamber. At the same time, he covertly told Gabriel to send a soldier down to find Sir John de Wolfe and get him up to the castle as soon as possible.

The new arrivals were Sir Walter de Ralegh, one of the Royal Justices and a member of the *Curia*, the King's Council, together with Sir Henry de Furnellis, a middle-aged knight whose father, Geoffrey de Furnellis, had been sheriff of Devon earlier in the century.

Both of them had strong Devon connections, as Walter had been born in East Budleigh and though de Furnellis was now a Somerset man, his family came from Venn Ottery, both manors being near each other about ten miles south-east of Exeter.

'I came in response to your message to Hubert Walter,' announced de Ralegh in his deep voice. 'I am due to hold an Assize of Gaol Delivery in Dorchester next week, so it was convenient for me to come here. I picked up my old friend Henry here on the way, as the Justiciar has plans for him!'

'Plans that I could well do without,' put in de Furnellis wryly. 'I want a quiet life these days, but my duty to the king comes first.'

They avoided further discussion while they ate and drank after their journey, the visitors saying that they would stay in the New Inn, the city's largest hostelry in the High Street, where visiting judges were usually accommodated.

When John de Wolfe arrived, he too was surprised by the rapid response to the messages to the Chief Justiciar about both his success in combating outlaws and in dealing with the killer

327

of the royal messenger, as well as the news that Prince John had flaunted the royal protocol in appointing his own sheriff. De Wolfe was already acquainted with both of the visitors, from various campaigns in Ireland and France, as well as at tournaments. Walter de Ralegh still had a Devonshire accent and because of his local knowledge, was often sent by the *Curia Regis* on matters concerning the west of England. When the platters and cups were cleared away, Walter got straight down to business.

'The *Curia* is concerned about the increasing level of violence all over the country and the lack of any proper means to deal with it. Hubert Walter has plans to set up Keepers of the Peace and other measures, but that's in the future, when the king is back in circulation.'

'It's bad down here, Sir Walter,' said Ralph Morin. 'The roads are getting so unsafe that it's dangerous for folk to travel anywhere.'

'Don't think you're alone in that, the Justiciar gets pleas from all over the country complaining of the same thing. But not having a sheriff here makes things worse.'

'We now have a self-appointed one!' said John cynically.

Walter de Ralegh turned his rough, weather-beaten face towards de Wolfe. 'Not for long, John! Where is the bloody man? We'll soon deal with him.'

'De Revelle has settled himself in the old sheriff's room here, but he's not shown up today,' advised the constable. 'The clerk he's brought with him says he's starting his duties tomorrow.'

De Ralegh scowled. 'What in hell is he doing settling in a royal castle, like a cuckoo in another bird's nest? Have him here in the morning, we'll soon stamp on another of Prince John's little schemes!'

The reign of Richard de Revelle as Sheriff of Devon was very short and not particularly sweet. When next morning he arrived at the castle from the house he was leasing in North Street, he had already heard from his steward about the unexpected arrival in the city of Walter de Ralegh and Henry de Furnellis, but had no idea of their mission. He knew both of them slightly, but as they were staunch supporters of the king, he had kept his distance from them ever since his sympathies had moved to Prince John.

It was with considerable surprise that he entered his chamber in the keep to find it already occupied by four men. Sir Walter was sitting in his own chair behind the table and the constable, Henry de Furnellis and his own brother-in-law occupied stools alongside him.

Richard's habitual arrogance and self-assurance soon surfaced. 'What are you doing in my room?' he demanded.

Walter jabbed a finger towards an empty chair. 'Sit down, de Revelle. Firstly, it's not your room, it belongs to the king – as will all Devonshire again be very soon.'

De Revelle's mouth opened to protest, then the significance of the remark came home to him. Rapidly, he began to reassess his fortunes in the light of a possible change of politics.

'The process of King Richard's release is under way,' continued Walter. 'Queen Eleanor should by now be at the Emperor's court in Mainz with the bulk of the ransom money, so his return home is only a matter of time – a very short time!'

'I'm delighted to hear it!' said de Revelle, after some rapid thought. 'I am the caretaker sheriff at present, but would be honoured to continue to serve the king in that post.'

De Ralegh glowered at him and thumped the table with a big fist. 'Not a chance, de Revelle! You are not the sheriff, you never were the sheriff – and if I have any say in the matter, you never will be the bloody sheriff!' He lifted a parchment from the table, which had a heavy seal dangling from ribbons at the bottom. 'This is a warrant signed and sealed by Archbishop Hubert Walter, Chief Justiciar of England, appointing Sir Henry de Furnellis as Sheriff in this county, as from the day of Christ Mass. It was issued by the Justiciar on behalf of the king, for whom he is acting in every capacity.'

'But the county belongs to Prince John!' howled de Revelle.

Walter de Ralegh jabbed a finger at the speaker. 'A word of advice, de Revelle! As soon as the king is released, all lands he unwisely gave to his brother will be forfeit. John's remaining castles will be attacked and seized and the prince himself will probably be charged with treason, along with those who are known to support him. If I were you and you wish to save your neck, I

330

would try to forget you'd ever heard of the Count of Mortain!' The tall judge got to his feet and pointed at the door. 'Now go, de Revelle! You have no business here. Go to your manors, hunt, eat and sleep, but stop meddling in affairs of state that will only bring ruin upon you!'

Richard went pale, then red as his chagrin at being so summarily dismissed, wounded his pride and his vanity. He stalked to the door, sweeping his green cloak around him. As he passed John, he glared at him venomously. 'This is your doing, de Wolfe! I'll never forget it!'

TWENTY-TWO

It was now early September and much had happened since the depths of winter. One warm afternoon, Nesta had moved two trestle tables and benches outside to flank the front door of the Bush. A pair of carpenters and a blacksmith sat on one, with John de Wolfe, Gwyn of Polruan and Nesta on the other. The only view was that of a bare patch opposite, where weeds covered the charred remains of the fire of some years ago, but it was pleasant to sit in the sun with a jug of ale and chat about the state of the world.

'Any news from across the Channel?' asked Gwyn, leaning back against the wall of the inn, with a quart pot in his hand.

'Ralph Morin's usual source passed through yesterday,' replied John. 'A courier from Winchester said that our king is making slow but steady progress against Philip's army in Touraine and that he is planning to build a huge castle on the Seine.'

'What about his traitorous brother?' demanded Nesta. 'He seems to have faded from sight since May, when the king pardoned him yet again.'

De Wolfe scowled at the memory. 'Yes, the Lionheart said he was like a naughty child and it was those men who led him astray who should be punished. But I don't trust him, he won't easily give up plotting to unseat Richard.'

After the collapse of John's rebellion in March, the main instigator, Hugh of Nonant, Bishop of Coventry, was fined heavily and went into exile in Normandy, where he died in disgrace. His brother, Robert Brito (who had refused to go to Germany as a hostage for the king) was thrown into the cells of Dover castle and was starved to death.

John himself had fled to Normandy and allied himself openly with King Philip, until he had crawled back to Liseaux to seek his brother's forgiveness. As Walter de Ralegh had foreseen, the *Curia Regis* had stripped him of his English possessions, including Devon, even before the king was released from Germany into his doughty mother's custody in February.

As the sun warmed them, they gave up talking politics in favour of things nearer home. Their sheriff, Henry de Furnellis, was liked well enough, but they were rather irked by his lack of enthusiasm for keeping the peace.

'He's not a well man,' said John, in mitigation. 'He suffered wounds in Ireland when we were there, but his main problem is this shaking fever he gets at intervals, picked up in the marshes of southern France, due to their foul air.'

'Whatever it is, he's not too keen on chasing trail robbers from the roads,' grunted Gwyn. 'We've had to go out with Ralph a few times on his behalf.'

'It keeps us from growing rusty,' countered John. 'And it's something to do to pass the time.'

333

John was becoming restless at his own inactivity. He had been back in Exeter now for a year and apart from some sporadic involvement with their wool business, had no real occupation. This was a common problem for knights who had neither a manor to administer nor a war to fight. Some of them even turned to banditry, but many more found little to occupy themselves – and of these, many were relatively poor, as an honourable rank does not fill an empty stomach. De Wolfe had even been considering entering the king's service again, but that would mean leaving Devon and almost certainly going to France to join the royal armies. Though he had no objection to this, he was now so enamoured of Nesta that it would be a great wrench to leave her. He looked at her now, smiling at him across the table, pretty and happy in her summer kirtle and lace coif.

'Why so solemn, John?' she asked gaily. 'It's a lovely day, the ale is perfect and Molly has a fine salmon to cook for our supper!'

He gave her one of his lopsided grins. 'Not solemn, *cariad* – just wondering how to spend the next thirty years? Maybe I should take up my lance and go tourneying again, now that the king has made it legal.'

Old King Henry had forbidden jousting and tournaments, concerned at the loss of life amongst his knights and the fear that it trained them to be more proficient at rebelling against him. However, one of the first acts that Richard had made after his return, was to authorize five sites in England where they could be held on payment of steep entrance fees – another ploy to raise money for his war against Philip.

Nesta sat pondering John's reply about the next thirty years, as it reminded her of the hopelessness of their relationship. She loved him and knew that he probably returned her love – but to what end? He was the mature son of a Norman knight, married to a woman from another notable Norman family – a marriage that was irrevocable in the eyes of the Church, one that only death could dissolve. And she was but a Welsh widow, a mere alewife of no social status whatsoever. There was no future for them other than an illicit affair, with furtive love-making and a dalliance virtually confined to the inside of a tavern. John could never be seen in public with her or even acknowledge her, outside the circle of those who frequented the Bush.

She sighed and wondered whether she should have left Exeter when Meredydd was taken from her – perhaps gone home to Gwent and lived with her mother and sisters, then found a nice local man and settled down to have children. But then Nesta rebelled and mentally straightened her back. Today was today, she was going to enjoy her romance while it lasted and be damned to the consequences.

She looked across at de Wolfe, wondering what he was thinking. Not as uncomplicated and unimaginative as many people thought, he was also troubled about his liaison with Nesta, but in a different way. He both loved her and lusted after her, enjoying every moment of her company. But he felt that he was cheating her, standing in the way of her getting on with her life. Like her, he knew they could never marry and that he was blocking her chances of becoming a wife and mother. He was not concerned about his own image or reputation – after almost eight months, most of Exeter knew that she was his mistress. Many of the others of Norman blood, both knights and rich merchants, openly had lovers, even bastard children. Some of the canons and parish priests had the same illicit habits and no great notice was taken of it.

Of course, Matilda kept up a barrage of invective against him, but her vindictiveness over the 'Welsh whore', as she usually called Nesta, had been overshadowed by a different hatred. This was her burning rage against her husband for his part in getting her wonderful brother so ignominiously dismissed as sheriff within days of being appointed. She had endlessly made it plain that for that, she would never forgive him. With this as the background to his life, what was to happen very soon, was all the more remarkable.

Richard the Lionheart was now firmly re-established as King of England, even to the extent of holding a second coronation at Winchester in April – to which he failed to invite his wife, Berengaria, who never set foot in the country of which she was queen. After landing at Sandwich in Kent with his mother in March, he was to spend only two months in the country, leaving with his fleet and army from Portsmouth in May, never to return.

Within days of landing, he had put on his armour and hurried to Nottingham, the last of Prince John's castles to hold out. The others had all surrendered, the castellan at St Michael's Mount having dropped dead of fright on hearing of the king's return!

Henry de la Pomeroy had also fled to the Mount, where to avoid the king's retribution, he had ordered his physician to open the veins in his wrists, so that he expired! At Nottingham, Richard fought his way into the barbican, then erected a gallows in full view of the defenders and hanged several men captured earlier, which rapidly caused the remaining men to surrender.

Under the expert guidance of Archbishop Hubert Walter, all the machinery of state regained its former pattern. The royal courts continued their rounds, the king's justices sitting at the Eyres of Assize and commissioners of lesser rank coming more frequently to clear the gaols of remand prisoners who had not either died or escaped. The day following John's ruminations outside the Bush, he learned of the arrival of a pair of these commissioners, due to hold a Court of Gaol Delivery the following week.

John had gone up to the castle to make a social call on the constable and the sheriff, mainly to catch up on recent gossip. He sat with the constable in the chamber of Henry de Furnellis, where the sheriff was bemoaning the fact that he would prefer to be back at his manor in Somerset, supervising the coming harvest.

'I never wanted this damned job, John,' he grumbled. 'My feelings of duty to the king persuaded me, but only on condition that it was temporary. My health is not good and I have petitioned the Chief Justiciar to relieve me of the task and appoint someone else.'

Ralph Morin said that they would all be sorry to see him leave, but he gave John a surreptitious wink, as they had often talked about having a younger, more active man as sheriff.

'Perhaps these commissioners who came today may have some news for me before they hold court next week,' said Henry, hopefully. 'They are at the bishop's palace at present, and I'm invited down to eat with them tonight.'

'Who are they this time?' asked Ralph.

'Simon Waring, the abbot of St Albans, who's staying with the bishop – and Sir Philip de Culleforde, a baron from Wiltshire. He's lodging at the New Inn.'

'How have you found the new bishop?' asked John, who had heard that Henry Marshal, enthroned in May, had been inclined towards Prince John when Dean of York.

The old sheriff held up his palms and shrugged. 'He's no jolly friar, John. A serious man with a serious face and somehow, a coldness about him. A different man to his brother William, that's for sure.'

This William was the Marshal of England, perhaps the best-known fighting man in the country, both on the tourney field and the battlefield. He had served two kings well and would serve two more during his long life. No doubt it was his influence with the king that gained his brother the bishop's mitre.

When John left Rougemont and walked back to his house in St Martin's Lane, he gloomily expected the usual frosty reception from his wife, who rarely spoke to him these days, except on the rare occasions when they were together in public, when she assumed a facade of normality for the benefit of her friends. But somewhat to his surprise and perhaps with a little apprehension, he found her in a more benign mood, as if she was concealing some pleasant secret. As they sat down to the usual light supper that Mary provided, he wondered what new spite Matilda was going to unleash on him.

But in the event, it was the sheriff's supper that night with the two judges, which would bring news of a great change in the life of John de Wolfe.

The following afternoon, John was in the farrier's opposite his home, preparing to get Bran saddled up for a canter around Bull Mead to give the old horse some exercise. Before he could leave, a young soldier appeared with a message from Ralph Morin, urgently requesting his presence at the castle within the hour 'for a meeting on the king's business'.

Intrigued, he loped up to Rougemont and found his friend in the sheriff's chamber. Two other men were present and Henry de Furnellis introduced them as the commissioners who were to preside in the Shire Hall, Sir Philip de Culleforde and Abbot Simon Waring. The latter was a jovial-looking monk, with a bland round face, but a pair of steely eyes that suggested a hard core under the soft skin. De Culleforde was a tall, handsome man of about fifty, with a calm, unruffled manner. He was a member of the King's Council and had the ear of Hubert Walter and the king himself. They all sat on benches around Henry's table and his chief clerk appeared with glass goblets, filling them from a large flask of good wine. He then stood behind his master in case he was needed, as he was the only one of the Exeter men who could read and write. When they had all settled, the sheriff took the lead.

'When I petitioned the Chief Justiciar about my desire to be relieved of this shrievalty, I had no idea that it would be acted on so quickly and so decisively,' he began. 'But these two gentlemen have brought instructions from Archbishop Walter – and hence from the king himself – which have left me both happy and also bewildered.'

De Wolfe wondered what in God's name the sheriff was talking about, but he was soon to be enlightened, as Henry picked up three parchment rolls from the table, each having impressive seals dangling from them.

Henry handed them up to his clerk. 'Tell them what they are, Elphin,' he commanded.

Elphin, a dried-up stick of a man, looked briefly at their headings before explaining their content. 'Sirs, the first is a relief for Sir Henry, expressing the thanks of the Justiciar and of the king for his faithful service and discharging him from further duties as from the eve of Michaelmas.'

He shuffled the parchments and moved to the second one. 'This is an appointment and commission for a new sheriff, as from Michaelmas itself.' He swallowed nervously before continuing. 'It is drawn in the name of Sir Richard de Revelle.'

There was a moment's silence as the words sank into the ears of Ralph Morin and John de Wolfe.

'De Revelle! Are you jesting?' demanded John. 'He was ejected from that office only months ago!'

'This cannot be true, surely!' barked the castle constable. 'He is the last man in England who deserves to be sheriff here!'

Henry de Furnellis looked appealing at Philip de Culleforde. 'Can you repeat the explanation you gave to me, Sir Philip?'

The tall, grave knight nodded. 'I fully realize your surprise and discomfort over this, but we have not finished explaining our arrangements. Firstly, there is no proof of any wrongdoing by de Revelle in relation to the revolt of a few months ago. The king has now fully pardoned his brother and is trying to put the whole sorry episode behind him.'

He paused and looked slightly embarrassed. 'Also, William Marshal, who, after Hubert Walter himself, is probably the most powerful man in the kingdom and very close to the Lionheart, has specifically requested de Revelle's reinstatement. This is no doubt at the behest of his brother Henry, now your bishop.'

Bitterly, John now saw the wheels-within-wheels, the power of nepotism that operated amongst the great families of the land.

But Philip de Culleforde had not yet finished his explanation. 'In addition, I must tell you that Archbishop Walter is well aware of the suspicion and hostility that surrounds de Revelle. He told me of his previous request to you, de Wolfe, to keep an eye on the situation in Devon, though with the crushing of the rebellion, this no longer seems so necessary. However, the Justiciar feels that it might be better to have de Revelle where he can be seen, rather than covertly causing trouble.' He paused and waved a hand at the clerk. 'Give us the gist of the third document, if you please. This is also relevant to our concerns.'

Elphin cleared his throat and unrolled the parchment. 'This is also a commission from the Archbishop, but adding the caveat that it is also the personal wish of King Richard that it be accepted. It offers the appointment of the King's Coroner for the County of Devon to Sir John de Wolfe, in recognition of his faithful service and bravery during the Crusade and afterwards to the person of the king himself. And furthermore, to his dedication to keeping the peace in the County of Devin.'

For a moment there was another profound silence. Dumbfounded, John could only stumble out a few words. 'What in God's name is a "coroner"?' he asked.

'So what is a coroner?' demanded Gwyn bluntly. He sat with Nesta at their usual table in the Bush, as they listened to John de Wolfe relating the extraordinary news from the castle. Matilda had gone to some special Mass in St Olave's, so John had not spoken to her and instead had come to his second home in Idle Lane.

'Coroner? I knew nothing of the name until I had a lecture from the two commissioners, especially the fat abbot, who seems more of a lawyer than a priest.' He paused for a swallow of ale. 'It comes from the Latin *custos placitorum coronae,* which means "keeper of the pleas of the crown".'

The Cornishman looked at him blankly. 'I'm none the wiser for hearing that,' he growled.

'Neither was I, until they explained that Hubert Walter has devised yet another scheme for both raising money – and also starting to improve the keeping of the king's peace.'

It was now Nesta's turn to look baffled. 'How's it going to do that, John?'

'It seems that it's a "Jack-of-all-trades" appointment. This coroner has to keep records of all serious crimes, deaths, rapes, fires, wrecks, robberies, finds of treasure and God knows what else, to present to the king's judges when they come on circuit. After an unnatural death, he has to hold an inquest, with a jury. He has to attend executions to confiscate the property of felons for the king, and all sorts of odd jobs, mainly directed at pushing as much business as he can to the royal courts, instead of the county, manor and burgess courts.'

'What's the point of that?' she asked.

'Money, that's what it's about! It's all about scraping every penny into the Exchequer to pay the last of the ransom and for his campaign against the French.'

He paused for a drink, and Nesta refilled his pot from the large jug on the table.

'And the king wants you to take up this appointment in Devon?' she asked doubtfully.

'It sounds as if he won't take no for an answer,' replied de Wolfe. 'Though I don't know if I want to be a glori-fied tax collector!'

'You were complaining that you were tired of inactivity and wanted something to occupy you,' said Nesta accusingly. 'This sounds ideal, it would keep you in Exeter with some aim in life and give you the status of a king's officer.'

He nodded slowly, as he considered his words. 'I think there is a deeper motive behind this. The commissioners hinted that the king was incensed at the widespread corruption amongst sheriffs and needed some curb placed on their excesses. Old King Henry dismissed them all for mal-feasance back in 1170, but they have crept back into their old ways. It's hoped that these new coroners can act as a check on sheriffs – and in Devon, given this extraordinary return of bloody de Revelle, it will be all the more vital to keep a sharp eye on him.'

Gwyn grinned. 'And knowing how you two men love each other, the Justiciar can be sure that you will watch him like a hawk!'

Nesta, pleased with any development that would prevent her lover from going off to find a war abroad, turned to practicalities. 'So, Sir John, are you going to accept this honour from a grateful king? And when would you take office

– and is there a salary?'

He put a long arm around her and pulled her to him. 'Hussy, is all that concerns you whether or not I get paid? The answer is "no"! In fact, coroners will be forbidden to accept anything other than expenses – and they will have to prove they already have an income of at least twenty pounds a year. This is to ensure that they are so rich that they would not be tempted to embezzle the funds, as do the sheriffs.'

Gwyn's booming laugh conveyed his cynicism. 'Some hope! Can you imagine de Revelle passing up the chance to dip his hand into the county taxes, even though he must be worth a hundred pounds a year?'

'And when would you begin, if you accept?' persisted Nesta.

'The whole scheme will be announced by the royal justices at the Kent Eyre to be held in Rochester Castle this month. Both the new sheriff and the coroners will take office at Michaelmas.'

Gwyn scratched his head to frighten away a few fleas. 'I suppose the king gave you this new job in gratitude for what you did for him on the journey home?' he said, with a note of pride in his voice.

John punched him on the arm. 'He's given you a job too, old friend! I want you to be my officer, my guard and the man who keeps me out of trouble – unless you have something better to do with your time!'

Gwyn grinned hugely and said he would give it a try to see if he liked it. 'But how could you cover a county as big as Devon on your own? You'd spend your life on horseback!'

John nodded his agreement. 'I asked them that, but it seems that each county is supposed to have three coroners, in different areas.'

'Who are the others, then?' demanded Nesta sharply, already acting as if John was being taken advantage of by the state.

'They have a knight from up Barnstaple way who may accept. Another should be recruited for the Plymouth area, but that's just wishful thinking at the moment. There has to be a clerk as well, as few of us can read or write.'

'Where are you going to get a clerk?' asked Gwyn. 'We don't know anyone who can read and write, apart from all the damned clergy.'

John shrugged. 'If it comes to pass, then I'll ask the archdeacon, he's sure to know someone.' He finished his ale and stood up. 'In fact, I'll call there now, on my way back to face my wife.'

As he kissed Nesta goodbye, he groaned at the prospect of returning home. 'Oh God, how she'll crow over me, now that her bloody brother is going to be sheriff again. Life won't be worth living in Martin's Lane!'

The archdeacon admitted to John that he had already heard rumours of de Revelle's return to favour.

'The bishop told me several weeks ago that his brother William had petitioned the archbishop and the *Curia* about it, but directed me not to speak publicly about the matter. But I had not heard about this offer to you, John. It's an honour to have this bestowed upon you by the king himself – a well-deserved honour, too.'

John described what he knew about the nature of the coroner's duties and the archdeacon, a very well-educated man, said that he had heard of such an officer in the past.

'There are several mentions of such an officer in Saxon times, right back to King Alfred and Athelstan,' the archdeacon observed. 'It seems to have died out, but Hubert Walter seems to be reviving it to his advantage.'

'If I do accept – and it looks as if I have little choice, given the royal command,' said John, 'I would need a clerk, someone who could keep all these records which have to be presented to the king's courts. Where could I find such a person?'

De Alencon raised a hand to his lips and tapped them for a moment as he thought, then raised a finger. 'I may have the answer, John!' He leaned across and rang a small bell on his table to summon his steward from the next room.

After a whispered request, the man left and came back leading a small young fellow of a most unprepossessing appearance. He had a slight limp and a small hump on his back, under a threadbare black cassock. His face was pathetically thin, with a long sharp nose and a receding chin, but relieved by a pair of bright, intelligent eyes. His sparse dark hair was unkempt and showed the remains of a clerical tonsure on top, though this was growing over again.

'This is my nephew, Thomas de Peyne, who has fallen on hard times and has walked from

Winchester to throw himself upon my mercy,' explained the archdeacon. 'He has found himself a bed in my servant's quarters but is in dire need of some employment. I can vouch for his literacy, as he taught at the cathedral school in Winchester, where he was in holy orders.'

John noticed the past tense in the last few words and was about to enquire further, when the sad-faced clerk spoke up.

'To save my uncle's embarrassment, sir, I will declare straight away that I was dismissed from the school and indeed, banned from any ecclesiastical post. It was because of an allegation that I made improper advances towards one of the female pupils. It was a false and malicious claim, but that is of no consequence now. I am cast out into the world and will either perish, as I almost did this past year – or find some occupation to give me food and shelter.'

There was something about Thomas's tone that rang true in John's ears. Perhaps it was the utter fatalism with which he stated his situation or the detachment from caring much what happened to him.

'It is premature for me to decide on employing a clerk at this stage,' John said to both of them. 'But if I accept this post, and it is confirmed, then I will certainly take you on for a trial period, which starts at Michaelmas.'

To John's great discomfort, Thomas de Peyne's eyes suddenly filled with tears and he dropped to his knees in front of him.

'Sir, your kindness is only matched by that of the archdeacon.' With a sob, he rose and hurried from the room, leaving his uncle to promise to tell John the whole sad story of Thomas de Peyne at some other time.

Finding no other excuse to delay confronting Matilda, John slowly walked the few hundred paces from Canon's Row to his house, where he found his wife sitting alone at the table, drinking hare stew from a wooden bowl with a spoon carved from a cow's horn. Bread and cheese lay in front of her, together with a large cup of wine. She looked up at him with a sly smile of triumph, but he decided to get in his attack first.

'Yes, I know all about it now, lady! Thanks to his friends in high places, your brother has wormed his way back into favour – though for how long, depends on how he behaves himself.'

Matilda raised her glass and drank, before replying. 'Jealousy, jealousy, always jealousy, John!' she sneered. 'My brother has attained high office, while my husband remains an unemployed wastrel, useless at anything but killing, drinking and whoring!'

A warm glow of satisfaction crept over him as he saw his chance. 'Your brother has not yet seen the king's commissioners, then?' he asked innocently.

Matilda looked at him suspiciously. 'He is at the castle now, receiving the official warrant of his appointment – though the bishop told him of it several days ago.'

John dropped into his cowled chair with assumed nonchalance. 'Then neither of you are aware that I have already received a warrant from the Archbishop of Canterbury, issued to me on the Lionheart's specific orders, to become the King's Coroner for the County of Devon, taking office on the same day as your dear brother!'

John had rarely seen his wife lost for a tart reply, but this was one of those delicious occasions. Making the most of it, he got up again and informed her harshly that he was taking the hound for some exercise.

'I don't know when I'll be home, I have much to think about,' he said, as he went to the door and slammed it behind him. Whistling for Brutus, he set off for the Bush again.

Historical Note

The sequence of sheriffs in Devon in the last decades of the twelfth century is something of a mystery. Several lists exist but the most reliable one records that William Brewer held the shrievalty until Michaelmas 1189, the year of Richard the Lionheart's accession. Then the Count of Mortain is listed, but with the brief comment that 'he did not account', that is, send the county taxes to Winchester.

At Christmas 1193, Richard Revel appears on the list, but immediately following, Henry de Furnellis is also recorded as being sheriff from Christmas. This is unusual, as almost all other changes over several centuries were at either Easter or Michaelmas.

Henry stays until Michaelmas 1194, then Richard Revel reappears, but a year later, Henry de Furnellis is back again at Michaelmas 1195 and remains in office until 1198. Though history offers us no explanation, the coincidence of dates with the rise and fall of Prince John seems very suggestive.

For those interested in the events portrayed in this book and the fascinating story of the Lionheart's reign, the following books are recommended:

Blondel's Song by David Boyle, Penguin Books (2006), paperback, ISBN 9780141015972. An excellent, very readable account of Richard's journey home from the Holy Land, from which many of the facts in this novel are taken – together with a wealth of other detail about life and politics at that time.

Richard I by John Gillingham, Yale University Press (2002), paperback, ISBN 9780300094046. The definitive text about the Lionheart in the *Yale English Monarch Series*.

Domesday Book to Magna Carta by A. L. Poole, Oxford University Press (1993), paperback, ISBN 9780192852878. This is the standard volume in the *Oxford History of England series*, covering the twelfth century.